CW00428020

STAR NEXUS (BOOK 1)

NEXUS EMPIRE

DOMINIQUE MONDESIR
C.W. TICKNER

BROKEN NATIVE

Copyright © 2023 by Dominique Mondesir

All rights reserved.

No part of this book may be reproduced in any form or by any electronic
or mechanical means, including information storage and retrieval systems,
without written permission from the author, except for the use of brief
quotations in a book review.

This is a work of fiction. Any similarity to actual persons, living or dead, or
actual events, is purely coincidental.

Thanks to Cheynne Edmonton for the amazing cover art as always info@standoutcovers.com
And lastly thanks to my proof readers Martin Ohearn, Brandon Sommerville and Bob Clarkson for making this book readable.

E ighteen years, four months and five days. That's how long it took to infiltrate the most secretive organization on the planet.

And now, after conquering countless challenges, battling his way from military oil rigs in Russia to presidential security details, Jason Korzon was finally in the one place he had always wanted to be.

From the day he joined, he knew it would end up here. It was always going to finish in the Nevada desert. The most top-secret facility in the world and ironically, the most well-known secret on the planet.

It had been a boyhood dream, like that of so many others, to find out if the government that ruled over them knew the secrets of the universe.

The thwopping of his transport helicopter leaving the facility under nightfall echoed through the doors as Jason waited in the reception room to meet his new commander. The air inside the bland room was dry and chill, tasting of the ever-present sand that had made a home in the corners.

Jason knew he would never have made it here by being

one of those smart physics types. He didn't have the mental capacity. He was more brawn than brains. Athletics had been his passion and when he'd realized he didn't need to be Einstein, his dreams to find out the truth became a faint hope once again. Of course, he'd kept them a complete and utter secret. If his peers knew he believed in aliens, UFOs, and black ops mysteries, then his career would be toast and he'd never get to find out the things he had tried so hard to discover.

For a moment, the corners of his mouth twitched and he wondered if the weird-looking receptionist woman had noticed it. He resumed the cold hard face of stone that had gotten him through so many difficult encounters.

Eighteen years. It was two life sentences, all combined into one. The things he'd done, many of which he regretted, now seemed to pale beside the future that was being presented to him. He was close, closer than he had ever been in his entire life, and he needed to keep his cool in case everything came undone.

He stared around the room, admiring the cold decor, a world away from the military secrets that he had guessed existed here. It was all a facade. He knew that somewhere beneath his feet lay secrets that the rest of the world wanted to know. Whether he would tell them, or keep them to himself, he hadn't yet decided. All that mattered was that he had found what he was looking for, and he would go on from there.

The doors at the back of the office opened, sliding silently apart to allow a man to pass through. He was tall, slim framed and dark-skinned, with a hawkish look. The regimental jacket, a standard military issue for anyone higher than a colonel, was decorated with more ribbons than a car crash memorial and enough medals to sink a navy transport ship in the Black Sea.

Jason waited patiently as the man entered and eyed him for several seconds without saying a word. The name 'Forrester' was patched beneath the braided silver aiguillette that looped under his medals.

When he spoke, his hawk-like features became animated as if seeking prey. He locked onto Jason. 'So you're the new recruit then?' he said, casting his brown eyes over Jason's civilian clothes.

Jason rose, conscious of his own lack of regalia, and threw the man a formal salute before standing promptly to attention.

'Not really new, sir,' Jason said, standing at ease when the man gave a wry smile at his words. 'Major Korzon, sir.'

The Colonel's smile dropped, and his face took on a serious note, tinged with the tone of someone who knows things most people don't.

Jason knew that look. He'd used it himself after dealing in the black ops projects of the military.

Colonel Forrester went on, indicating for Jason to follow him through the doors. 'Anyone who's not been around here for ten years is new,' he said. 'Everything you see here is going to be new and everything that you don't see here is probably going to be new as well.'

The corridor that they entered gave way from the metal siding of the office to the solid concrete of military installations around the globe. The air changed from a dry chill to the tinged smell of air conditioning. Ahead of them was a single doorway and, as they passed through it, they were presented with a security checkpoint.

Two stoney-faced guards stood silent watch on either side of the corridor. Between them was an MRI scanner and beyond that, a single heavy-set titanium door. A single soldier was waiting in front, holding a SCAR rifle and eyeing their approach.

'I hear you've done work with the President?' the Colonel said as they passed through the scanner. A moment later, there was a pinging noise and the door opened onto a wide elevator. The sentry lowered the rifle.

'Two years as head of field protection and one as a senior security executive,' Jason said, his eyes locked onto the rotating turret in the elevator's ceiling and the cameras from four angles pointing down at them. For a second, the hairs on the back of his neck stood on end until he realized that within the next day he would be in charge of those turrets and the soldiers keeping the base secure. It was rare that a position so high up on base was given to someone who had no on-site experience, but Jason had covered every type of operation and he knew he was qualified for the post, regardless of what this colonel might think.

'And I've headed up several black ops security details,' Jason finished.

Colonel Forrester chuckled. 'Those black ops are barely gray compared to here. More like an off-white.'

The lift descended with a smooth motion and seemed to go down for minutes.

'I've upped your security clearance from ultra top secret to ultra high top secret,' Forrester said.

'I didn't know it went any higher,' Jason said, taking a proffered identity card from the Colonel as the elevator finally slowed to a stop and the doors peeled open.

They opened up onto a blank wall.

Jason looked at the Colonel, suspecting something had gone wrong. Forrester confidently stepped forwards and pressed his hand against the wall in the top right corner, almost out of reach.

His hand was lit up by a thin line of bright red light coming from inside the featureless concrete.

As if by magic, the bare concrete wall cracked apart at waist height and the top half slid up.

The barrel of an assault rifle was thrust through the half opening, aimed directly at their faces. Jason instinctively ducked, ready to clamber over the half door before the rifle fired, but he knew he would be too late. He'd let his guard down for a second and would now pay for his slip-up with his life.

'Hold, Major!' Colonel Forrester shouted, putting a vice-like hand on Jason's shoulder.

When no shots rang out in the confined space, Jason froze, the bony hand on his shoulder forcing him to stillness.

The rifle barrel retreated and the Colonel gave a nod to the stoney-faced man behind the weapon. With a beep, the lower half of the door slid down. Jason realized it was another security checkpoint. There would be no risks taken here. This was dangerous territory.

There were no scanners this time, just a semicircle of well-armed soldiers who stepped aside to let them pass into a corridor lined with doors on either side.

They strode down the tunnel. Jason glanced left and right through any of the doors that were open, peering inside to see laboratories and instruments being worked on by bespectacled men and women dressed in the white frocks of scientists, all of which were a complete mystery.

There were canteens, barracks and offices. This layer of the facility was set out in a circular pattern: a big loop that came back on itself. Along the inner wall of the ringed tunnel at the opposite end from the entrance was a huge hangar door, and this was where the Colonel led him. They had seen relatively few people on route, with rooms they passed seemingly abandoned.

'Beyond this door is what you will be charged with guarding,' Colonel Forrester said. You and the team of fifty men stationed across the facility will be constantly on alert to protect what lies behind these doors. Only a small portion of you will ever set foot inside the hangar. The rest will be charged with duties above ground and protecting this facility from attacks.'

'Should we expect enemies?' Jason asked.

The Colonel seemed put out for a second but quickly regained his composure.

'There are always those that wish to know what we have here,' he said. 'Who knows? The Russians, the Chinese, the Koreans? Any of a dozen other countries want to have control of the things we keep safe. If they knew even a fraction of what we have here, they would descend on this facility like a plague, or expose it. Thankfully, it's a well-kept secret, and you're going to keep it that way.'

'So what's the secret?' Jason asked. A sudden feeling of worry struck him. What if they didn't have any extraterrestrial things here at all? What if it was something entirely unrelated to space exploration? Some secret fusion power or a dark secret program like that of MK Ultra in the sixties?

Forrester didn't respond, just pressed his hands to two separate parts of the large hangar door. Both palms glowed with a moving red line before amber lights flashed above the door. The thick titanium construction split diagonally apart, revealing a cramped room beyond, like an airlock.

Along one side of the white-tiled wall were yellow

hazmat suits hanging from hooks. Beneath them were rows of gray lockers.

'Should we put one on?' Jason asked, giving a nod to the suits as the door behind was sealed with a hiss and a rush of air flooded the room from small vents set in the ceiling.

The Colonel glanced contemptuously at the suits. 'We'll leave those for the science folks,' he said. 'We've got more important work to do. Their work may never yield any results, but we have to make sure no one else gets the chance to excel where they have failed. We keep our distance from everything in there and we make sure it's safe. *You* make sure it's safe, Major.'

'Make sure what's safe?' Jason asked.

Before Colonel Forrester could answer, the rush of air ceased and the gray metal door in front of them rose slowly up, revealing a sight that would forever be etched in Jason's mind.

J ason barely noted the vast hangar, surrounded by computer-laden covered terminals and the army of hazmat-covered scientists. His palms were sweaty and his senses heightened, taking in every strange detail.

Perched in the centre was his most treasured hope. Clamps from the steel floor rose like three metal arms, clasping in their midst a ship. Nothing could have prepared him for the reality of the situation—the truth. It was an alien spacecraft; it had to be. No man had ever made anything so singular and sleek. The initial outline was that of a giant manta ray, the size of a modest house, sleek and stretched to perfection. Its hull was a single smooth metal piece, without a bolt or cable to break it up, sweeping out to two thin curving wings.

They had erected scaffolding around the manta, allowing the constant host of scientists to conduct experiments at every curve and bump. There seemed to be no doors or windows, nothing that even resembled an engine or thruster.

A thousand questions rose in Jason's mind and it seemed the Colonel had heard them all before. He cut him off without pausing to let the answers begin.

'We found it in the nineteen forties,' he said. 'Close to Roswell, New Mexico. So yeah, the crazies had it right.'

Jason was one of those who had read up everything about that finding, not to mention a hundred others. He kept his face emotionless, but his insides roiled like a sack of snakes.

'J-just one?' Jason stammered.

'One, and one alone,' Forrester said.

'What do we know about it?'

'That is not your remit, recruit,' Forrester said, his tone changing again. Jason stifled himself as the Colonel went on. 'All you need to know is nothing gets into the ship and nothing has ever come out, and while you're in charge, nothing gets into this facility without my say-so, and it goes without saying that nothing about this gets out.'

Jason tore his gaze from the alien ship and managed to finally snatch a look around the rest of the room. Away from the scaffolding, towards the side of the hangar, were rows of machines. The room was more than large enough to house the rows of excavators and diggers with drill bits attached and various attachments lined up on racks waiting to be swapped out.

Hundreds of cables snaked across the floor, twisting and winding, leading from the ship to a dozen computer terminals, like a sick patient undergoing critical surgery and hooked up to life-saving devices.

Beneath the three clamping arms ran a railed track leading to one side of the hangar that was clear of machinery. Beyond was another set of doors, stretching the entire length of the three-hundred-foot hangar. It was obvious the ship could be slid across into another adjoining hangar.

'What's on the other side?' Jason asked, gesturing to the far door.

'Weapons testing,' Forrester said.

Jason had assumed that with no doors, there would be no way to use the craft. Had they hacked the hull and got the ship to fire shots? 'You can use its weapons?'

Forrester shook his head. 'To test how defensive it is against our weapons.'

'And?' Jason probed.

'Not a god-damned scratch,' Forrester sighed.

The Colonel seemed to remember something and checked his watch. He frowned. 'I need to be going,' he said. 'Find yourself a bunk, settle down for the night and tomorrow I'll give you the lowdown on everything you need to make this place more secure.'

'What about a weapon?' Jason asked, eyeing the Glock at Forrester's hip.

'Tomorrow,' Forrester said. 'It's getting too late to be checking firearms in and out and most likely the quarter-master is already asleep.'

'Is there anything I can do in the meantime?' Jason asked, 'I don't want to be sitting around like a dead weight.'

'Grab yourself a radio from stores. Set it to frequency 846. That one is direct to me. Tomorrow I'll give you the frequencies of all the patrols and you can start gathering them together and working out how you want to go about your job. Remember that some guards under your command do not know what goes on in here. So pick your men carefully, ten only inside the facility below level six and the rest above ground.' He took another glance at his watch.

'I've got to be going. You know how to get back to the barracks?'

Jason nodded. 'I'll figure it out.'

'Good,' the Colonel said, marching away almost at the double. 'See you tomorrow.'

Jason stood there watching the scene before him for nearly half an hour. Even this late at night scientists were constantly running tests on the ship. How many years had they had to test things, and still there was more to do? He guessed technology jumped ahead every few years and that meant they could always complete more tests.

He dragged his feet down the steps leading to the hangar floor, anticipation trying to overwhelm him. Some of the scientists looked up as he approached, before turning away to concentrate on their work again.

The fact he wasn't wearing a hazmat suit didn't seem to faze them. Perhaps the Colonel often came in just wearing a uniform.

Needing to approach the ship, he stayed at least ten feet away, but one scientist started excitedly calling over several others. Something on her terminal had jumped to life. Jason wasn't going to miss anything new happening.

Several scientists gathered around the one woman who was manning the station.

'Just had a power surge,' she said, tapping away on the keyboard in front of her, 'and it didn't come from one of our batteries or generators.'

'Something from the ship?' one of the supervisors asked.

'Who knows?' she said. 'But we need to do more tests tomorrow to find out.'

'If it came from the ship, then that's a first.'

The supervisor flicked through a tablet in his hands, swiping the small screen. 'There were several power outputs in the eighties that were measured at about a quarter of what we just got here. We'll need to run comparison experiments to duplicate whatever just happened.' He looked around at all of them, Jason seemed to be included in the find. 'Good work, guys. The day shift will be working their asses off to explain this one—'

A tremendous alarm erupted from speakers set high in the ceiling, cutting off the supervisor mid-sentence. Red lights flared to life at all stations, and radios around the room crackled with static and panicked voices.

The radio on Jason's belt broke out with frantic voices, calling for reinforcements to some unknown location he had yet to discover.

'We're being attacked,' a voice broke through the chaotic babble.

What a shitty first day on the job.

4

Yelling to be heard above the noise of the alarms and shouting scientists, Jason tried to respond, but his radio did not have a return frequency to let him communicate with any of the base guards. He only had the Colonel's number.

Squeezing the call button with 846, he tried to get answers.

'Colonel, come in, this is Major Korzon. What the hell is going on?' There was no answer.

He raced to the door, through the security checkpoint, calling for the guards nearest to hold stations until further orders were given. Whether the soldiers knew he was their new commander or not wasn't clear, but none of them followed him.

Reaching the barracks, he was hoping to find some sort of weapon. He found speakers blaring a new warning. 'Enemies approaching, all personnel to your combat stations. Repeat, all personnel to combat stations.'

Jason headed to the main elevator shaft and through the agonizing wait as it slid up to ground level. Damn it, was taking an age. 'Come on,' he said, slamming a hand against the buttons as if it might make a difference.

The main office was empty, but as he burst from the door into the cold desert night, he could finally see soldiers piling into Humvees and racing for the nearest helicopters parked beside an empty runway.

Lights filled the air, automatically scanning the wispy clouds above. In the distance, he could see a patch of flickering lights coming towards them beyond the wire perimeter fence. He guessed they were not friendly.

Why hadn't he taken a weapon from one of the guards below? Shit, why was he so unprepared?

He spotted a radio tower on the edge of the runway and made a beeline through the darkness towards it. Any height would be an advantage. As he neared the metal construction, a soldier broke cover, gun raised at him.

'Identify yourself!' the soldier screamed.

Jason threw his hands up but kept walking forwards. 'Major Jason Korzon. The new head of security detachment, fifty-one. Stand down, soldier.'

'Bullshit,' the man said, sighting down the rifle.

There wasn't any time to negotiate. The lights in the distance were growing and his adrenaline was up. Jason had to risk it. He ducked and rolled, closing the gap between them and sweeping the man's legs out from underneath him in one smooth motion. He found his footing and snatched up the man's rifle, pointing it down at him whilst using his lead foot to pin the man's pistol to its holster as he tried to yank it free.

'I'm not against you.' Jason said, lowering the rifle. 'I mean it. Colonel Forrester just appointed me today.' He offered the soldier a hand and after a huff, the man accepted the proffered limb.

'Look,' Jason said, helping him up and patting him down. ' I'm new to this place, but if you can find me a weapon, some men and a decent radio frequency, then we can do something about whatever is happening.'

'The long-range troops picked up helicopters coming in from the east,' the man said, spitting a gob of sand on the tarmac. 'Most of our guys are out by the western fence line on a training op. There's nobody here, compared to what there should be.'

The helicopters by the runway thundered to life and spun to face the incoming attackers. But it was so dark that Jason couldn't make out much more than the lights and noise of both forces.

There was a bright flash and deafening boom as explosions tore into the hangars alongside the runway.

'Christ! They're fucking bombing us!,' the soldier cried, sprinting for the tower entrance.

Jason scanned the sky above as a whooshing noise drowned out the man's cries to join him.

Fighter jets. Damned fast ones. They were too high to make out, but his ears knew the noise. More explosions tore through the base, levelling shadowed buildings in the distance. His only chance was to get back to the underground part of the facility. This was no small attack. Those helicopters would breach the airspace in minutes just as the last bombs were deployed, and that meant an organised attack.

All he had to defend himself was his wits, and against a determined force, that was hardly anything at all.

The Humvee he had seen drive off was long gone, plunged into darkness with everything else in the aftermath of the bombs.

Trails of thick black smoke drifted across the base from

the bombed-out buildings, obscuring everything for minutes at a time.

Shots rang out across the base, flickers of gunfire lighting up the watchtowers with temporary silhouettes, but there was no resistance, not even a group of men to throw into combat.

'This way,' he shouted, hoping the man he had just convinced would have the sense to follow him before they were blown to pieces or the helicopters arrived to deliver an extra layer of death.

Why weren't there any base defenses returning fire? Did they think that being so deep in the center of the country they would not be needed? Some turrets wouldn't have been a help.

A stream of explosions tore across the base, forcing them both to duck as they hauled ass towards the underground entrance. What a shitty first day.

5

The facility entrance was still intact, but it couldn't hold out forever. The thought that the enemy were leaving it untouched was nerve-wracking. They would be seeking a way in.

Jason's years of fighting kicked in, getting him ready for the task ahead. But as he eyed the incoming lights crossing the smokey sky and the vehicles piling up behind the perimeter fence, he knew it was not a fight he would win.

He slammed into the door, hoping to barge in, but the locks had been thrown and he was tossed backwards. Groaning, he readied himself to find another way in.

The soldier with him thrust a keycard at a small pad beside the door and a red light set within turned bright green, letting them open the door and roll inside as more bombs flared flames at their backs.

Jason didn't wait. He knew this territory and how to get places. He reached the first door and shoved a hand against the door's security reader. It didn't open. Did he still not have clearance?

'Damn!'

The soldier with him tried and after his palm had been scanned, they were through into the security checkpoint.

They found themselves in front of a firing squad of five men, all patiently waiting for the enemy to come through.

'Don't fire!' they both yelled in unison, stumbling inside.

'Hold!' the group leader said, recognising Jason from earlier and ushering them both past.

'Lister, isn't it?' he asked the panicked soldier who had joined Jason.

Lister nodded, pausing to wipe a smear of black soot and rubble dust from his face.

'Get down and grab a weapon from security. Then get back up here. And you?' the leading soldier asked, eyeing Jason.

'Major Korzon,' Jason said.

The man straightened at the rank. 'Go with Lister, sir, and he'll show you where it is. If things get too hairy before you get back here, then stay down below and protect what matters. Try to find the Colonel. There should be reinforcements en route from Edwards and drones from Area Six. But we have to wait it out. Maybe the training troops will return. Go!'

A series of explosions rocked the building as they ran for the security room, before a sinister silence descended on the facility.

Jason didn't wait. He had a sinking feeling that he knew what was coming and it was headed straight this way. This was an invasion. Maybe not of the country, but of the facility at least. Those half-dozen men couldn't hold off a determined attack for more than a few minutes.

Lister stumbled ahead of him, weariness telling Jason that these men did not have regular training, regardless of the fact that most of them were away at such a crucial time.

They made it through the next checkpoint and into the main facility loop.

'Damn,' Lister said, banging on a door with 'Security' stamped across it. 'Has the base been sealed internally?'

Something wasn't adding up. 'How often do the base soldiers go on training exercises?' Jason asked.

Gunfire echoed from the opposite side of the ringed tunnel, making Lister flinch. 'Can't remember the last one I went on,' he said, attempting another hammering on the door using the butt of his rifle. 'Maybe they could train us how to break down doors when we need to.'

Jason grabbed his arm as he wound up for another whack. 'Don't,' he said with a shake of his head. If the rifle discharged, then they might end up in a bigger mess. He considered taking the weapon and making better use of it than this foolish amateur.

'Does this place have any automated defenses? Turrets that should be firing? Drones that should be launching? Anything like that?'

'Of course,' Lister said. 'Should have tons of them up above ground. I don't know why they aren't firing.'

'I think I might,' Jason said. 'There's an insider.'

The gunfire from within the facility died down. Several small explosions forced motes of dust to flutter down from the concrete cracks in the ceiling. They both gave up trying to beat the door down. The sound of boots scudding on the floor echoed down the corridor.

'Quick,' Jason said, 'we got to get to the hangar. We need to go down.'

'Never been down there,' Lister saids. 'Is there a way out?'

Jason shrugged. 'I honestly don't know,' he said, 'but

there might be more weapons and other people we can use. There's no going back up top. Those guys are gone.'

'I will not leave them,' Lister said. He turned to head for the elevator in a show of bravado that Jason did not expect.

Jason grabbed his arm, spinning him in place. 'They've already gone. Don't you hear them?'

'Hear what? Lister asked.

'No more gunfire,' Jason shouted, realizing the man must have gone partially deaf from the explosions. 'Those guys are gone. Let's go.'

His gaze locked on to Lister's belt and the holstered pistol there. He tugged it free and checked the magazine.

A series of bangs and pops echoed down the corridor.

'They've breached the door,' Jason said. 'We need to get to the hangar now or they'll come from both sides of this loop.'

Gunfire pinged off the walls around them as two soldiers rounded the curve. Jason fired back instinctively. Between the shots, he caught a glimpse of two soldiers in silver-plated armor. They certainly weren't Russian uniforms. They didn't look Chinese and there was no god-damned way they were Korean.

Lister knelt and fired, forcing the invaders to retreat and take cover.

'Come on,' Jason said, sprinting further around the loop, away from the soldiers.

They rounded the corner and faced the huge door.

Running footsteps were coming their way. Jason fired a few random shots at a nearby wall and the footfalls stopped amidst cries to take cover.

It took Jason a second to realize what he needed to do. He placed both hands on the door in the same positions as Forrester and, to his surprise, the hangar doors opened, revealing the airlock inside. For some reason, they had keyed him into these but not the other doors. What the hell was going on?

They stepped inside and the door sealed shut just as the soldiers reached it.

Gas filled the room from the vents in the ceiling. Gunfire echoed outside in single shots and short bursts as the enemy filled the facility.

'Who the hell are they?' Lister asked, checking his magazine. 'Never seen a uniform like it. Russians? Japanese?'

'No idea,' Jason said, pressing a finger to a cut on his arm that he'd not noticed before. 'I'm just a damn recruit.'

Lister seemed confused, but the doors opened and the sight of the alien ship before him took his breath away.

Several scientists were huddled under desks and behind some of the heavier machinery, while a few had managed to get inside some of the diggers. All of them looked afraid, and none of them had a gun.

He remembered Forrester telling him about the weapons testing on the other side of the large door. He screamed at one of the scientists, causing the man to back away, hands up in supplication. 'Can you open the door to the weapons testing facility?'

The perplexed man shook his head.

'N-never been in there, sir,' he said. 'None of us have. It's a different division that deals with weapons testing.'

Jason looked around trying to remain calm. If these people knew what was coming, they might turn on each other and even him. 'We should be safe in here,' he said 'They won't get through that door in a hurry. Is there another way out?'

Most of the scientists shook their heads.

'Like rats in a damned barrel,' Jason muttered.

He couldn't believe it. Here he was trapped in an underground bunker with no way out, waiting to die at the hands of people he didn't know, whilst standing in front of the one thing that he'd always wanted to discover. It was a sick irony, as a feeling of ridicule rumbled deep in the pit of his stomach.

He walked slowly towards the ship, staring up at the manta-ray-like outline. It was as if the ship had been hammered from a solid piece of the purest chrome. He hadn't even touched it yet, and he knew that before he died, he wanted to. If it was the last thing he did.

Several of the scientists started muttering as computers burst into activation. Beeps and sounds emanated from some of the testing instruments scattered around the room.

'Are they activating it from outside?' someone asked.

'Must be aliens,' another said, rushing to the nearest terminal, eyes wide in astonishment. 'They've come back for it!'

'Relax, Smith,' another said, 'it could be any of a hundred things and those attacking are more likely Russian than alien.'

'Damn Russkies,' one put in, testing the weight of a heavy set wrench and eyeing the hangar door.

There was a hissing sound which could only have been the exterior airlock door closing.

'They're inside,' one of the scientists said.

Jason hunkered down beside a steel crate, back against the cold metal, and gripped the pistol tightly between his sweaty fingers.

He called out orders for them to hide and be ready to fight, but it was pointless. These men were not soldiers. Even Lister wasn't what he would call a real soldier.

Jason leant out from the side of the crate as the doors

split apart. A dozen soldiers, kitted out in bright chrome armor, lined the width of the airlock. Their faces were grim with determination and before anyone inside could react, they opened fire on the unarmed scientists scattering across the room.

Jason fired back several shots, twisting and coming out on the other side of the crate, before rolling to a new position and firing again. He'd hit two of the soldiers, but only one was floored, grabbing limply at his neck where the bullet had burrowed between the armor plates.

Lister's rifle rattled off, forcing the enemy to spread out behind cover. Soon, though, that was drowned out by the firing weapons of the strange attackers.

Why didn't you take the damn rifle? Jason scolded himself. Idiot. He was too busy trying to stay alive to do anything else about it.

'Focus,' he murmured, trying to calm his nerves and concentrate.

Lister let loose a tremulous scream as they gunned him down. Jason peeked out to see the soldier's lifeless form on the floor, blood pooling around him.

Standing in the doorway, as the soldiers fanned out around the room, was Colonel Forrester, Glock in hand.

'I know you're there, recruit,' he said, giving the men around him time to spread out further.

Jason had two bullets; the counting was a subconscious talent he'd developed through a hundred firefights.

'It's Major Korzon, Colonel,' Jason said, speaking away from the entrance so it wouldn't be obvious exactly where he was.

'Well, whatever it is,' the Colonel said, 'it's over, boy.'

'So you're with the Russians, then?' Jason said, scanning around for his options.

'Ha,' Forrester said, 'they wouldn't be smart enough to get this far, no country would. It's a shame you had to come along the day before the climax of my time here.'

'You disabled the defenses?' Jason said, risking a dash towards a stack of barrels closer to the ship.

Bullets tore through the air around his head as one soldier spotted him and opened fire. It stopped abruptly as Jason pushed his back against the cool, curving steel.

'Yes,' Colonel Forrester said, his voice calm as ever in the sudden quiet.

'And sent the men on a training exercise just before?'

Forrester laughed. 'Of course, recruit, and secured the weapons room, and made sure you couldn't interfere with our plans, and cut the cables on the base's comms line and a hundred other things, all culminating in everyone at this facility being obliterated and the place being wiped off the face of this planet. Including you.'

Jason had the man's location pinpointed. He would have to run and shoot, make it behind the ship, then sprint in a direct line for the diggers. If he could get inside one and drive to the door, he might make it out alive, if not uninjured.

He had two shots. Should he fire both at the Colonel or wait until the others closed in on him and try to take one of their rifles?

A voice yelled from close beside him. 'Got him!' Jason dived towards the ship, pivoting to plant a single bullet in the man's head before twisting to face the Colonel. In his periphery, he spotted the traitor raising his Glock. Jason fired, missing as his foot clipped a tangle of cables.

He staggered towards the ship, ready to crawl underneath the bracing clamps for cover. He was too late. The Colonel fired and the Glock's bullet slammed into him like a punch in the shoulder, throwing him forwards against the ship. He slapped a hand to the wound to stem the blood flow and ducked, trying to get underneath before a second bullet could end him.

Pain seared through his body but he pushed through, shifting on his belly beneath the alien spacecraft. The Colonel's laughter echoed behind him in between the fire from his soldiers shooting from different angles. When he made it to the other side, he stood and turned. Pain was shooting through his arm, and he placed his bloody hand against the side of the ship to steady himself.

'You would have made a good leader to these men,' the Colonel said, when the staccato of bullets faded to a harsh ringing in Jason's ears. 'Clearly, you know how to fight and how to crawl away while you still can. Unfortunately, this is one tactical retreat you cannot win. There's nowhere to go, recruit.'

The ringing in Jason's ears became a deep buzzing. He knew the Colonel was making his way around the ship. It was only a matter of time. He was clean out of bullets. Perhaps he could wrestle the man? No, the others would shoot before he had time to get close. He knew then that his end had come. He breathed a sigh of relief and looked up at the alien ship. There was a little comfort in knowing he had accomplished his dream. It had been worth the years of effort. He just wished he'd had more of a chance to figure it out. But life was full of mysteries, most of which people just took for granted.

He had achieved a dream and as if in a dream, a door opened up in front of him. The hole was getting wider and wider until it formed an elliptical circle in the side of the ship. Was he imagining it, or was he delirious? How much blood had drained from the wound? The noise of gunfire around him shrunk to a distant glooping, like bubbles in a boiling stew.

Perhaps the bullets were striking him and he didn't even feel it anymore. He looked at his bloody handprint, stained on the gleaming exterior of the ship. The black doorway had opened up in front of him, big enough for a man to step through. The hull of the ship seemed to have morphed ever so slightly. A set of two steps had extruded from the hull near his feet.

His vision blurred as sweat trickled into his eyes. The blood felt warm on his chest. A look behind him confused things even more. The soldiers, a dozen of them and the Colonel, were all shooting at him, as if in a final firing squad. The tips of their weapons flared, but a barrier had formed across his vision and the bullets struck it, causing ripples like the surface of a puddle in a heavy summer rain. Dizziness at the display made him twist away, and he entered the ship feeling a cool breeze from inside.

If this was death, he thought, he couldn't think of a better way to go out.

J ason walked into the black circle feeling disorientated. A cool breeze washed over him, mingling with the hot fluids that dripped down his torso. He stared into a wide circular space, the same smooth plastering of metal. Like liquid silver poured against the walls it coated the entire interior.

A chest-height window encircled the entire room, giving him a three-hundred-and-sixty-degree view of the soldiers surrounding the ship.

He staggered forwards, wondering if there were any commands or controls he needed to deal with, or whether he should just lie down and die.

A tinny voice echoed within the small room. 'How can I help you?'

Jason stared around, expecting to see a female figure standing over him like some lost angel and welcoming him to the abyss, or possibly one of the soldiers outside, leveling a rifle at him for the final bullet.

There was no one there.

'Please get me out of here,' he begged.

The pain was overtaking every sensation that his body could conjure.

'You've got it,' the voice replied. It sounded cheery, as if it was enjoying his pain.

The interior of the ship hummed around him, drowning out the headache that threatened his sanity.

Something bumped into the back of his knees. He sat back, falling into a chair that had appeared from the floor.

He felt gravity pull him back as the humming grew in intensity. The view to the front of the ship tilted towards the hangar ceiling. The ship was leaning backwards, aimed at the roof.

'Shit,' Jason said. 'I hope you're not planning to do what I think you're gonna do.' Then he realized he was talking to nobody at all. He really was going mad! At least it involved his dreams of going on the spacecraft. This was a fun way to die.

What he assumed was the engine noise rose to a crescendo. The clamps holding the spacecraft were shaking. Cracks formed in the metal as the ship tried to break free of their hold.

A grinding sound echoed above the infernal humming. A flash of blue lights seared Jason's retinas as four bright beams exited the front of the ship. They bored into the roof of the hangar, before it shattered into a thousand red-hot fragments and sent the soldiers below diving for cover.

Jason barely managed a breath as his spine and internal organs were sucked into the back of the seat and the world around him became a blur. The ship accelerated at an unprecedented rate, up through the hole it had made in the hangar roof, through a hundred feet of solid rock and out into the blackness of the Nevada night sky.

Distance and time became a blur. All Jason could do was

hold on for dear life to the sides of the chair, praying to a god that he'd never believed in, that everything was going to be alright. In reality, he knew, deep down, that he was bleeding out and that if it didn't stop soon, everything would be over, dream or not.

The intense forward motion slowed and the alien ship slowed to a halt. Through the window, Jason could see the speckled pinpricks of stars on all sides and a bright glow behind the ship. He dared not turn around to look at the glow for fear of what he might see.

He knew it, but did not want to believe that he was in space, miles above the earth, in a ship that he had spent eighteen years, four months and five days trying to see. Twisting in the seat, which swivelled with his motion, he sucked in a sharp breath at the sight he knew he would see. Earth. The entire globe gently spinning below in its orbit of the sun.

It was either too much to take in or he'd lost too much blood, but his vision dimmed to match the blackness of space around him and his consciousness drifted away to the stars.

J ason was still bleeding when he awoke. It was much more of a trickle now, rather than the constant pumping that he had endured before blacking out. He'd expected to wake up in a hospital somewhere or in a place where the nightmare about an alien spaceship flying away from Earth had never happened.

Instead, he was on the warm floor of that strange ship, in a round room surrounded by curving walls, with only the chair he had sat on and a table that had not been there when he'd first entered.

Everything still had that poured molten metal look to it, except now his blood coated most of the surfaces. At some point, he must have lain on the table, which, looking at it now, seemed more like a bed.

'Hello?' he said to the room. Staring around, he thought he remembered a voice. He couldn't be sure though; everything had been such a blur.

'Good morning,' a woman's voice said, cheery and clipped. 'Are you still dying?'

Jason tried not to laugh, but it escaped him regardless.

'Probably,' he chuckled. The calculations flitted through his mind and if it was even close to morning, as the voice implied, then he'd escaped the worst. He would have to bind the wound and before he even finished the thought, he had torn off his shirt and ripped a strip from the blood-speckled cloth.

'Nice abs,' the female voice said.

Jason couldn't believe what he was hearing. 'I need medical supplies, please. Whoever you are.'

There was a long pause. 'Fascinating—I mean, fabricating.'

There was a rumbling from one part of the room. A portion of the wall slid forward like a cube being pushed through a silver plastic bag and a box, complete with a door, formed in front of Jason's eyes.

'Nice trick,' he said, stumbling over to the box. It opened easily enough, hinging down and revealing a jumbled medical kit within a bright white hollow. It looked more advanced than what he was used to on the battlefield. There was a needle and thread for stitches, several syringes of different coloured liquids he didn't trust, and a host of bandages and suction devices, besides an array of other bits that he didn't know what to do with.

Immediately he set to work on his shoulder. Some sort of work had been done to his injuries; they were flecked with a dark brown powder, possibly a clotting agent.

Halfway through the process and between cringing grimaces of pain, he managed to speak. 'Perhaps you can formulate a gun with that machine if you can make anything I ask for. Finish myself off nice and clean without all this horrible needlework. Not to mention the post-traumatic stress of having been flown out to space on an alien spacecraft by a female entity that refuses to show itself. Oh, and betrayal by my higher-ups and failing in my duty on the first day.'

'That would be a waste of resources,' the voice said.

'Of course,' Jason said, trying to calm himself before he exploded into a confused fury. Now he knew he wasn't going to die, he needed answers. 'What the hell is going on? This ship hasn't moved for eighty years and now it decides to fly my dying ass out beyond the damn atmosphere. With the exception of the entire base being attacked thing, I think I deserve an explanation.'

'This ship can only be activated by someone with a partially direct lineage from a former owner.' The voice said. ' I sensed you were in danger and to help preserve your DNA, I was able to program the navigation systems to escape from your home planet.'

Former owner? Had one of his ancestors found this thing? 'Who owned it?'

'That is classified information,' the voice said after a second of hesitation.

Jason heaved a sigh and sat in the chair. 'And you are?'

'I am Roo. A fully equipped and unlinked artificial intelligence program.'

'Unlinked?'

'It means not attached,' Roo said simply. 'Who are you?'

'Major Korzon,' Jason said, not knowing why he was engaging with voices in his head. 'Jason Korzon. Human,' he added, just in case. 'But I guess now I'm either a fugitive awaiting sentence, or some kind of traumatized incident survivor. Or I died, and this is the universe's idea of a cosmic joke.

'Korzon?' Roo asked.

'Yes. What of it?'

There was no answer.

'Why?' Jason pressed.

'Are you related to Korzon The Wise, a seventh-century Mongolian war general?'

'Yeah, sure, why not,' Jason said. 'Now, are you going to take me back down or am I being held hostage?'

'I haven't decided yet,' Roo said.

'Great,' he said, tearing himself out of the chair, which seemed to have moulded itself to his buttocks, and moved to stare at the stars all around the ship.

'I knew something like this was real,' he said. 'Who would have guessed I'd be the first one to discover it?' The recognition would be unparalleled, assuming Colonel Forrester and his cronies didn't show up to take him out. A thought struck him.

'If you can take me back down to another Air Force base, then I can inform them what happened and they'll give me a promotion and hopefully put me in charge of...' He drifted into his thoughts. What the hell could he even want now? A promotion to what? He had achieved his goal, discovered an alien life form and used an alien ship to fly above the Earth's atmosphere. He'd potentially made first contact. Where did it go from here?

8

'Roo?'

'Yes, Jason Human?'

He'd had time to think now. There were many things he had a responsibility to find out. And he had thought of them for years, but like all fantasies, when it gets real, it changes. 'Where do you come from?'

'I am linked to this ship.'

'And where does this ship come from?'

'From the binary galaxies NGC Four six seven six. Located two hundred and ninety million light-years away from this location.'

'Holy shit!' He jumped up from the seat, wincing at the pain in his shoulder but ecstatic. There was no doubt now, he had made the biggest discovery in the history of the Earth.

'How did you get here?'

'There are no database details on this subject. I'm sorry, Jason Human. Do you require fresher clothing?'

He tilted his head, feeling the aches emerging, and

stared down at his grubby—burnt—blood-stained uniform. 'If you've got it.'

There was a buzzing from the small box, which had yet to retract into the ship. Once it was finished, he walked over, opened the door and pulled out a heap of soft, gray clothing.

He dragged the top over his head, then made to fumble at his belt. He paused and looked around. The circular space was empty. As he undid the belt and let his pants slide down, the ship made a strange humming noise.

'What's that noise?'

'Processing video and x-ray for future reference on human anatomy.'

'Hang on! Wait,' he said, you can't just—'

'I can,' she blurted out.

Attempting to move at speed, he yanked the new pants up and reveled in the comfort against his skin.

'Can this machine make anything then?' he said, enjoying the feel of fresh cloth.

'No, Roo said. 'Its options are very limited. Basic survival and sustenance.'

'Food?' Jason suggested.

'Yep,' Roo said. 'Coming up.' The door to the box closed by itself and a rumbling vibration started up from within.

He withdrew something akin to a hard lump of condensed beef jerky. ''Don't I get to choose?'

'The nano materials needed to create this food have been in storage for over ten thousand years,' Roo declared. 'So, no. I cannot provide fresh food on your journey.'

'They'll be no journey, Roo,' he said. 'I need you to take me right back down to the surface. We've got a lot of work to do to figure this thing out.'

'Thing?'

'I mean you,' he stumbled, 'or—whatever this ship is. I

just need a moment to figure out where would be the safest place to go to figure that out.'

'Safety alert,' Roo said. 'Incoming.'

'Safety what?' Jason said, spitting out the meaty lump he had been slowly chewing.

'Incoming projectiles.'

'Wait, where?'

'Please take your seat, Jason Human,' Roo said. 'Initiating quantum jump.'

'Wait, no, hang on, what the—'

'Don't look behind you!' Roo chimed.

Jason spun, and through the rear part of the ship's window, he could just about make out a dozen small flaring objects, gaining speed and growing in size.

'Quantum jump in three—two—'

'Shit no, stop!' Jason screamed. The chair he was sitting on twisted him around to face forward.

For a split second, he only saw the blackness of space before it twisted into a mirage of colors, and a circular spiral appeared connected to the ship by a beam of intense golden light.

9

The vortex in front of the ship expanded in size until Jason thought it was going to swallow his entire vision. His feet and fingers felt tingly. Something was happening inside him. Butterflies in his stomach turned to the sensation of being on a roller coaster, except a hundred times worse. He wanted to throw up. He needed it to stop. He begged for it to stop, but the intense feeling grew, until all he could do was hold on to the stumpy sides of the chair and hope this wasn't his actual death.

Space became a cylinder around the ship, swirling with intense colors as if he had been flushed down a multicolored water slide whilst being injected directly to the highest point of an LSD trip.

He could barely keep his eyes open, yet something compelled him to watch the unique event that was happening in front of him.

The feeling reached a crescendo. Slowly, then faster, as if someone was slamming on the brakes of the roller coaster, the feeling was projected out of his body. The darkness of space reappeared as the vortex shrunk in size before the ship.

He had expected to see the darkness of space and the pinpricks of starlight around him. He guessed what had happened, that he had traveled... somewhere. But looking around, he saw something must have gone horribly wrong. Beams of light remained in the space around them. Dozens of red and blue beams, appearing then disappearing. He blinked, but they were still happening. For a long moment, he just stared out at the patch of darkness in front of the ship.

Something moved in the distance, a pinprick that swelled to encompass much of the forward-facing window. It grew until he could make out a trail of light behind and then came the realization that it was another ship, much, much larger than his. It rocketed towards him, closing the gap with tremendous speed.

He dived from habit as the ship swept right over them, giving Jason a chance to study the crater-pocked hull far too close for comfort. His little ship rattled as the titan passed so close he could have opened a window and touched it.

As it flew over, he glanced around, eyes wide, tracking the ship as it grew faint again.

'That was close,' Roo said. 'My sensors failed to pick that one up so soon after the Nexus jump.'

More things moved in the darkness beyond the window. Silvery-shaped metallic objects whizzed around, followed by trails of popping light. They were smaller crafts, similar in size to his.

It was then that an enormous triangular ship tore across the front of the craft. His tiny ship rocked in the titan's wake. Another ship passed them in the distance. Huge turrets at the front of it flared in the darkness of space, like a battery of ocean warships in combat at night. The blazing tips of the barrels forced him to squint. Bright red beams from a third, even larger ship struck its hull, opening a huge gash in the metallic hull. The smaller ship ripped apart, like a man slowly tearing a baguette of bread in half. Jason was sure he could see bodies and items being sucked out from inside the gaping holes on either end of the broken ship.

The inside was layered into decks, like bricks in a wall, exposing the innards as it drifted away. All of this seemed to happen in slow motion. Flitting around every large space-ship were hundreds of small craft, maybe even smaller than what he was in. A squadron of them peeled away from the split ship and flew towards him.

'What the hell is going on?' Jason screamed, holding onto the seat even tighter than he had during the wormhole experience.

Roo's voice was barely audible above the alarms still ringing out. 'I'm afraid we've arrived in the middle of a battle, Jason Human. I apologize. My calculations should have meant that this part of the Divide would be clear of inhabitants. Maybe I'll have better luck next time. It's been so long, I'm still rusty.'

'What do you mean, better luck next time?' Jason said, staring behind him through the rear of the ship as the squadron of fighters encircled the craft, firing directly at them. Just beyond the glass, there was a flare-up, the same as there had been when Forrester was shooting at him. Were they shields?

The nimble ships zipped off as a series of smaller craft exited another large carrier that lumbered into view below them, dwarfing all the ships he had seen so far.

There was so much to understand and to take note of. Blue and red laser beams shredded the sides of great black and blue cruisers that looked as if they had been made from a mishmash of scrap ships, sewn together to make something serviceable. Ballistic projectiles cannoned across his vision, punching rows of holes in the other vessel. It was chaos. Everything—everywhere was either being attacked or attacking.

Jason tried to calm himself by counting the ships around him. He ignored the laser beams that were flickering left and right, searing blisters into his retinas, and focused on trying to count each ship and work out what the hell was going on.

There were now at least ten large ships lining up on one side of his craft and fifteen large ships on the other side. In between, exactly where he was, were smaller squadrons, darting about in some sort of fighting skirmish. As soon as the larger vessels got close together, the explosions and general chaos grew in intensity. Watching such monstrosities obliterate each other with enormous weapons made him fear for his puny little ship, which he had no control over.

'Roo, we need to get the hell out of here, right now,' he said, unable to tear his gaze from another group of fighters twisting around to come for them after taking out a rival squadron. Yellow streaks trailed them, showing where they had been, like the taillights of a vehicle, etched into the blackness before thinning out into vapor.

'Engaging evasive maneuvers,' Roo's voice calmly announced.

The ship lurched left, then right, tilting up in a looping flip and throwing Jason back into his seat. He could barely crane his neck around to see whether the other ships were still following them. The maneuvers kept on going and going and he felt nausea growing inside. The only thing that stopped him from throwing up was the fact that he needed to scream at Roo to stop.

'Danger avoided,' Roo said.

'Who's trying to kill us?' Jason managed between lungfuls of panicked breaths.

'According to my database, these ships roughly resemble those from the Vistar and the Harken. This is a battle.'

'No shit, Roo,' Jason cried 'Could you be more helpful?'

'I have just performed a Pugachev's cobra, crossed with a three hundred and sixty-degree Kulbit maneuver, effectively saving your life.'

'Great,' Jason scoffed. 'Perhaps get me the hell out of here and back to Earth instead of showing off?'

'We are out of Nexus fuel, Jason Human.'

'Nexus fuel?' Jason asked, struggling not to lose his temper with the ship's snarky attitude.

'A rare element, once found in the system beyond Nexus Gate two.'

'OK,' Jason said. 'I need to get home, so we need fuel. How long would it take to get to this system's gate thing from here?'

'Calculating...' Roo said. 'Without the ability to jump, it will take approximately one year, three months and six days to arrive at Nexus Gate two.

'Oh, great,' Jason said, pounding a fist into the armrest of the uncomfortable chair.

10

J ust a year and three months. No problem,' Jason said, fighting the dark realization of being stranded in deep space.

'And six days...'

'And six days. How could I forget? I hope you've got more of that crappy jerky stashed away somewhere then, Roo? Also, I'll be needing a doctor who can fix my arm before it falls off, or can a one-handed captain pilot this heap of crap? I swear if you don't—'

'Incoming transmission,' Roo said.

A portion of the window at the front of the ship turned black, displaying several strange runes or something out of a Lord of the Rings novel, that Jason had no idea how to decipher.

The grizzled face of an old man in his fifties or sixties appeared on the screen.

Out of all the things in the middle of an alien space battle, a human face was the last thing Jason had expected to see. He must be going out of his mind. Or was this actually another human from Earth?

'This is Captain Partel,' the man said.

'Er, hello, Captain,' Jason stammered, his words turning into a flurry of questions. 'You've got to help with what's going on. Why and how are you up here? Can you stop those ships from coming for me again? Will you get me back home?'

The questions rolled off his tongue, not giving the man on the screen a chance to answer until the wrinkled forehead topped with a balding scalp creased in a deep frown.

Jason paused his rapid-fire monologue of questions.

'Slow down, boy,' Captain Partel said. 'Why are you asking me how I got here? *You're* the one who appeared out of nowhere and nearly crashed into me! I've burned up sixteen percent more of my fuel allowance for this run, using the overclock booster to get out of your way, and I damn well expect you to cover the costs, boy.'

Jason tried to think; it was all getting too much for him. 'As soon as I get back to Earth,' he said, 'and they know about what's going on up here—' he looked around—'all of this, then I can pay you back.'

'I don't care which pitiful little Seeder planet that you came from. They're springing up like moon barons in the Jilter system. You're going to need to pay me back much sooner than that.'

'OK, OK,' Jason said. 'I can get you the money or whatever it is you use up here. But first I need to get to Earth and to get back to Earth, all you need to do is give me some Nexus fuel and I swear I will bring anything you want back with me.'

'First off,' the captain said. 'I have no damn idea what Nexus fuel is and second, there is no way I'm going to sit here in the middle of this battle waiting for you to come back and repay me what you owe.' The captain seemed to think for a moment. His face lightened at the thought of something.

'I can see you're in a spot of bother here.' He looked around at the battle off-screen. 'Me too, as I didn't expect to get caught up in this mess on my usual run. So instead of standing here and bickering like two old Fang females, I propose that if you don't want your ship to be destroyed in a blast of Vistar lasers or Harken ballistics, then I suggest you fly into our cargo bay.'

'No problem,' Jason said, wondering what the old man was on about and how he was going to pilot the ship into another.

'Smart move, boy,' Partel said. 'Hold on a moment and I'll bring us alongside. And make it quick before these lasers tear us apart.' Someone was talking to him and he turned to face them, getting angry at whoever was on the receiving end. He turned back to the screen. 'We've got another squadron of Vistar elite fighters heading for us. My cargo ain't worth risking today. Two minutes to intercept. Hurry, boy.'

The screen went blank.

'Roo,' Jason said. 'Where are you? We need to do this. Help me. I can't pilot this ship by myself. Tell me how to do it or do it for me.'

'Any manners with that? Roo asked.

'Please,' Jason said, not caring about groveling to a computer. 'Thank you and you're amazing.'

'A bit too much,' Roo replied, 'but it's been a while since anyone called me such things, so you have a deal, Jason Human. One docking maneuver coming up. Also, did you know we are being tracked by a titan cruiser off our starboard bow?'

'No,' Jason said. 'What can we do about it?'

'I can perform some maneuvers before we dock,' she said. 'Might throw them off our case?'

'No, not that again,' Jason said, putting a hand to his stomach. 'Just dock with Captain Partel's ship.'

Captain Partel's scarred ship cruised around them, and Jason followed it with his gaze. It was fifty times bigger than his little ship, dwarfing the view from his bridge window. Roo's little ship, he corrected himself.

A pair of enormous hangar doors, set central to the captain's ship, slid smoothly apart in front of them. A series of green lights around the dark metal door frame flashed as they parted in silence. The lack of sound in space was eerie. His entire experience of battle had been a noisy, chaotic affair, that pummeled the senses, forcing him to adapt or die. This ponderous muted destruction was something entirely new to him.

There was no video feed this time, but Captain Partel's voice cracked from speakers hidden in the walls of Roo's ship. 'Hurry, boy,' he said, 'park next to the broken class two Vistar command ship and stay there until we're out of this messy excuse for a battle.'

'The class what?' Jason said, but there was no answer. 'Roo?'

'I have it,' she said. 'Please be aware that this is not a normal flight ship. Scans indicate there are dozens of different illegal items on board. Unless the delay in my updates have been so slow that they have introduced new empire laws that I'm unaware of. Although there has been some lag, as I cannot identify all the ships present in this battle.'

'Just focus on setting us down,' Jason said, taking in the strange interior of Partel's ship.

Half of the cargo bay was filled with wrecks, broken and

mangled portions of ships, and piles of containers that looked like they had been long lost and yet never opened. The walls were padded as if the heaps of miscellaneous cargo were patients in an insane asylum.

The other half of the bay was stacked with metal crates, containers, barrels and boxes packed from the furthest walls right up to where two run-down ships lay like wounded soldiers.

The front of Jason's ship pivoted in the narrow space toward the pair of ships.

Piles of shining scrap metal had been packed into some of the furthest corners, but even with all the cargo, there was still more than enough space to park several dozen like his own ship.

There was a heavy banging sound and a second ring of windows, lower down in the bridge, opened, showing clamps latching onto the bottom of their ship. A dizzy sensation of movement rumbled through the cargo bay and Jason waited to find out if they had made it out of the battle alive. Was the captain also performing a cobra maneuver to escape?

'Roo?' Jason said, realizing that he may have to convince the captain of his ability to get back to Earth. He couldn't admit some disembodied voice had guided him from the start. 'What's the name of this ship?

'*Nexus One,*' Roo said.

'Anything I should know about it before I speak with this Captain Partel?'

'There are around sixty-one thousand things you should know,' Roo said.

'Great,' Jason said.

'This Partel is likely a smuggler,' Roo went on. 'I have been able to download some basic details from his ship's system and it seems like a lot has changed in the empire since I was last an active part of it. I could give you some advice, but it will be outdated.'

'So I'm on my own then?' Jason muttered. 'What happens if—'

There was a banging on the hull of the ship. It rang out like a gong.

It felt stupid, but Jason said, 'come in.'

An airlock door from the inside of the ship materialized and swung open. Captain Partel strode in, dressed in a tight-fitting, aged gray uniform.

A female, who, unlike the captain, was not a human followed him in. Her slender features were humanoid, dressed in a scale-textured one-piece jumpsuit. Similar to the captain's uniform, it was tight but not for the same reasons. The gut on Partel had nothing on the slender curves of the woman. If that was what she was.

Like a mismatch of genetics between a cat and a woman, she eyed him warily. It wasn't the fact that she held a large and futuristic-looking rifle that made her seem predatory, or the short, sleek hair that covered part of her body and could only be described as fur. There was something in her poise. Something that made Jason want to run away, yet not turn his back on her. Her pupils were a hypnotic purple and bored into him with as much curiosity as suspicion.

'So then,' Captain Partel said, his eyes roving greedily over the circular bridge. 'You really are alone?'

'Well, except for the computer,' Jason said. 'I'm sorry about the cost to your mission or whatever it was,' he said, trying hard to cover his losses. 'But I need to get back home to Earth.'

'Ah yes,' Partel said, 'one of the Seeder's worlds, no doubt. Is that where you got this ship from?'

'Yes,' Jason said, 'and I can pay you when we get back there.'

'And,' the captain's voice took on a note of curiosity as he eyed the smooth contours of the interior, 'there are more Ancient Empire ships there?'

'Erm.' Jason hesitated. Would a lie get this captain to take him home? Judging by the sound of disbelief in the old man's scratchy voice, he doubted it. The truth would suffice. 'Maybe.'

'And these ships can all jump through space like a Nexus gate?'

'Maybe,' Jason muttered, feeling things getting well out of his control.

'He lies,' the cat woman said, twitching the rifle at Jason. 'This ship is special.' She partly hissed the last word.

'I can see that, Silver,' Partel said, 'That was blindingly obvious when he nearly crashed into us.'

'Didn't mean that,' Jason said quickly. 'Roo was in control.'

'Roo?' Silver asked, panning the rifle around the room as if expecting someone to jump out and attack her.

'The computer,' Jason said, looking up. 'Roo, you there?'

There was no answer.

'Roo?'

Nothing. What the hell? Was she not working?

'That's enough games,' Partel said, pulling a pistol tucked into the back of his uniform pants.

Years of training kicked in. Jason bolted forwards, rushing the captain before he could pull the weapon completely free. He slammed into the man's large bulk, thrusting him back against the wall. As he raised his fist to punch, the cold hard press of a barrel against his temple stopped him.

'Don't you dare,' Silver said, kicking Partel's exotic pistol away from Jason's reach.

Jason froze. He wasn't willing to risk his life any further. She hadn't shot him yet, so perhaps he could get out of this mess.

He let go of the captain's tunic and without hesitation, Captain Partel slammed a fist into his face, knocking him to the floor. Before Jason could rise, Silver's boot was planted firmly against his chest. The thin-plated boots ended at her thighs, giving a look similar to that of stockings. He turned his head and spat out the blood that filled his mouth.

'Should I finish him, Captain?' she asked, squinting down at Jason. He noticed her white teeth were pointed, like those of an animal.

'No,' Partel said. 'Can't see any controls in here. Maybe he knows how to use this ship. We'll keep him for the moment. Throw him in the brig.'

The foot was removed, something tight was corded around his hands, and Silver yanked Jason to his feet.

'What do you think you're doing? Jason asked as Silver bustled him towards the door. 'You told me to come in here. Here I am, and you want to throw me in a cell? You're a liar and a cheat, Partel!'

'No,' Partel said, calmly, 'what I said was that if you don't want your ship to be destroyed in a blast of Harken ballistics or Vistar lasers, then fly inside. This ship is armed with both. If you didn't do as I said, I would have destroyed you. Do not blame me for your stupidity.'

11

Silver jabbed Jason in the small of his back, forcing him to take a staggered step out onto the cargo bay.

'Hey, take it easy, lady,' Jason said, stumbling to the nearest corridor. 'You always work for a backstabber or is this a first?'

Jason could hear a small hiss escape Silver's mouth. 'He is no backstabber. He told you the truth, and you interpreted it differently to what he meant.'

'So not the first time,' Jason said.

'Just keep moving,' Silver said.

The corridors leading through the ship were tightly packed with goods and cargo hold overspill. Whatever this captain intended, he meant to make a profit wherever he was heading. There were a few others on the ship. One or two soldiers rushed past and a small team of engineers headed towards the cargo bay.

Jason had determined how close the cat woman was behind him, and even though his hands were tied, he reckoned he could spin and take her out before she could fire the rifle at the small of his back.

As if sensing his thoughts, the predatory woman had let a gap widen between them when he looked over his shoulder.

A voice echoed down the corridor. 'Commander Silver, Commander?'

Silver broke off her challenging stare at their little showdown and stopped to look at the man who had raced up to them.

'Ensign Hicks,' she said, 'what now?'

'Sorry to disturb you, commander,' Hicks said. 'There's a Harken destroyer out, searching for us. It's picked up our signal and it's been on our tail for the last twenty minutes. They've been scanning us. They must know that we have that strange ship on board. Is it true what the men are saying about it?'

Silver hissed, giving no vocal answer, but her scowl told the story.

'Just get back to it, Hicks,' she said. 'Make sure that the captain knows. He's in the cargo bay, so tell him I'll meet him on the bridge once this man is secure in the brig.'

Hicks ran his gaze over Jason. 'He's from the ship?'

'Just get on with it,' Silver said, her teeth gritted in anger.

They continued the rest of the journey in near silence, stepping aside as men and women ran past them.

It was obvious when they reached the prison block as there was a single guard on the door and, as if a universal law had been accepted, there were bars on the main entranceway. He wondered why prison bars were always vertical. Was there something to it?

Inside, the area was even more run down than the rest of the ship. Rust, grime and debris had built up on the walls, like a coating of paint over decades of service. He couldn't tell if that meant it was well-used or not used at all.

The guard opened the door using some sort of code pad set in the frame.

'Throw him in with the other one, Commander?' the guard asked.

'No,' Silver said. 'This one goes in alone.'

He nodded. 'I hear there's trouble coming, Commander. Is it true?'

'There was always trouble on this ship. Just be ready for it.'

'Treachery too,' said Jason.

'Shut it, ball brains,' the man said, taking hold of Jason, clearly reveling in the power play and shoving him down a double row of cells.

The ten-foot square cells lined either side of the wide corridor. There weren't any doors or bars on them, and Jason wondered if they were all empty. Hadn't they said something about another prisoner?

Before he had a chance to look around, the guard thrust him at the nearest opening and slammed a hand on a screen outside before Jason coiled and spun on him. A slender beam of blue light flashed in front of the doorway, rising, then falling in a line before disappearing.

As the man turned to walk away, Jason took his chance. He leapt through the open doorway, ready to strangle the man from behind. His face met something hard and painful, and his entire body was thrown back into the cell, reeling from the unexpected resistance.

Silver poked her head around the corner and shook her head in disappointment as he lurched to his feet. 'Not as clever as you seemed to be, are you?'

A beeping alarm echoed twice throughout the ship and she looked away, eyes wide, before sprinting off without another word.

'What a shitty first day,' Jason said, eyeing his rust-coated cell.

'Could be worse,' a hushed voice said from across the corridor.

'Oh yeah?' Jason asked, trying to see who the speaker was, but failing.

'Could be dead,' a figure said, moving into the door-frame so they were face to face across the corridor.

Dressed in a tank top and pocket pants, the figure was not human. He was humanoid or nearly human, except for the dozens of electronic pieces that seemed either fused to his body or connected via wires and cables. Patches of bare skin on his arms were implanted with circuit boards and sockets, like the motherboard of a computer, before merging back to flesh. His right cheek had a square cut out and a metal plate had been inserted into where the flesh should have been. Three slots that reminded Jason of a retro Nintendo 64 cartridge slot could be seen in the metal plate. Two were already full, with the last one empty, showing a connector within.

A maze of wires mixed with hair looped in and out of his skull. His thin frame was enhanced with a myriad of mismatched metal plates, sockets, and what could only be processors pressed into his taut gray skin. One of his eyes glowed green and up one side of his neck were slots for what looked like car fuses to Jason.

'You know it's rude to stare, or do you just find me that attractive?'

'Sorry,' Jason said. 'It's just I'm not used to... well, to any of this.'

'So what did you do to get in here? Or not do, for that matter?'

'I refused to give the captain my ship.'

The computer man chuckled at Jason's reply.

'What about you?' Jason asked.

'Well. He's a smuggler and I guess I'm a worthwhile prize.'

The alarms flared up in the distance again before dying down. 'How so?' Jason asked.

'I'm a Humdroid. Too smart for my own good. Cocky too, if you hadn't noticed. But I don't care. Do you have a name, or will it not be worth my limited time to bother finding out?'

'I'm Jason Korzon,' Jason said. 'Major, if that's even important out here.'

'Someone in your family had a sense of humor,' the robot man said. 'I don't care if you're a major or a minor in the scheme of things, as long as you're not a pain in my ass.'

The man was odd, no doubt Jason thought. There were some mental issues, but nothing too close to madness. He decided it was better to get some information than stew over the last few hours. 'And your name?'

'Calculator,' the Humdroid said. 'Friends call me Calc. You might even be privileged enough to, if we can get to that ship of yours. What is it? A class three Harken junk blaster or a class six Vistar elite military juggernaut?'

'Er,' Jason stammered, 'I don't know.'

'Well, whatever it is, I can fly it,' Calc said, oozing confidence. 'I could fly a rogue comet with a fire extinguisher. Nearly did once, but that's another story. My speciality is navigation as well as being a bloody clever bastard, but I guess it's the former that Captain Partel wants to use as a trading chip. Heck, he might even recruit me.' He chuckled. 'Nah, too late for that. The fat, balding, smelly old git will have to watch me crash the thing before I agree to fly this heap of space debris, after what he did.'

'Which was?'

Calc stayed silent. 'Got lucky, was all,' he said myste-riously.

The rusting metal floor shook violently as more alarms sounded. The guard at the main door called out for infor-mation from the corridor as the sound of a dozen feet pounded the metal floor and ran past.

'Someone's putting up a fight,' Calc said. 'But if I was to put my thinking cap on, I would say they're not trying to capture this ship with its useless cargo. Instead, there's a seventy percent chance they're looking for something more valuable. It could be me, but I don't think so this time.' He glanced up at Jason. 'Where did you come from?' he mused. 'Someone said something about a ship suddenly appearing, and if that's the case and you turned up a few minutes later, then you must have arrived on said appearing ship.' He went on, toying with the cartridges on his cheek, then twirling a loose wire by his ear as if in thought.

'Only the Vistar elite ships have cloaking abilities, at least good enough to avoid detection by a smuggler.'

Jason opened his mouth to answer, hoping this half-human would know something about Earth or the Nexus fuel he needed so badly.

'Wait!' Calc said, holding up a palm. 'Don't tell me. It's something to do with your ship, or its cargo. The Harken don't trouble professional smugglers like Partel unless it means them salvaging something special...'

The ship rumbled, groaning as they felt the tilting of an attempt to maneuver away from incoming fire.

'Those Harkens are going to tear this ship to pieces,' Calc said. 'They won't leave a trace for others to find. They'll either disintegrate it to plates and rivets or it'll turn up in a fleet, heavily modified with pieces missing and replaced with whatever they thought would be superior in combat.'

'How do you know all this?' Jason asked.

'A blind baby could tell the difference between Harken ballistic fire and that of Vistar lasers.' He shrugged. 'It may be another faction altogether, but considering the battle we have been crossing, the chance would be less than point five of a percentile that any would risk it.'

The ship gave a violent shudder. This time, the noise was deafening. The lights above them set in the ceiling flickered. The guard at the main door could be heard running away.

The lights continued to flicker. Most of the time they were on and stable, but every few seconds they would go out.

Calc stared up at the light above him before looking back at Jason.

Jason frowned at the scrutiny. 'Something on my face?'

Calc chuckled. 'More important than that,' he said, 'the barriers, they're intermittent.'

'What do you mean?' Jason asked, holding onto the wall as another tremor shook the ship.

'The force fields on your side of the brig are not permanently on.'

Jason studied the door frame. He could see a hole through the middle of the force field.

'You can jump through,' Calc said

'I thought you said you were clever?' Jason said.

'I can get you through,' Calc said. 'In exchange for that, you get me out. Then we find your ship and leave these fools to it.'

Jason could see the air shimmer in front of him as the

invisible barrier turned on and off, in time with the flickering of the lights above them.'

'It's not off permanently,' he said.

'It doesn't need to be,' Calc said. 'I need you to do something for me and it's going to sound silly, but trust me.'

'That does sound silly,' Jason said. 'I don't trust anyone, let alone Johnny Five.'

'Not a joke I understand,' Calc said. 'Trust me or not?'

Jason sighed. 'What other choice have I got?'

'Several actually,' Calc said. 'Would you like me to take you through your options?'

Jason grunted. 'No, just tell me what you want me to do.'

'Jump up and down,' Calc said.

Jason did not.

'Come on,' Calc said, as if he was being a spoilsport on the playground.

Jason jumped once.

'Not now!' Calc said, as if he was being ridiculous. 'Only when I say jump.'

'Explain to me first,' Jason said, 'then I'll be your dog.'

'Does dog mean slave?' Calc asked, but didn't wait for an answer. 'I need to calculate your response time to my commands. When I have established a ninety percent error free margin, I will tell you when to jump through the doorway. If you get it wrong, you might end up cut in half, so be prepared.'

'Just ninety percent?' Jason said.

'Go on then,' Calc said, scowling so the wires on his forehead scrunched up.

'What?' Jason asked.

'Do it yourself.'

Jason was put out. He needed to get out of here, back on

his ship, and find the stupid Nexus fuel stuff to get back to Earth.

'Look,' he said, ' I didn't mean it, Calc. I need your help.'

'Of course, you do,' Calc said, smugly. 'I'm your best option.'

'Yes,' Jason growled, 'so tell me when.'

Without more than a second passing, Calc yelled, 'Now!'

It was too soon, too sudden. Jason hadn't expected the navigator to say it so quickly. He hesitated, then jumped, knowing he was far too slow.

12

Death felt pretty normal, like leaping forward into the unknown. It was dark, pitch black, with an eternal laughter that echoed in his head.

Something wasn't right. Or at least something *was* right. He was breathing. Not the pure air of heavenly places, but the recycled whiff of a ship's atmosphere.

The perpetual blackness that had swallowed him was merely his eyelids. He had scrunched his eyes shut, before leaping, and as he now realized, opening them, the eternal cackling was merely Calc, bent double with uncontrollable laughter.

'Not funny,' Jason said, feeling relieved and extremely foolish at the same time.

'Incredibly comical,' Calc said, 'like watching a fish try to swim on land, only to realize it is in water.'

Jason recovered and approached the doorway to Calc's cell.

'How did I even manage that?' Jason asked, hearing several more deep percussive booms reverberate through the hull.

'I figured you would hesitate if I gave a sudden command and that the chances of you reacting on impulse were twenty-one point six percent higher than if I gave you time to think about it.'

The half-man, half-robot was much more complicated up close. His green eye had a tiny reticule imprinted on the lens, and what Jason had assumed to be three cartridge spaces in his cheek were three rows of a dozen smaller ones.

Jason just shook his head. 'What now?'

'Open this infernal trapping device,' Calc said, 'and let's get going.'

Jason found the keypad in the wall beside the door. It had English numbers, which boggled his mind. Was there some sort of universal numerical system?

'There must be a code,' he said. Hopelessness crushed him. He had expected a simple lever or an emergency open button.

'Try four zeros,' Calc said.

Jason raised an eyebrow and punched in the numbers. Could it be so simple?

There was a sharp buzz. *Incorrect* flashed on the screen.

'No,' Jason said.

'Well, it was worth a shot,' Calc said.

Jason glanced around, as if the number might be stamped like graffiti on a rust-pitted wall somewhere. 'Really?'

'There was a fourteen percent chance it would be that combination. Given that most computer systems have backup accounts or are reset often, not to mention the pure laziness of their operators.' Calc said. 'And fourteen percent is nothing to be scoffed at.'

'I'm going to have to leave you,' Jason said, trying to regain his balance against the keypad wall as the ship pitched sharply to one side, making them both stagger. 'I'm sorry, Calc.'

'Like hell, asshole,' Calc said. 'You're not leaving me after what I've done for you. I just need time to think.'

More bangs rocked the ship. 'Not much of that left around here,' Jason said.

Calc frowned, then closed his eyes.

The green eye glowed and his normal one flitted left and right as if scanning reams of information displayed behind the eyelid.

After what seemed an eternity but was only half a minute, Calc opened his eyes, a tight smile toying his lips. 'Two, Eight, Four, Four,' he said.

'Huh?'

'Two, Eight, Four, Four, that's the code.'

This time, Jason knew he was making it up. But perhaps the Humdroid deserved a chance, and if Jason gave him one, he'd feel less bad about having to leave him here.

The ship shook violently, causing flaking paint to rain down on him, almost making his fingers miss the keypad. It was time to go.

He tapped the numbers in and turned, ready to sprint off. 'Sorry, Calc!' he said.

'Hey, I can't move that fast yet.'

Jason took several long strides, then stopped and looked over his shoulder. Calc stepped out into the corridor and brushed himself down.

'No goddamn way did that random code work,' Jason said, scratching his head in pure disbelief.

'Random code?' Calc said, with a scornful huff. 'Random code,' he muttered again, as if he'd been cheated.

'You knew it all along then,' Jason said, eager to get going but also eager to find out how this Humdroid knew it.

'No, not at all,' Calc said. 'I knew the jailor was born on Calden's largest moon, Jin, and from that I surmised it.'

'Just from that?'

'Well, no,' Calc said. 'He was wearing a jeweled Rangor pendant, the moon's largest predator. Those were wiped out fifty-two standard years ago and exactly three standard years afterward, the authorities dispersed the medals among the populace as an ecological reminder. They gave every child one and from that, I knew roughly what his age was and backdated that to give me a birth year.'

'From a pendant?' Jason said, still not believing.

'No,' Calc said, impatiently. 'Combined with the fact that he did not have a missing finger, which was dished out to all unruly families during the famine war there six years later, I guessed he was born in the years after. Out of those years, the government only allowed the populace to have one child, but changed that law on a specific year. I would not have guessed so if he had not been on a lightwave call with his brother last night.'

'And you knew he would choose his birth year?'

'A high proportion of lesser-witted creatures often do. A staggering percentage, in fact.'

'So to the ship?' Jason said, stunned by Calc's skills at deduction.

'Not yet,' Calc said, hobbling towards a small office used by the jailor. 'Keep watch on the door while I get something.'

He was walking so slowly that Jason wondered if they could even make it to the cargo bay before the smuggler's ship blew up.

'Is your leg injured?' Jason asked.

'No,' Calc said, 'not quite.'

Jason rushed for the door, peered around it and slunk

back as he spotted the old jailor coming back down the hallway towards the door.

'Oi!' he heard as he headed for the office. He found Calc rummaging amidst lockers.

'He's coming,'

'Take this.' Calc tossed him what might have been a pistol. It was shaped like one, but looked as if it was made from pipes and bent, welded metal pieces. Just behind the crude grip was a small gas-looking cylinder with a pressure dial labeled with alien characters.

There were several twistable screws along the side. Did they have safety switches?

A pistol poked around the corner and Jason dived behind the nearest cover, which was the office door. The pistol let loose, blasting bullets towards the office. The barrage stopped for a second when the old guard peered around to see what damage he'd done.

Jason took advantage of the rookie mistake, leveled his pistol and squeezed the cold trigger. Of course nothing happened. He cursed and spun away, back into the office.

'How'd you work this damned thing?'

In the space of a few seconds, Calc had turned the office inside out. He had pulled out all the drawers in the ceramic-looking desk and was rummaging inside a trio of lockers.

'Calc!'

The Humdroid stopped pulling clothes out from within and turned.

Jason waved the pistol like a flag in front of Calc's face. 'The DIY weapon?'

Calc clearly didn't know the acronym but guessed the question. 'Turn the dials on the side to the same position.'

The three screws he'd noticed were marked with lines

carved into the tips. He twisted them to align with the barrel.

As he turned, the old man made to fire again, and it was only pure reflex that allowed Jason to raise his pistol and fire faster. The old guard's shot had gone wide but Jason's struck home, throwing the old man back dead, into the corridor with a surprising force.

'Got it!' Calc said, opening a hinged box that resembled a lunchbox. He plunged a circuited hand in and drew out a small cartridge. With a hard slap, he inserted it into an empty slot on his cheek and grinned. 'Bastards tried to slow me down,' he said; 'not anymore.'

He ran to the door, bustling past Jason. The slow limp from the cell had become a speedy jaunt. Like giving coffee to a toddler and speeding up the video of them racing around.

Jason followed, but as they both turned into the corridor a trio of the captain's guards were running towards the cell block. Jason opened fire, giving Calc time to pick up the weapon of the dead guard.

Jason continued firing, forcing the three guards into an adjacent room along the corridor about forty feet away. 'You going to fire that or what?' Jason called, waiting as Calc sighted down the pistol. Calc muttered something about unknown variables and fired. The shot went so wide that Jason thought it had malfunctioned. Calc shot again and this time he was forced to jump back, knocking into Jason as his shot hit the wall right beside them.

The trio down the corridor had ceased firing and Jason assumed they were just as amazed as him at Calc's tragic aim. Before he could resume firing, he saw they were fixated on a section of the wall lit up like a welder's torch beside them.

It hurt the eyes to stare at it, but it was fascinating watching as a line in the steel corridor wall melted in rivulets and pooled on the floor like molten silver.

The light stopped and so did a sinister background hiss that had gone undetected during the chaos of the firefight.

With a loud bang, the cut section of the wall burst inwards, crushing one of the trio and blinding the others as smoke poured in.

A dozen soldiers, dressed like scrap-laden homeless people, trudged through. They shot the last two bewildered guards and stepped over the portion of the wall lying on the floor. They turned to face Jason and Calc, and it was clear they were dangerous. Their faces were covered with scraps of rag or ill-fitted helmets that resembled something out of a medieval blacksmith's shop. Beneath that were furs and skins, covering random-sized plates of armor all crudely stitched together. Jason was sure they had taken the plates from the sides of ships. He could even see rivets and old burn marks as the soldiers roared and stampeded towards them.

A vice-like grip clenched around Jason's arm and before he could fire, the hand was yanked, tugging him back into the prison block doorway.

'No chance,' Calc said. He reversed his pistol in his hands and   thumped the handle at a keypad in the doorframe. The rusted pad sparked and the two halves of a door slid in from either side, just as the first grubby soldiers reached the entrance.

'Harkens,' Calc said, staring around the room, searching for something.

'Space hobos is more like it,' Jason said.

'Exactly,' Calc said in agreement.

'There's too many of them for us to take,' Jason said, as a

click sounded behind the sealed door. A bright flare of light punctured the thick steel as the tip of a gas cutter pierced the barrier and began slicing through.

They both backpedaled deeper into the prison block, their eyes never leaving the door.

'No ammunition in that,' Calc said, glancing at Jason's sorry excuse for a pistol.

He was right. The small gauge on the side was in the red and a tiny flashing symbol pulsed beside it.

The cutter was halfway through the door, searing their eyes like a fireworks display in a sensory deprivation room.

Jason tossed the DIY pistol and as Calc gave a whoop and sped past him, the Humdroid thrust his pistol at him. It was much more than a collection of pipes and metal pieces. It was once smooth and solid, but time seemed to have etched its way deep into the handle and along the ribbed barrel.

It was similar to an Earth pistol, with spaces for attachments along the top. The only major difference, other than its aged appearance, was that instead of a magazine inserted into the handle, a tube stuck out of the back of the barrel like the stick in a glue gun. A strip of green light lined the tube, hopefully denoting that the clip was just under half full.

'Follow, human,' Calc screamed from the far side of the prison block at the end of the hallway between the cells as far from the door as possible.

There was a wheeled box trolley at waist height and crammed with food bars and bottles of water for feeding the inmates. Jason took cover behind it with Calc crouched behind him, scratching at the wall like a demented prisoner.

Jason didn't have time to panic. He leant out, ready to fire as the main doorway tumbled in from an external blast.

He ducked back behind cover, realizing that with Calc hunched behind him, the soldiers might not see them immediately.

'Spread out and find them,' one of the tramp soldiers said, in the gruff voice of someone that must have smoked a thousand cigarettes during a week-long illness to sound so rough.

Jason risked a tiny peek around the trolley. The leader was taller than the others, with a wide-bladed sword in one hand, chipped and notched, and a pipe pistol in the other. His head was covered in a fur hood, tainted with the stains of dried blood. A pauldron of heavy scrap metal protected one shoulder in a display of rank and was painted with a red symbol.

The man seemed to sense Jason's watchfulness and looked straight at him. 'There!' he shouted, pointing. 'Kill him!'

A dozen weapons all fired at Jason. The trolley was no match for such an onslaught. He was ready to face his doom, but not without taking one or two of them out. He tensed, ready to push the cart and wheel it along, using it as cover.

13

The shots hammered the trolley. Parts blew off it, ringing as they hit the floor, but instead of running with it in front of him, he was jerked backwards by strong hands and thrown unceremoniously into a tight, coffin-sized tunnel.

Calc had thrown him inside and followed behind, tugging a thick panel into place and sealing them in.

'Crawl for all you're worth,' Calc said as shots burrowed into the panel. Jason didn't wait to be told again and scurried as fast as he could on all fours into the darkness.

A green light beamed ahead after a while of straight crawling and Jason slowed as they neared a T junction. 'Left or right?' he asked.

A green haze, emanating from a flat bulb embedded in the back of Calc's hand, illuminated a sign written in complete gibberish. 'Right,' Calc said. 'Cargo bay is just through engineering and around the medibay.'

'What is all this?' Jason asked, staring around at wires and small computer screens every few feet along the tube-like run.

'Maintenance tunnels,' Calc said. 'There are always some on every ship and they go to most places. I'm guessing this one is not trapped, but most ships have defenses in their tunnels for just this scenario.'

'Why not?'

'Captain Partel's a smuggler, so he needs all the hiding space he can get. Some smugglers use the tunnels to transport the most valuable items or the most dangerous without alerting the crew.'

'Or any snooping officials,' Jason put in.

'Exactly,' Calc said. 'Here.'

He offered Jason a bottle of water and a handful of the snack bars, which Calc had at the last minute pilfered from the trolley.

There was no sign of their pursuers, so they stopped for a minute to rest, monitoring the way they had come.

Jason wolfed down the bars after peeling a clear rubber skin from them. He washed it down with water and offered the rest to Calc.

'I ate just before you arrived,' Calc said, 'and I've no desire for more of those bloody prison food bars.'

'How long were you in there for?'

'Twenty-four days,' Calc said. 'They picked me up on Gold Plain after hunting me down.'

'Gold Plain?'

'A pathetic planet in the B-three system,' Calc sneered. 'The Harken home system. Captain Partel had been using the Harken war fleet as cover for moving through space, hoping to remain undetected among the hundreds of smaller vessels passing between the cruisers. Maybe he had a deal with them for protection? I don't know, but your turning up sure changed things for him.'

One of the many small screens along the tunnel walls

lit up. "*Hull breach, section six-zero.*" A moment later, another warning joined the first. "*Hull breach, section five-five.*"

'They're breaking the ship up,' Calc said, getting ready to crawl again. 'Hurry. There's not much time.'

The heat inside the tunnels was building as Jason followed him, twisting left then right in the confined space. They stopped every minute or two and he would wait for Calc to access the small screens, checking the ship's systems before choosing a safer route to their goal.

'The medibay,' Calc said, sliding open a panel to a small room with several beds watched over by large lamps and a wall of drawers and lockers. 'We'll have to go on foot from now on. It's only a short walk from here.'

Together they sidled up to the door, each taking a side before Calc pressed the open button. The door split in two, revealing an empty hallway lined with dead crew. Smoke lingered at the top of the hallway, the fumes drifting over the lights and making them cast a dull gray sheen over everything.

'It's dead ahead,' Calc said.

'I can see that,' Jason said, staring at the open eyes of a dead engineer, his leather tool bag split open beside his bloody form.

'I mean, the cargo bay is through the end of the hallway,' Calc said. 'Just keep an eye on the corridors we pass. There'll be Harken troops everywhere by now.'

They passed two more corridors and Jason was feeling confident that they might just make it safely to the ship.

He ducked and dived, shoving Calc forwards as bullets peppered the walls and ceiling. The next corridor was host to a patrol that opened fire on the pair before they could retaliate. Jason twisted back to the corridor and flung his arm around the corner, elbow hinging around it. He squeezed the trigger furiously, praying he hit something.

'Go!' he yelled at Calc.

The pistol clicked. A croaking metallic voice emanated from the weapon. '*Empty.*'

Jason cursed and joined the fleeing Humdroid as the ship shook. A pipe running along the top of the ceiling burst and a stream of hissing vapor forced them to bend double and rush through a growing cloud. More pipes burst further on, making the space around them like a white-out fog. They didn't slow. Jason kept one arm extended out in front, ready to touch the cargo bay door, for fear of crashing into it.

Something slammed into him from a joining corridor. Someone, that is. The person hissed in the mist and Jason jumped up, ready to grapple. He saw the face of Captain Partel beside him wrestling with Calc, and Jason found himself staring into the predatory eyes of Silver.

She didn't hesitate and pounced on him. He dodged, hitting the wall and bouncing back. He swung a leg out to trip her. She tumbled to her back and rolled away, fumbling for a pistol at her belt. She brought it up, leant on one knee, and took aim straight at Jason. He couldn't avoid this one.

Captain Partel and Calc crashed into her and the shot went wide. Jason slipped around the two and before Silver could recover, hit her full force in the face. She dropped like a sack to the floor. A series of bullets tore into the walls around them, twitching the smoke as they passed.

The Harkens had caught up with them and the group were firing blindly into the fog.

Captain Partel was hammering down blows on Calc, and Jason made ready to shove him out of the way and run from the incoming death.

A bullet struck Partel, throwing him to the floor. He cried out in anguish at the pain, clawing at the floor to get away from any more projectiles.

'Damn,' Jason said, looking down at the prone form of Silver. There was no doubt the Harken soldiers would kill her, or worse. Partel was writhing on the floor, a hollow wound in his stomach. Jason had seen wounds like that before. He'd be dead soon enough.

The rate of fire increased, and so did their speed for the door. Calc hit it first and in the smoky fog found the door's keypad. The keypad buzzed and flashed red in the darkness.

'Not working,' Calc said, trying twice more, before attempting to prise up the keypad to get to the innards beneath.

The moans of the captain echoed like a haunting ghost behind them. The boots of the soldiers pounded the floor. Jason glimpsed them through the mist and knew they would bring death.

14

The Harken soldiers were coming. The outline of their furs and sewn-together plates were visible through the fog. 'Hurry, Calc,' Jason said.

'I can't do it in time. It's a biolock and a five-point encryption. There are too many wires for me to test!'

'Just keep trying,' Jason said, looking around for a half-decent plan of action. He slapped himself on the forehead as the answer stared him in the face. 'Ah! You idiot.'

'Hey!' Calc said. 'I'm doing my best. Why don't you figure it out if you're so smart?'

Jason ignored him, racing back into the fog. He rolled and found what he was looking for. She was heavy enough, but he dragged Silver's limp form back to the door and slapped her hand down on the pad's screen. It lit green under her palm. One of the Harken had spotted their movement. Bullets shattered the frame above them, showering them both with metal fragments. Jason shielded his eyes. Thankfully the door opened, and they staggered through. Calc closed it behind with a deep sigh and slumped against the door.

'Good thinking,' Calc said, 'for an unaugmented human.'

Jason looked around the cargo hold. Calc joined him after catching his breath. The familiar sound of a cutting tool echoed on the far side until the gleaming light pierced the door.

'Let's go,' Calc said, then stopped. 'What on the moon of Kaleo are you doing?' he asked, as Jason stooped to lift Silver from the ground.

'Not being an asshole,' he said, straining to throw her over his shoulder. She wasn't really heavy, but he was weak from lack of rest and it took a steadying hand from Calc to stop him from slouching back against the door.

'This way.' Jason said, roughly remembering where the ship had been docked amidst the chaos of cargo boxes stacked up like a hoarder's living room.

They came to a ceiling-high pile of barrels and huge containers wrapped together with chains, and the row of derelict ships came into view.

Nexus One stood out like a naked ballerina in a sumo wrestling ring.

The sleek manta curves and the unbroken one-piece hull contrasted with the cobbled-together remains of the other ships.

Calc froze in shock.

'Solder my circuits,' he said. 'Is that your ship?'

Yes,' Jason said. 'Well, sort of.'

'Sort of is good enough,' Calc said, gazing in wonder at the smooth vessel. 'Let's just use it to get out of here first and then establish what is whose.'

He sped up and walked over to touch the hull, running a circuit-covered hand along the hull, searching for the way in. 'No wonder Partel wanted it and no wonder the Harkens would kill him to get it. Who wouldn't want this?'

'Why?' Jason asked, glancing back as the sound of the door crashed in and echoed through the cargo bay.

'This is the single biggest piece of Ancient Empire tech I've ever seen,' Calc said.

'Ancient Empire?'

'Yes,' Calc said, 'before the Unfathomable Split.'

Jason shrugged.

'Hang on,' Calc said, seeing his reaction. 'So what are you telling me? That you have no idea what the empire is?'

'Not an inkling,' Jason said, shifting Silver to a more comfortable position.

Calc threw his hands up. 'Have you been living under a rock on Gedi Six?'

'On Earth,' Jason said. 'So, something like that.'

'Never heard of it,' Calc said.

The dreaded sound of heavy footfalls echoed through the cargo bay. The Harken soldiers had made it inside, and from the sound of clanking armor and guttural shouts, there were a lot of them.

'OK, no more joking,' Calc asked, rounding the ship again. 'Where's the door? We need to get in.'

Jason hesitated. 'Roo,' he called. 'Door!'

Calc looked at him sidelong.

Placing Silver on the floor, Jason raced around the ship. No door had appeared. What was she playing at? Was she even inside? Did she even exist at all?

'Damn, Roo,' he said, punching his hand against the hull. Shots rang out in the cargo bay. They'd been spotted and there was no way inside.

15

'Not a second too late,' Calc said, ducking the gunfire and gratefully eyeing the opening that had suddenly appeared on the side of the ship.

Jason was sure the door had been on the other side last time. The cursed vessel was trouble, but staying outside waiting to be torn apart by space savages was more immediate trouble.

He scooped up Silver and followed in behind Calc.

The doors molded together behind them, sealing the three of them inside an airlock. A second door ahead was already open. He lowered Silver to the floor and walked through. They could keep her in here until she woke up.

Lights glowed from pin holes all across the ceiling, which curved to eight feet overhead. The hull pinged with bullets, but judging by the fact the entirety of Earth's military couldn't break it earlier, Jason took a second to relax.

Center of the room was his chair, still uncomfortable as ever as he sank into it, breathing a sigh of relief.

'This is truly bizarre,' Calc said, gawking at the circular

space. He just stood in the center and spun in place, taking in the rather bland, silvery curves.

'Thought you could pilot any ship,' Jason said.

'Don't you get it?' Calc said. 'This isn't just any old ship. I mean, it's old, really old. Like nothing I've ever set foot on and I've set foot on a *lot* of ships. The tech looks like all Ancient Empire stuff but I've only seen artifacts, small trinkets and once a rifle, which I used to buy a harem of Lonestar milkmaids and a galactic supercruiser, but that's another story.'

'Go on,' Jason said, eager to hear more.

'Well, for a start, there's no navigation terminal, no sign of an engineering bay or anything. And where's the rest of it?'

'The rest?' Jason asked.

'Yes, idiot,' Calc said, gesturing wildly. 'This room is only one-eighth of the potential interior space given the size of the exterior curvature.'

'You mean there're more rooms?' asked Jason slowly.

'Yes,' said Calc, like he was speaking to a slow child.

'Don't take that tone with me. If you didn't always speak like you swallowed a dictionary, maybe I'd understand you better.'

Calc waved the comment away. 'Who knows what's in here?' he said, poking a small hole along the edge of the three-hundred-and-sixty-degree window. 'Think of the upgrades that could be stashed away in here.'

The soldiers outside were circling the ship, searching for a way in. Every now and then one would stop and start whacking it with a crude rusted tool, or open fire.

The second time one tried to fire up close, the bullet ricocheted off and punctured his forehead. He stumbled back a single pace, then dropped straight down like a puppet after having its strings cut.

'Upgrades?' asked Jason.

'Of course. First off, if this ship is yours, which, judging by the fact you haven't done anything since we got in here, is doubtful, then you're rich. Not just rich, but filthy rich. That rifle I acquired was worth a hundred thousand credits, and that was cheap! This is a whole Ancient Empire ship.' He gave the chair Jason was on a kick. 'That alone, if you could detach the thing, would be worth fifty thousand in the markets of the Traversai merchant fleet.'

'So what now? Worth a fortune, but not if these animals get it.'

'Fly time,' Calc said.

'Thought you could fly anything?'

Calc looked around again at the room. 'I would, if there was the usual navigation seat. Or any seat other than the one you're sitting on.'

'Come on, Roo. Get us out of here.'

'Who or what the hell is Roo?'

They hadn't noticed the Harken soldiers fleeing in all directions until a huge explosion rocked *Nexus One*. They had planted charges along the hull in an attempt to blow it open. The ship rocked, but this time there was just a bubbly shimmer. The shields had activated.

'Roo is the computer.'

Calc threw his arms wide and spun around. 'Which is located where, exactly?'

Jason ignored him. The frustration was too much. 'Roo! Listen up. We need a navigation terminal right now to get the hell out of here. If not, I'm leaving the ship and letting those nice smelly men inside to break the ship up and sell it to strange merchants.'

Nothing happened.

'To hell with this!'

Jason walked for the door.

16

Calling the bluff of a computer that hadn't responded was about the height of stupidity. But he didn't care. Jason stepped into the cool airlock, glanced down at the unconscious form of the catwoman and went straight to the exterior door. He put his hand on the wall and it opened a fraction before stopping. Harkens called excitedly from outside, seeing the opening. Gunfire erupted again, but the shield absorbed the bullets.

'Jason!' Calc called from the bridge, his voice brimming with excitement. 'It worked!'

Jason spun. A second seat was rising from the floor, molding itself into shape. The chair, much more comfortable looking than Jason's, grew from the floor. Two small flat-screen computers were recessed in the ends of the armrests.

A curving desk arched, like a flattened rainbow, over the seat's footrest and a series of holographic screens hovered above the surface. Calc didn't hesitate. He gave a whoop of delight and jumped into the seat, scanning the screens that curved in front of him.

Jason ran for his seat.

'I knew it was worth learning Ancient Empirical,' Calc said, hands swiping the screens and tapping away at the controls on the tips of the armrests. 'I've got impulse and secondary thruster controls. There's quite a lot that has been removed from use, judging by missing options.' He looked up. 'Not that I'm complaining, Ruse.'

'Roo,' Jason corrected him, but Calc wasn't paying attention.

'Powering up,' Calc said, his voice taking on a serious tone. 'We need a way out though.'

A singular, high-pitched whine grew from a distant background noise to a deafening wail. The ship rocked and a pair of purple lasers shot from within both wings of the ship. They cut in opposite directions, burning a molten square into the hull of the larger ship. Air rushed out from the breach as the perfect square, the size of *Nexus One*, was sucked out into the blackness of space. All the screaming soldiers in the cargo bay, along with the entire smuggled contents, vacated as if in a hurricane through the void, leaving enough space for *Nexus One* to fly out.

Calc's face was a rictus of pure joy as the engines buzzed to life and the ship hovered up.

Nexus One bolted forwards, straight out of the hole, perfectly fitting the gap. The backdrop of galactic nebulae surrounded them and the remnants of Captain Partel's ship shrunk to insignificance far behind them. 'Whoa!' Calc cried. 'This thing is fast.'

'Shame your reactions aren't,' a female voice mused from just behind Jason's ear. 'Don't move!' she hissed, pressing the razor point of a blade into Jason's throat. 'Now take me back to the *Garda*.'

'*Garda?*'

'Partel's ship,' Silver said. 'And make it quick, my patience is thinner than the blood that's soon going to spill down your clothes.'

'Why didn't you search her, idiot?' Calc said.

'Hey, that's not fair,' Jason said, tensing in frustration. 'You're the one that did it in *reverse*.'

'When?' Calc countered.

'When I *checked her?*'

'Fine!' Calc said, ignoring Silver's demand that they shut up. 'But you should have found the knife, stupid amateur.'

'I took all her clothes off to *check*!'

'What?' Silver said, shocked.

Calc swept a palm across the pad by his right hand and the ship jolted backwards.

Jason slipped his hand up between the small gap that the maneuver had put between his throat and the deadly weapon. He rotated his wrist, caught Silver's hand that clasped the blade and kicked up from his chair, cracking the back of his skull into her face. She toppled backwards. Only Jason's hold on the weapon hand kept her from hitting the floor hard. She was unconscious and he lowered her slowly down.

He tore off a strip of a sleeve of his white clothing and used it to bind her hands.

'Close one, that,' Calc said.

'At least we have an understanding between us, Calc. That's a good start.'

'To what?'

'Friendship?'

'The chances of that are slim, extremely slim.'

'What odds?' Jason asked.

Calc seemed to think for a moment. 'About four thousand to one, given the encounters I've had and not formed relationships within a similar timeframe.'

'Calc, what are the odds of us two meeting and having this conversation? And of me asking these questions?'

'One point eight billion, nine million, three thousand two hundred to one.'

'Surely the logic dictates that as we made it this far into the conversation we should be friends as the chance is so much higher than those you originally said?'

Calc raised an eyebrow.

Jason thought he was grasping at straws but something he'd just said must have made logical sense, as the Humdroid didn't immediately shut him down.

'What's that?' Calc asked, pointing over to Jason's central chair. A tiny screen had popped up glowing yellow.

Jason rushed over and squinted at the tiny screen. 'There's a ship following us.'

17

'Why is this screen so small, Roo?' Jason said. 'I can't make out more than basic details.'

'I can't access it from here,' Calc said. 'Needs captain's permission.'

'It says a class four Harken interceptor. Whatever the hell that is.'

'Not something we want to hang around for,' Calc said. 'I know this ship can take a beating, but those interceptors will track this thing and bring the entire Harken military down on us.'

'I know a place we can hide,' a husky voice said from behind them both.

Silver had managed to sit up and was rubbing her head.

'Sorry about that,' Jason said.

'You should be,' she said, touching her split lip.

'Well, you might have startled me with that sharp knife thing,' Jason mocked.

'Where?' Calc asked. 'We've got one minute before they get within weapons range. Just be glad it's not a class six. Those things have got a disastrous range.'

'What's the difference?' Jason asked, not taking his eyes off Silver.

'The higher the class, the larger the ship,' Calc said.

'Has he been living under a rock on—'

'Gedi Six?' Jason finished.

'Maybe not,' Calc said, giving a light chuckle. His voice turned serious. 'Thirty seconds, Captain, where are we going?'

Jason hadn't considered he might be a deciding factor in anything that went on in this strange after-Earth experience. 'We'll go with Silver's suggestion,' he said, quickly shifting the uncomfortable feeling to someone else.

'Which is?' Calc asked. 'Fifteen seconds...'

Silver seemed taken aback by being asked.

'Head for Aquinia, in the Coreton system along the edge of the Great Divide. I have a friend there who may give us shelter for a while.'

'Will there be a cost?' Calc asked, priming the engines and plotting in a course.

'Of course,' Silver said. 'No one likes fugitives. But this one hates Harkens more, so that may be in our favor.'

The ship swiveled to face a random patch of space before the engines kicked in, forcing Jason back into his incommodious seat. Silver was shunted back against a wall where she slid down, knees to her chin.

'How long?' Jason asked.

'Fifteen hours or so,' Calc said. 'I would suggest we all get some well-deserved sleep, but the floor doesn't look or feel too appealing.'

'Roo,' Jason said, 'beds please.'

He had expected nothing from the A.I., but to the left of the room, a door spiraled open, leading to a new section of the ship.

'Where does that go?' Calc asked.

Jason rose, finally taking his eyes off Silver. 'Who knows with this ship? Could lead straight outside for all I know. Never seen it before.' He crept over to the door and looked through.

A short corridor split to half a dozen doors, each with a bed, lockers and writing desks, all shaped from the silvery hull of the ship. There were blankets and pillows adorning each room and—it couldn't be... a pot of hot coffee and a stack of cups rested on a kitchen counter in one of the rooms. He snatched the coffeepot and poured half a cup, before bringing it to his mouth. It was hot, but he didn't care.

Coffee!

'Thank you, Roo,' he said, to the room at large.

He found a slightly bigger room than the others at the end of the corridor and claimed it as his own, exploring whilst enjoying the succulent yet bitter taste of the drink. It might not have been exactly coffee, but it was close enough to relish.

A sliding cupboard door in his room grabbed his attention. Inside, he found three sets of simple clothing, all the same pale gray. Two pairs of boots lay at the bottom of the cupboard beside a pair of trainer-like soft shoes.

The desk had a single drawer and within he fished out a small tablet and half a dozen food bars, the same as he had when he first came on board.

'If we stock up on basic foodstuffs, Captain,' Roo said, 'I can use them to create a menu which can be ordered from the tablet.'

'Roo?' Jason said. 'I thought you had stopped talking, or you'd abandoned us...'

Footsteps sounded down the corridor. Jason turned to

find Silver, looking into each room until she found him. 'So you didn't know this was here then?' she asked.

Jason eyed her hands, still tied by the strips of cloth that he had torn from his shirt.

'I will not try anything again,' she said. 'I'm guessing Partel is dead?'

Jason nodded slowly. 'I'm sorry,' he said, sitting on the bed. 'He was hit in the smoke. It was a stomach wound.'

She sat next to him, without waiting to be invited, and sighed. 'Ten years I've been with him.'

'You were partners?' Jason asked.

She chuckled. 'Not at all. I'll give it to him, he tried. But he wasn't a nice man. He wasn't horrible, but there was always something slightly... off with him. Plus, he wasn't my type. Fat, balding and barely bothered to shave.'

It was Jason's turn to laugh. 'I would have thought with the fur and shaving thing, you might prefer it.'

'Not in a human.'

'So you're not gonna try to kill me again, then?'

'As long as you don't grow a beard.'

Jason couldn't tell if she was serious or not. He twisted to face her. She was startlingly attractive, even with the fur that curved up her face like a delicate tattoo.

He fumbled with her bonds, unraveling the tight knot.

She didn't thank him, just stood, turned and left the room, heading for the direction of the bridge.

Jason followed, making sure she wasn't going to strangle Calc when he least expected it.

Calc was already at the entrance to the bridge, mid-showdown with Silver.

'You can let her pass, Calc,' Jason said. 'She's going to be on our side.'

'What side?' Silver asked. They both ignored her.

'There's a higher chance that she has you in her power and is forcing you to say this,' Calc said coldly. 'Rather than the slim and idiotic chance that you set someone who put a knife to your neck free to roam the ship.'

'I'm taking a chance, Calc.' Jason said, catching Silver's eye. 'We're thin on friends at the moment and our list of enemies grows larger every time we're not on the run. Perhaps Silver can enlighten me on our current enemies?'

She shrugged, turning her back on Calc to explain, a trusting move that didn't go unnoticed by the Humdroid. The navigator's fingers flexed as if holding back the opportunity to strangle her.

'The Harken?' she said.

'Yes.' Jason said. 'Living under a rock, remember?'

'The Harkens are arguably the second most powerful faction in the two galaxies.'

'Right behind the Vistar,' Calc put in.

'They rule their territory purely by military might,' Silver continued. 'As you may have noticed, they are scavengers. They take out other ships that they like the look of and aren't associated with larger factions, breaking them into pieces which are shipped back to Harken prime in the B three system of the second galaxy. Everything they have is pieced together from other less useful things. Although they're stupid enough to take something apart that works perfectly well to try to improve it.'

'More often than not,' Calc snorted.

'Second galaxy?' Jason tried.

Silver rolled her purple eyes. 'That was one large rock you were under,' she said.

'Amnesia,' Jason said, trying in vain to cover his ignorance.

'There are two galaxies that are inhabited. Both are

slowly colliding and between them is the Great Divide. When you showed up, that's where we were.'

'All big battles happen in the Divide,' said Calc.

Jason felt like he finally was working things out. 'Between who?'

'Usually the Harkens and their eternal nemeses, the Vistar,' Silver said, licking her wrists where the bonds had ruffled the short hair. Jason tried not to stare. It was discomforting, yet alluring.

'Far too much info all at once,' Jason said. 'But two more questions before I go straight to bed.'

They both stared at him.

'Are you two going to help me get back to Earth?' he asked, shifting from one leg to another, 'and where is the goddamned toilet on this ship?'

18

J   ason woke, feeling refreshed, until he looked at the door, realized he was on a strange spaceship, in the middle of some galaxy that did not contain Earth, and was being eyed by a feline woman staring at him from the doorway.

'Shit, what is it?' he snapped.

Silver raised a perfectly manicured eyebrow.

'Sorry. I'm a bit confused right now.'

'Amnesia?' she asked.

'Something like that.' Jason said, rubbing his eyes and swinging his legs out of the bed. He had eventually found the toilet before sleeping, after much cursing of Roo. It had been hidden behind a locker door in his quarters, opening into a toilet and shower area. It was compact but convenient. He'd taken a wonderful warm shower and pondered if it was the same in each room or if they changed to suit the guest's needs.

'We're about to arrive at Aquinia,' Silver said. 'Last time I was here, it got a bit jumpy on the way down, so don't panic if things go bang.'

She left without another word.

'Anything to eat, apart from those crappy bars, Roo?' Jason asked.

'We need to stock up on inventory, Captain,' she said quietly. 'Until then, there are plenty of healthy vitamin biscuits. They have all you need to survive.'

'Except taste,' Jason scoffed, opening a drawer beside his bed. He began munching down on several of the pasty, flavorless bars and gently massaged his shoulder. The wound was healing surprisingly well. He wondered if the ship influenced that or if it was something else entirely. He had changed the bandages twice now and—

Calc's voice crackled from the small pinholes in the ceiling. 'Hold on to something, we're going to enter the atmosphere, but first I need to navigate these bloody ice blocks.'

Jason gulped the last mouthful down and strode to the command room. He looked out at a sea of icy asteroids tumbling past them as Calc made the ship dance between the rolling boulders, all much bigger than the ship.

'Good flying,' Jason said, taking a seat and trying to realign his bottom to fit the chair's unsavory contours.

'Easy,' Calc said. 'Just got to stay on top of the math.' With one hand he was using a calculator on one arm of the chair, punching in numbers like a secretary on a typewriter. The other swiped power bars and pushed buttons on the trio of holoscreens in front of him. A cartridge on his face, and several along his arms, were glowing gently green as if running at full capacity.

'Those two will collide,' Silver said, pointing to two huge asteroids darting in from opposite sides of them.

Calc gritted his teeth. 'I know.'

'And that one,' Jason said, watching two others break

into each other. The crystalline shards spread out in all directions, the largest one knocking another off course so the two breaking up became five, the debris causing a chain reaction.

'Too much to calculate!' Calc cried, giving up on the math and using a control stick between the screens to turn the ship into a sharp dive. 'It's going to hit us!'

Jason held on, wishing his round-based chair had proper armrests to grab. Silver was sitting in a newly formed seat beside him. Hers had armrests; was it also padded?

Bangs clattered on the hull from smaller pieces of asteroid, but even some of the larger ones were moving too fast for Calc to avoid.

Nexus One's engines whined, shrieking in a new sound like a hearing test, getting more high-pitched until a roaring hiss punctured the air in a tremendous release of power. The ship barrel-rolled, then turned flat on towards an asteroid as if to land on it. All engines underneath thrusted, and it looked to be either pushing the asteroid away or firing so hard that it bounced the ship off the surface, melting the icy exterior of the asteroid at the same time.

They were all screaming until the ship pushed back in a vertical takeoff, and was in clearer space facing the planet and ready to enter Aquinia's atmosphere.

'That was freaking amazing,' Jason said. Even Silver looked shocked at Calc's abilities.

Calc, on the other hand, seemed in awe of his skills, staring open-mouthed at the screens.

In seconds, the exterior of the ship was shrouded in a golden haze as the air around them reached astronomical temperatures.

The haze cleared as they descended through the atmosphere, and instead of eye-numbing yellow, the planet was coated with a clear blue. Water covered its entire surface. As far as the eye could see, the blue desert stretched on without interruption.

'OK,' Calc said. 'So where are we going?'

'Latitude, forty-nine point six six,' Silver said. 'Longitude one, one, two, point one-two-seven. Distortion. Two point four four.'

Calc punched in the numbers. 'Sixteen minutes,' he said.

Jason was expecting to see land somewhere in the vast blue abyss. Instead, it was all water. As the ship skimmed, creatures from the water would jump up from the waves before plunging back down.

'Why is it endless water?' Jason asked.

'Failed Seedar planet,' Silver said. 'Too many asteroids nearby. Every time they entered the atmosphere, the water content increased. After a few hundred years, the surface was just water, fifteen thousand feet deep. When they realized their mistake, they sold it cheap to colonists who now live on boats and flotillas that drift across the surface.'

'Bloody good fishing, though,' Calc said.

Silver nodded. 'They import fish from both galaxies to help preserve species from dying planets.'

'For those with large wallets to catch you mean,' Calc said.

'I imagine the sushi is the best in the galaxy.' Jason said.

'Sushi?' Calc said. 'Never heard of that fish, but I'm not a galactic marine biologist. You know I once caught a Bayan terror shark as big as a class six destroyer with only a stick and a piece of Algean cheese. But that's another story.'

'Sure,' Silver said, rolling her eyes.

'This should be the location,' Calc said, ignoring her as the screen flashed up in front of him, displaying the local area. 'We're not receiving a comms prompt unless your coordinates are wrong.'

'Not likely,' Silver said. 'He may have moved, though. But it would be unlike him to leave behind a relay. Put a signal out anyway.'

Calc flipped through several screens. 'Not on this computer.'

Jason looked up. 'We need a communications terminal.'

Time stretched from awkward silence to awkward looks from the other two. 'Please.'

Like magic, a small, thin pedestal rose slowly from the floor beside Silver's chair. She lifted a foot to stomp down on the odd apparition.

'Wait,' Jason said. She moved her heel.

It stretched up on one side of her seat, curving in front to form a quarter circle that curved around her right side.

She gave a little hiss, eyeing the new control panel with deep suspicion. After a few moments, she gave in and began swiping the little screens. She plucked a thin curving slice from beside the computer screens and examined it. It was an earpiece. She sniffed it, then hooked the contraption behind her ear.

'I'm guessing that's for you to make sure there are no signals,' Calc said.

'How would you know that?' she asked.

'The most logical reason for an earpiece for someone who has a universal translator is to receive incoming data,' Calc started, ' is to—'

'Wait. Hang on. I'm getting something. Damn. It's gone. Turn around and go back over the last patch of water again.' She tapped some controls and spoke. 'Return call sign is Silver,' she said. 'Repeat, Silver. Xen, are you there?'

There were several long moments of silence before a

husky voice, either belonging to an old man or someone who suffered from a long-term lung illness, broke the call sign.

'Silver?'

'Yes, Xen, I'm here. I need a little help.'

'Again?' Xen asked.

'What do you mean again?' Silver growled, 'Last time I saved *you* from that pack of pirates demanding you give back their—'

'Yes, yes,' Xen said quickly. 'I remember. Hold on a minute and I'll be with you.'

From the ocean directly below them, a black bubble broke the surface. It was dotted with a panoply of bright corals. At first the dome was small, then like a ball rising, it grew larger and larger, until at the halfway point of the sphere, just before it would curve back, it stopped.

The glass dome split open like a clam, its sides arching back and retracting, until no trace of the coral dome was visible.

Inside was a circle of floating huts, sheds, and general small buildings, all brimming with rust and in dire need of repair. The buildings were linked by bridges and pontoons, shifting back and forth in a gentle tide that meandered inside the circle.

At the center was a square landing pad, tied by heavy chains and anchored to nearly every other shack that was close by. A series of green lights showed an invitation to land. At its center was a frizzy-bearded man waving at them as if beckoning them down.

He was dressed in ragged fur-patched clothes, half covered in grease and oil, long black hair piled over his broad shoulders, giving Jason the impression of a modern-day Viking warrior who had been midway through changing the boat's engine oil.

Calc lowered *Nexus One* gently down, forcing Xen to backpedal out of the ship's engine radius. Once the ship was powered down, an exit appeared on the side nearest to where Xen had been standing.

They made quick introductions while Xen eyed the ship.

'What in the Great Divide is that vessel?' Xen asked, his rough voice, deeper and gruffer in person.

'Not important,' Silver said. 'We need some place to lay low.' She looked around. 'Where are Gallway, Liss and Nimmit?'

Xen pulled a small oblong flask from beneath a fur-covered pocket and took a swig. 'The old team have gone their own ways.'

'Why?' she asked.

'Gallway left because of money problems,' Xen said, escorting them across the landing pad to the nearest building that didn't look like it would collapse in the face of the next gentle sea breeze. 'In fact, so did Nimmit a few weeks later.'

'And Liss?' Silver asked, ducking under a low door into a square room that would once have been a nice living space. Now, though, the tables that had once entertained diners were laden with old metal machine parts and a selection of weapons.

'Liss left complaining that I complained too much about money problems. Come to think of it, now that we're on the subject... You're going to need to pay your way if you're going to stay here. I'm sure you're going to be needing things?'

'We do,' Jason, said. 'Basic resources for food production. Maybe some weapons?' He eyed the armaments on the table. 'Seems like you've got plenty lying around, and some Nexus fuel if you've got it.'

Xen seemed to think for a moment. 'It's going to cost a hundred credits each per night,' he said. 'If I order up the resources, a local merchant can get most of them here tomorrow. For, say, two thousand credits?'

Jason wasn't sure if he even had one credit to his name.

'You've got a deal,' Silver said.

Xen looked put out. 'What? No haggling? No negotiations?' He raised a bushy eyebrow..

Silver didn't say anything and he seemed to understand.

He laughed. 'You haven't got any money, have you? You still with that bloody Captain Partel? I know he was always a couple of months behind in arrears, and that was on a good run. You want food, shelter and resources and you got no money? The only thing free on Aquinia is water and even that's salty.'

'I'll get the money,' Silver said. 'Trust me.'

Xen shook his head. 'No, no, no. You guys get back on your shiny ship and get out of here before you bring trouble. If you haven't got the money, you don't get to stay.'

Silver let out a sharp hiss, snatched up a pistol from the table and armed it with a press of a button. It hummed to life, and she pressed the barrel tip to Xen's forehead.

'Do you not remember the time I saved you from that Scribe? That little thing who was going to chop you up for cheating him about having acquired Ancient Empire tech?'

'Wibbles,' Xen said.

'That's not his real name,' Silver said.

'Well, I can't pronounce it,' Xen said, 'but yes.' Silver's dominant attitude dropped when a small click sounded. 'Don't think you've got the drop on me, Fang,' Xen said, a grin just showing beneath his beard.

Clasped in one oil-stained hand close to Xen's chest was a small pistol, which he must have had concealed up his sleeve. It was aimed at Silver's midriff. 'I wasn't rated first marksman in the imperial guard for not keeping vigilant, even against so-called friends.'

'A truce then,' Jason said, before things got out of hand. 'We've got bigger enemies to worry about with those Harkins or whatever they are.'

Silver let Xen go.

'Harkens,' Calc corrected.

Instead of making a fuss, Xen scowled and moved to a small computer. After swiping the coating of dust and grime from its monitor, he turned it on. 'I swear if you've led Harkens here then they'll not only kill you lot, but they'll try to extract what they think I owe them.'

'Which is?' Silver asked, moving to the only window in the room and peering out through the scum-covered glass at the blue sky.

Xen breathed a sigh of relief when nothing dramatic happened on the screen and drank from his flask. 'Somewhere around a hundred and eighteen thousand credits,' he said. 'Though that was before I sold that class one fighter of theirs, which had washed up nearby. Thing was a death trap, so I probably did them a favor.'

'Doubt they'll see it like that,' Calc said, examining a small cassette he'd found on a dusty shelf.

'Grub?' Xen asked, heading into a tight room beyond and coming back out with some sort of portable cooker and a large blue and gray striped fish.

They helped him clear some space on the table, placing machine and gun parts up on the cluttered shelves which had likely once housed them.

Silver found a square of cloth that looked relatively

clean compared to all the others and buffed some metal plates to usable condition, placing one each in front of Jason, Calc, and Xen.

Xen lit the cooker and laid the fish reverently across a once shiny grill, turning it every few minutes. He then tapped away on a small computer pad. 'I've ordered the supplies you wanted. The courier owes me a favor or two. But you need to take me with you when you go.'

'No,' Silver said simply.

'You don't even know where we're going,' Calc said, accepting a large slice of fish that Xen hacked off for him. 'Ah, Sweetshark. Perfect with green wine.

'No poncy wine around here,' Xen said, taking another flask swig. 'Hard stuff only.'

'You can't come,' Silver said, folding her arms at the table.

'Then you need to get me the money for the resources,' Xen said, sliding a hunk of Sweetshark onto Jason's plate. 'Two thousand credits.'

Jason didn't know if he trusted this old warrior man, and waited for Calc to sample the fish before he couldn't resist the temptation anymore. Compared to the sustenance bars on board *Nexus One*, the fish, tasting like caramelized onions and seasoned salmon, was heavenly.

'You owe me for saving you from the Scribe,' Silver said. 'And the pirates with that whole woman-stealing thing. I'll take the resources as payment and call it quits. I'll never bother you again after.'

Xen seemed to ponder this between huge fish bites that sent grease cascading into his frizzy black beard. 'Half the resources in exchange,' he said, finishing a mouthful with a belch, 'and you pay back the other thousand credits whenever you sell that odd ship out there. Must be worth something.'

'Deal,' Silver said, before Jason could interject.

'It's not yours to sell,' Jason scolded her.

Before her hiss finished, a siren echoed in from outside.

Xen stood, kicking his chair out, and raced to the old computer, flicking switches on a box behind it and changing the display to something like a radar crossed with a GPS tracker.

'Shit!'

'Harken?' Jason asked, reluctant to put the food down.

'A great gobbler.'

'A fish?' Silver asked.

'The granddaddy of all fish,' Xen said, staring intently at the screen. 'And by the size of it, this one might be a great granddaddy.'

19

More sirens went off, combining into a cacophony of wailing that echoed over the platform. 'It's too late to sink the base below to the safety of the rock formations,' Xen said. 'Follow me. We need weapons to stop this if it decides to attack the base.' He raced out the door, giving them only a second to choose to pursue or not.

All three of them trailed him, wobbling across several wave-rocked pontoons to a rickety shed. Opening the rusted door revealed a solid, new door behind. Xen placed a palm on the door and it slid open onto a room stacked with boxes and heavy metal racks laden with rifles, pistols and dozens of weapons Jason couldn't begin to fathom the uses for.

'Grab one and get up on the perimeter,' Xen said, snatching up a large scoped weapon. 'If it crests the surface, aim for the eye or back of the mouth.'

Jason took a pistol, knowing at least how to use it, assuming the same button pressing as before. Calc and Silver armed themselves and Jason followed them as they sped outside, up a shoddy set of rust-caked steps to a railed walkway that encircled the perimeter.

They found Xen was staring at a point-on wave sailing towards their section of the base at an incredible speed.

From five hundred feet away, a jet-black fin peaked from the crest of the wave. It grew from the size of a blue whale fin to as big as a 747 wing, tilted on edge. A second fin extended up behind it, followed by a third and then a row of a dozen fins, finally showing the titanic size of a monster fish two hundred feet long and fifty feet wide snaking towards them.

Although Xen shouted for them to fire, Jason was well ahead of him. He hammered the trigger in fear, shooting laser blast after laser blast at the incoming monster.

The Gulper fish lifted from the water as it neared the platform. The mouth, sixty feet wide, was a scaly frame for a thousand deadly teeth. Front on, it was big enough to swallow most navy ships that Jason had seen.

A single cyclopean eye jutted out above the upper jaw, eyeing them with malice.

To Jason, it was a perfect target.

The pistol didn't kick back like the one he had used on Partel's ship. This one had no recoil and blasted red lasers, like something out of a science fiction film. Of course, to him, all of this was science fiction.

Even with the combined effort and shots of the four of them, the creature did not slow or flinch away. Its mouth slammed hard into the side of the floating platform, biting down with thousands of serrated teeth, shredding the outer buildings and tearing them to pieces as it wounded the structure.

The platform shuddered violently. Jason snatched at a railing to steady himself. Calc had dropped his weapon and was holding on with both hands while Silver was riding the undulations and taking potshots at the monster as it turned side-on, finishing off a mouthful of sharp metal and plastic.

'Bastard!' Xen shouted, still firing at the tail end of the colossal fish as huge chunks of the platform floated away.

Jason still couldn't get over the size of the thing. The mouth, the fins. The scale of it was bigger than anything he'd ever seen.

The Gulper wasn't ready to flee. It turned back, curving around in the water like a submarine-sized snake to surge at them again.

Jason knew this part of the platform would not survive another strike like the previous one.

'Not this time,' Xen said, rushing down the broken steps. He leapt over a buckled bridge leading to the weapon shed. Disappearing inside, he came back out after five seconds with an enormous gun like a bazooka weighted over one shoulder. He climbed to the top of another shack, giving him a reasonable view, and waited with the gun hefted over one shoulder. Tilting his head to aim down the sight, he sent a blue laser point skimming the water. He was calmly awaiting the inevitable.

'We need to get away from this section,' Calc called, skipping over a trio of broken pipes to the nearest platform that looked partially stable. Silver followed, but from down there, there would be no view of the incoming fish.

The Gulper closed in and reared up as before, ready to slam down on the platform. Its mouth was like a black abyss speckled with stalactite teeth.

Jason's shots took out teeth by the dozen, barely making the monster flinch. It was like shooting a rhinoceros with a pellet gun, mid-stampede. He was about to leap down behind the crumpled walkway, but as the

Gulper crashed into the platforms, Xen opened fire. Four streaks of smoke left the tip of the weapon. The force threw the burly man backwards against a rusting steel plate.

The missiles spiraled around each other, trailing red smoke. The shot hit home, plunging directly into the Gulper's mouth. There was a second of gloopy noise as the projectiles burrowed through the thick flesh, then the creature's entire mouth burst open in an explosion of clear, jellified liquid. There was a deafening roar as it flopped down onto the platform, twitching as the last throes of life abandoned it. Xen scrambled over to the bulbous body and began kicking it in fury.

'Ruined everything!' he screamed. 'My home,' he kicked again, 'my life!' He stared at the weapons from the now shredded building, floating away and sinking. He gave the carcass another kick. 'And my weapons!'

Jason, Calc, and Silver were all caked in gelatinous lumps, each of them trying to wipe it off before washing briefly in the salty water. The platform was a mangled wreck. Only the central platform with *Nexus One* had survived untouched along with the far side of the floating platform, which was a collection of old, battered boats huddled together as if in fear of a rope fraying and being cast off.

The sky slowly filled with dark angry clouds, threatening a dreadful tempest.

'What now?' Calc asked, carefully washing around his computer parts with scoops of seawater.

'Are those waterproof?' Silver asked, watching him and casting a glance up to the sky.

'Yes,' Calc said. 'Not acid proof though.'

'Well, that's good to know,' Jason said, looking up at a

flock of seabirds heading towards them, fleeing the oncoming weather system.

'I'm surprised you think so,' Calc said.

The birds were moving fast. He had so much to discover away from Earth. 'Huh, why?' he said, not paying attention to Calc.

'Aquinia is famous for its acid rain storms,' Calc said. 'And judging by the orange tint in the lining of those cumulus clouds above us, that storm has a ninety-four percent chance of being just that.'

The first speck of rain hit Calc's shoulder at that exact moment, causing a small spark where it splashed over a bare circuit board.

A drop, like scalding water, struck the bare skin on Jason's neck. He ignored it. He was about to run for cover like Calc and Silver, but the cluster of birds in the sky held his attention.

They may have been giant birds, like the sea monster, but the angles on them shifted to lines instead of wings. They were wings but—

'Spaceships!' he called out.

Calc poked his head out from under cover. 'Harken,' he said. 'Six class three search vessels and one class five interceptor. How did they find us?'

'Xen!' Silver hissed.

The central ship must have been the class five. Almost twice the size of its wingmen, it dominated the sky as it closed in.

Jason cursed as the rain came down, stinging and burning.

'We need to get on board *Nexus One*,' he said and sprinted for their ship, not caring to find out where Xen was sulking. Silver and Calc followed, Calc holding a sheet of metal over his head and weaving a path towards the central landing pad.

Shots raked the ground in front of them and all three dived aside, narrowly missing the explosive bullets that tore holes right through the platform. Water pooled up through the holes, making them slip as they crossed the final few steps to the door on the side of their ship. The bullets raked the *Nexus One*, denting the exterior and leaving black smears across it. A shot caused Jason to duck, sending a splinter from below into his leg.

Jason crumpled against the steps. He cursed Xen, who had sold him out. But in reality, he cursed himself. How did it get to this? Getting killed on some godforsaken planet by the alien equivalent of hobos.

20

Silver's hand shot out, clasped Jason's and yanked him up the step and into the ship.

The door sealed behind them.

'Got him,' Silver shouted. 'Let's get out of here, Calc.'

Jason felt woozy. His stomach was trying its best to empty its contents.

'Hold on,' Calc called, 'going to be a close one.'

The Harken ship had circled and was lining up for another strafe.

The ship lurched, throwing Jason backwards. His balance was gone.

He felt someone catch him. It was Silver. She half carried him to a room, looping an arm under his. He caught sight of the patches of her fur that had been burnt in the acid rain.

She laid him down and started to tend to him, Roo making the first aid supplies slide out next to them.

'This ship,' Silver said in frustrated wonder as she sorted through a clinking selection of medical apparatus.

Coldness spread through Jason before something spiked

into his arm and a sensation of bliss overtook him, followed by sweet blackness.

There was no way to tell how long had passed since his injury, but it was more than a few hours.

'Damn,' he mumbled, feeling his old arm wound throb as well as the one in his leg. 'How long have I been out?' There was no one there and he expected no answer until a female voice replied.

'Two days, eight hours and three minutes, Jason Human,' Roo said.

'What happened?'

'You received a minor injury, combined with a two-point three P.H. acid rain damaging your old wound and speeding up the infection.'

'Infection?'

'Yes,' Roo said.

Jason sat up. The bed seemed softer than before. A cup of water had been placed on the bedside table. He gulped it back in one.

'You did well to avoid the Gulper fish,' Roo said. 'I wasn't sure you'd be able to defeat it. Well done.'

Jason choked on the water. 'What do you mean, you weren't sure?'

'The signal was only intended to summon a smaller specimen.'

Anger flushed through Jason. 'A signal you sent out?'

'Of course,' Roo said casually.

Could he believe her? His pulse raced. He was ready to explode at the sheer-

'Just kidding, Jason Human,' she said quickly. 'I need to inform you of an intruder hiding on board, Captain.'

'I don't have time for jokes like that,' he said.

'It is not a jest. There is someone else on board. Someone new.'

Jason surged to his feet. His hand slapped the wall to steady himself. The bedrooms were the only option. Once he was ready, he went straight across to the opposite room, checked under the bed, the shower and the locker area, and then continued the search into the next room.

He went from room to room until there was only one remaining.

Sliding the door aside, he found the main living space empty. He marched straight for the shower cubicle and thrust a hand inside, hauling up a half-asleep Xen from the floor.

Judging by his clenched fists, the man considered fighting back but seemed to think twice about it.

'Hang on,' he cried, as Jason dragged him out into the corridor. 'I can explain. Wait!'

'You'll explain to all of us,' Jason growled, 'you piece of treacherous scum.'

Calc and Silver stood as Jason tugged Xen in front of them.

'Found him inside the shower cubicle in room three.'

'You sold us out to the Harkens,' Calc said.

'How much were they offering?' Silver asked, tying Xen's hands together.

Xen shook his head. 'I don't know.'

Jason drew back a hand to hit him.

'Ten thousand!' Xen screamed.

Jason sighed. 'I knew it. Good luck outside the airlock, Xen.'

'No, I didn't though. I mean, I was going to, but they arrived before I could. I only heard the amount on the radio before that bloody Gulper attacked.'

'Sure,' Jason said, shoving him towards the inner airlock door.

'They found out another way, trust me. The Gulper broke the radio!'

'Trust you?' Silver said, shaking her head.

'Do we have to kill him, though?' Calc asked.

'No!' Xen cried. 'You owe me for taking you in.'

Jason tightened his grip on the man, reaching for the inner door. It now had a small porthole, showing an airlock inside.

'Please, there's no need for this.'

Jason was beyond caring. He would not get stabbed in the back again. When he pressed the button to open the door, it slid silently open.

'I can get you the Nexus fuel you want!' Xen hollered.

21

J ason stopped.

Xen perked up at the possibility of redemption.

'Explain,' Jason said, 'and be damned quick about it. What do you know about it?'

'He's lying,' Calc said. 'I've never heard of it and there's a three percent chance this double-crosser knows anything.'

'Good odds,' Xen said quickly. 'I might know a guy who might know.'

Silver stepped in. 'If this is a "you might know a guy who might know a guy", then forget it.'

'I know him directly. We are close friends.'

Jason snorted.

'Surprised you have many left,' Silver said.

'I am not saying I know what it is, but if anyone does, he will. It's your only shot, or go back to being chased by the Harken.'

'Lies,' Silver spat. 'He'd say anything to save his own skin and make a profit.'

Xen was open-mouthed but did not contradict her.

'If you don't deliver,' Jason said, 'or you contact the

Harken again, then you'll be praying for that airlock.'

Xen grimaced. 'I believe you. But what if my contact doesn't know about it?'

'You'd better hope he does,' Jason said. 'In the meantime, you'll pitch in on board, cleaning until we get there.'

Xen looked down at his bonds.

Jason untied them and took a step back. 'You can begin with that shower cubicle you haunted. You might find some cleaning supplies in that room.' He hoped Roo was listening.

'Where are we going first?' Calc asked, taking up his seat again, eager to get back to it.

'Nexus Gate ten thousand, seven hundred and seventy-five,' said Xen.

'That's three days of solid travel,' Calc said, inputting the data onto his computer.

'Nexus gate?' Jason askede. 'Someone explain please.'

Xen gave him a stupefied look. 'Is he still injured?'

'Been living on Gedi Six,' Jason said. 'And amnesia. So tell me about them, please.'

Silver smiled at the in-joke. 'There are twelve thousand and ten gates discovered so far within both the Harken and Vistar galaxies,' she said. 'Even some within the Great Divide between the two.'

'If we bring our lovely ship inside one,' Calc said, 'it will transport us instantly to the corresponding gate across immense spans of space and time.'

Sliver nodded. 'One gate to one gate only. There is a waiting time at many gates, although most are nearly instant. Some can take hours of waiting, though.'

'Combine that with a waiting list for ships, and there can be quite a backlog,' Xen put in, producing a flask and gulping down the contents. 'Paying off the ones in front helps to speed things up a bit... if you have any credits?' He gave Silver a questioning look.

'None,' she said. 'Which we need to fix before we head for your gate.' She hovered over Calc's shoulder, daring to swipe a hand through his holoscreen to bring up a start chart. He looked to be holding back, but she went on regardless. 'There's a simple trade run between two planets close to the first gate we need to pass.'

'It would be nice to eat something other than those damn bars,' Jason said.

'And the coffee ran out while you were sleeping,' Calc said.

Jason growled at the thought.

'We need credits to resupply our basic resources,' Silver said, highlighting a planet on the holoscreen. 'We'll need them to get to Gate ten thousand, seven hundred and seventy-five.'

'Setting a course for the planet B eight prime,' Calc said, 'three hours travel time. Should be a desert planet.'

'What are we trading?' Xen asked.

'There's always someone wanting to deliver resources to Urdu four.'

'Urdu four is pirate territory,' Xen said.

'That's why it pays well,' Silver said, 'unless you have a better idea?'

'Bloody pirates.'

Jason laughed.

'What?' Xen said.

Jason couldn't keep it in. 'Actual space pirates? Pull the other one.'

Xen was clearly confused, almost angry that Jason might be mocking him.

'Pull the other what?'

22

J ason sat in the canteen, which reminded him of an eighties sci-fi movie. Everything silver and chrome took time for his eyes to adjust. He sat on a long bench that made it feel like his butt was being tortured, just for the simple fact of existing.

He looked up as the door slid open and Silver and Calc walked in.

'What's to eat?' asked Calc.

Jason held up his bowl, which showed a brown substance mixed with water.

Calc groaned. 'I can't force myself to eat another bowl of protein gruel. My circuits need better nourishment.'

'Stop your bellyaching,' said Silver. 'When you were a prisoner of Partel, you were lucky to get water.' She grabbed two bowls and two spoons and waited while the food processor filled them. Walking back to the table, she slid one bowl in front of Calc and sat opposite both of the men.

Calc looked at the bowl with disdain. 'You know I once dated a Valkai princess, who used to have her chefs make me the most mouth-watering meals you've ever had. The smell alone put me in a food coma. We had to part ways because she found out about her mother and me—'

'How much of that story is even true?' asked Silver with an eye-roll.

'I'll have you know I am something of a legend on Valkai. The man who brought down a kingdom with his penis. Anyway, every time I take a bite out of this gray sludge, it reminds me of better times. Times where I was feasting like a king.'

Jason grimaced as he swallowed another mouthful. 'At least it does that for you. Every time I eat this, I think of my days as an army cadet.' He shook his head. 'Those were dark days. Days filled with uncertainty—heartache and doubt.'

'Why did you stay in the army if you didn't enjoy it?' asked Silver.

'I...' Jason looked off into the distance, mind taking him back to dark thoughts he had wanted to leave back on Earth. 'Growing up as a child, there weren't that many options for me. It was either go into the army, work a dead-end job or turn to a life of crime. Don't get me wrong, the army is great for most who join. They teach you life skills, give you confidence, routine and even offering to pay for any degree or course you want. But... I saw far too many of my friends chewed up and spit out. Left with nothing but PTSD and an empty bank balance. Many became homeless because they couldn't keep down a job because of the things they saw, the things they were ordered to do. Things I did... maybe I'm bitter.'

The only sound was the clinking of spoons against bowls.

Calc looked at Jason over his spoon. 'What stopped you from going down that path?'

'Aliens. It was an obsession that kept my mind preoccupied. Kept it from thinking those dark thoughts that had caused my friends to go down a path they could never recover from. Thinking about it now, I don't even know if I believed life existed outside of Earth. It was just an obsession that took over my life. I can't even tell you how it started. I just remember being parked in the mountains, lying back on the hood of my car drinking a beer, looking up at the stars and thinking, there must be something more to this. I didn't know what "more to this" was, but I just had a gut feeling that there was more to life than getting drunk on the weekends, so I could forget about my past.

"I started reading a few websites and before you knew it, I'm fighting for my life because people I don't know want this ship.'

Calc chewed dramatically before swallowing. 'That seems to be a theme, doesn't it? People wanting this ship.'

Calc and Silver both looked at Jason, their stares drilling into him. He gave them a clueless shrug. 'What can I say? It's a nice ship.'

'Yeah,' said Calc with an eye-roll, 'that must be it.'

'What about you?' Silver said, nodding at Calc. 'How did you come to be on Partel's ship?'

Calc's eyes went dark as he finished chewing on his meal. 'It's a story of betrayal—love lost—hopelessness and good old-fashioned greed. But that's a story for another time. I knew someone like Partel would catch me eventually. There was a sixty-nine percent chance someone like him would catch me if I continued living how I lived.'

'How did you live?' asked Jason.

'Always looking for the next upgrade. It's a blessing and curse of all Humdroids. We are constantly looking to improve, looking to be smarter—faster—stronger. Some Humdroids tame the urge and live normal lives, while others... like me... are never satisfied. We keep on pushing until madness takes us.'

Jason and Silver shared a look.

'Don't worry,' said Calc. 'I have calculated when that will happen to me and we are some years away from that yet.'

The shared look between Jason and Silver grew more worried before they turned to him.

'Don't give me that look. If I keep upgrading at the rate I am, I know down to the second when it all goes wrong.'

'Why keep upgrading if it only leads to madness?' asked Silver.

'Because of The Mainframe.' They both gave him a clueless look. 'Eons ago, during the time of the Emperor, there was a man—woman—being, who was a Humdroid. They reached a God level of intelligence. Able to calculate events so precisely, it was like they could foretell the future.'

'Did this person work for the Emperor?' asked Jason.

'Yes. They were part of the Emperor's collective. A group of individuals who were part of the Emperor's crew. Each person in that crew is legendary in their own right. Every member of that crew could have ruled planets, which speaks to the power the Emperor had to all rein them in under one banner.'

'They sounded like worthy foes,' said Silver.

'I would say terrifying,' said Jason. 'But it's not surprising since they helped the Emperor rule all of known space.'

Calc nodded. 'And that is why there are factions of Humdroids who kill or imprison Humdroids who get too powerful. They fear the second coming of The Mainframe.'

Another wave of silence, this one deeper than the last as each retreated into their own thoughts. Jason was the first to break it. 'Speaking of which, how well do you trust Xen?' he asked, looking at Silver.

'He's a drunken asshole who I would like nothing better than to shoot out of an airlock. But... he has his uses. I don't know how he does it, but he knows everyone. It's a weird trait. But if you need anything, and I mean anything, he knows someone or knows someone who knows someone that can get it. I've known him for more years than I would like to admit. He is one of the most capable fighters I have ever met, and I would rather fight with him than against him. But... do I trust him? No. Do I think he'll double-cross us the first chance he gets? Yes.

'It just all comes down to how valuable you believe him to be. There may come a time when he is more useful to us dead than alive. When that time is, I don't know. But it will come, trust me.'

23

Their destination was an insignificant moon orbiting a titanic blue and green gas giant. The system was a jumbled mass of asteroid fields and space clouds, a strange phenomenon that Calc identified as drifting particles of colored ice. It gave the system a beauty that was unrivaled by anything Jason had seen before.

He could barely look away from the panoramic window as they descended to the gray barren landscape. When he did look at the moon below, a vast complex of glass-sided buildings, linked by dome-topped tunnels, stretched out across the horizon.

As they neared, Jason could see down into the glass complex. Farms ran in rows under one section while another had large hangar doors, opening and closing, letting through a near-constant stream of shuttles and small ships. Like a dockyard, there were several large vessels, like yachts, lined up inside, clearly intended as a display of wealth and power. They were clean and tidy amid the smaller rugged ships that did the heavy-duty work.

Calc circled *Nexus One* behind a white, cigar-shaped ship as they waited for Silver to get confirmation to land.

'When we get down,' Calc said, 'just head straight for the marketplace. Find the first Blim sugar dealer you can and arrange a shipment from them. They'll stack the boxes by the door and I'll bring them in. Don't hang around. This ship draws far too much attention for that.'

Jason drew his gaze away from the rows of ships. 'Blim sugar?'

'From the Blimmin tree,' Calc said. 'It is an incredibly potent sweetener, a thousand times more than most sugars.'

'Perfect for homemade explosives,' Xen put in. 'Just what pirates need when no one wants to sell weapons to them directly.'

'I know where to find a trustworthy dealer here,' Silver said, 'and they know my previous record. So there'll be no questioning.'

'In and out,' Calc said. 'Get across to Urdu four and make the swap.'

'No security?' Jason asked. It sounded too simple.

'Not yet,' Silver said, 'and if we have Harkens on our tail anyway, then what does it matter?'

Jason shrugged. 'Ready to go.'

Calc brought the ship down perfectly, lining up with an empty space beside a large black triangular ship covered in little maintenance robots buffing the exterior.

The airlock door opened onto an inflated tunnel, leading to a second airlock. Jason, Silver and Xen went together, leaving Calc behind to man the ship and await the Blim delivery.

Stepping out onto a main concourse was like a trip to the galactic zoo crossed with a trip to Tokyo. The place was packed with creatures. Jason didn't baulk at the feline Fang who Silver eyed with a natural curiosity, or the humans marching about, caught in the throes of trading and market selling. But the others were something to behold.

An alien hopped past on one thick trunk-like leg. Three appendage-like tubes were protruding from its lower chest, each using a computer tablet. The alien was in mid-conversation with someone on the other end of an earpiece. 'Of course I know about the Vista embargo, but that doesn't mean we can't make a profit.'

A slender human passed the other way, nearly barging into them in a hurry. 'Mom, please don't be mad—' he said, speaking into something like a watch on his arm. 'It's like a holiday on Kaleo but more... permanent. She's a nice Fang. You'll like her. Well, maybe not Dad but...' The voice faded into the hubbub.

There were two more species that Jason had not seen so far on his bewildering adventure. One was a four-legged muscle-bound creature, half a head taller than most humans. Their legs were spread in four directions for balance and to match their quadruped legs there were four stout arms, triple-jointed and split in two pairs. The upper pair of seven-fingered hands worked on a small holoscreen, and the second pair seemed to transform into a range of strange ends, depending on what the creatures were doing —from flat stumps for pushing to curving tentacles that carried barrels or lifted crates.

'Jason?' Silver asked. Unconsciously, he had stopped and was staring as one clumped past, using its normal hands for smoking some sort of tubular pipe while the other two carved wooden furniture effortlessly, all while walking along talking to a companion.

'Seedars,' Silver said.

'Who?' Jason said, unable to look away

'Seedars build things. They're most well known for terraforming uninhabitable planets into lush worlds and selling them off to new colonies looking for a home. When they're not sourcing resources, they make useful items.'

'Are they a faction then?' Jason asked, following behind Silver as she wound through the crowds, into lifts, traversing the station.

'More like the manufacturing workforce. Well paid for what they do though. No one would dare give them trouble unless they were keen for a long-term supply shortage of nearly everything.'

'Doesn't everyone use the makers, like on the ship, to produce things?'

'Only good for simple and small recipes. Nothing complex; and even slightly complicated items, with a hinge or a moving part, takes hours to fabricate from basic resources, and will break quickly.'

'And what about—'

'Up ahead,' she said, cutting him off mid-query.

A row of booths lined a glass-paned room, overlooked by the starry sky above and the constant flyover of ships circling overhead. Each boxed booth seemed to offer something different, with most displaying wares he could only guess at.

Computer salesmen showed off their best holodisplays, encouraging passers-by to upgrade their digital world or try on reality-adjusting goggles.

On the opposite side a Fang was handing out model ships of the latest craft. 'Only twenty thousand credits for a class two!' they said, tossing one to Jason. Jason caught the model as well as a glimpse of a Seedar carving them out of metal blocks in the booth's rear.

'How much is twenty thousand?' Jason asked, walking past so the alien didn't follow up with a pitch.

Xen seemed to think about it. 'About a year's wages working in some backwards cafe somewhere in the Harken galaxy. Or a bloody good night out on Vistar Prime.'

They approached a gloomy-looking booth, run down and filled with green-painted boxes stacked near the ceiling.

'Silver?' a huge-weighted man said, running a thick-fingered hand through a chest-length beard. 'Been a while.'

'It has, Allet. We're looking to do a delivery. Special, as we've done before.' Allet glanced up at a booth raised above the others, close to the glass ceiling. A security guard watched over the marketplace from the vantage place. He was busy eyeing an argument between two Fang over a heavy ship part.

'Straight to business then, hey?' Allet said, plonking his weight on a bar stool that groaned under the sudden burden. 'Where's Partel? Is he too lazy to come himself now?'

'I'm not with him. This one's for me alone.'

'Hmm.' Allet weighed the new information. 'Is it safe then? Partel was a solid captain. You think you're going to make it through any checkpoints without him?'

Silver nodded. 'Easy. I don't need Partel.'

Allet seemed swayed by her confidence. 'How many cubits can you hold?'

'We're in bay nine-four. Silver ship. Bring twenty cubits, but we'll cram as much in as possible.' She put a hand out to seal the deal. 'Half credits now though.'

'Half credits?' Allet laughed, slapping a hand on the thin table between them, ignoring the gesture. 'Doesn't work like that, Silver. I need confirmation first. How do I know you're not just burning bridges after ditching Partel?'

Silver gave a short hiss. 'Forget it,' she said, turning away. 'Plenty more Blimmers out there.'

Allet frowned, but stood up from the stool and held his hand out for her to wait. 'Fine. Half now, half after confirmation from the receivers. I'll pay three hundred per cubit. Six thousand total. Three now and three after confirmation.'

Silver smirked, before turning around to face him, hands on hips, face serious. 'Deal,' she said, handing him a small tablet. 'Deposit the credits in this account. We need to stock up on supplies before we leave.'

Allet nodded, handing the tablet to a small wiry man in the back of the booth whose pockets were stuffed with receipts and number tables, like an overloaded accountant.

The transfer was made and the three of them headed back to *Nexus One*.

Two men and a stocky woman were unloading green crates from a hovering cart in front of the ship's main door.

Jason ducked inside, clambering over the crates in the airlock. The bridge was crowded with more containers, spilling over the consoles and chairs. Calc was staring at an opening beside the hallway to the crew quarters. It hadn't been there before.

'What is it?' Jason asked, standing beside him.

'I think we have a cargo bay.' He led them all through a heavy-duty door.

There was indeed a new room, rectangular and about the size of the bridge, empty but with a small rectangular hangar door which must have led outside.

'I love this ship,' Calc said, nearly jumping with enthusiasm.

'Let's get it loaded up and get out of here,' Xen said. 'They'll be coming for us if we stay here.'

'You seem to know a lot about it,' Jason said.

'News travels fast,' Silver said, agreeing with Xen. 'Especially along the edge of the Divide.'

'We still need the resources,' Calc said. 'Did you get an up-front payment?'

Silver reached inside a pocket and waved a small blue glowing card at Calc.

'Let me guess,' Jason said. 'Credit card?'

She nodded. 'Exactly.'

Jason had to laugh. 'Right, let's get those supplies loaded and go sugar these space pirates.'

24

'W e're in the Great Divide,' Calc said after several hours at a speed he called maximum impulse. 'Home to pirates, outlaws, and thousands of derelict ships.'

They had got a basic stock of resources from the moon and were currently all enjoying snacks on the bridge, courtesy of the ship's fabricator.

'Which in turn,' Silver said, 'bring in the treasure hunters.'

They'd passed asteroid fields littered with drifting parts of ships and vast swathes of drifting space clouds. 'Why so many derelicts?' Jason asked, watching Calc guide them effortlessly between two huge, wrecked carriers that seemed to circle each other whilst being bombarded with tiny fragments of debris from the artificial asteroid field of parts floating nearby.

'War,' Xen chimed in from the door to the newly discovered storage bay.

'Between the Vistar and the Harkens,' Silver said, clearly guessing that Jason would likely not know about it. 'The

Ancient Empire was around thousands of years ago. The Emperor ruled over both galaxies until something divided the two. It was known as the Unfathomable Split. The Emperor disappeared along with his family, and the Empire was divided roughly into two. They left behind the Nexus gates, but everything else was systematically destroyed.'

'Those ships over there,' Calc said, pointing out the window to a small collection of shuttles, roaming around an immense engine floating freely in space, 'are treasure hunters. Always on the hunt for the few Ancient Empire artifacts left over from before the split.'

'Scum,' Xen grumbled.

'After the Unfathomable Split,' Silver said, 'both factions declared war over who should be the rightful empire. Both had different ideas.'

'They still fight?' Jason asked.

'Whenever they get the chance,' Xen said.

'Not compared to the old days,' Silver said. 'They destroyed entire systems with hyper atomics in the dark centuries. Nowhere was safe. Over time, they pushed out towards the Great Divide and the battles are all fought there now. Like the one we found you in.'

'And these treasure hunters search the wreckage?' Jason asked.

'Searching for the scraps left behind that the Harkens didn't scoop up to reuse,' Xen said. 'But they're all seeking the real prize.'

'The Emperor's lost treasure,' Calc said, his voice dripping with longing.

'Gold?' Jason guessed.

'Upgrades,' Calc replied.

'Weapons,' said Xen.

Silver gave a small smile, revealing her pointed teeth.

'You'll find no end of guesses. Infinite wealth, time travel, everlasting life. Truth is, no one knows what the secret treasure was and everyone guesses it is the thing that they seek the most.'

'How does anyone know about it?' Jason asked, imagining a furious Emperor being overthrown and forced to hide the things that had given him power.

'There are old records in ancient libraries of the Vistar and Harken,' Calc said. 'Probably elsewhere too. Maybe if someone had access to both archives, they might find it. Then again, it may not have existed at all and was just the Emperor's final joke before he disappeared.'

'He wasn't killed then?'

Calc's console beeped and he turned back to give it his full attention. 'We're coming up on our delivery planet. Putting coordinates in now.'

From this distance, the planet was gray, cloaked in a constantly shifting pattern of dark swirls, hinting at a rocky land mass below.

The ship dived through a heavy layer of black clouds before emerging only two hundred feet above a bleak stone surface, unbroken by green or water. Its key features across the rocky plain were uncountable craters. Jason knew that only something with the power of a nuclear bomb could produce such cavities down to bedrock. Even the craters had craters, curving together to form an undulating surface as if a child had bounced a giant ball across a sand pit, then tossed a hundred tennis balls on top.

A jagged mountain range edged the horizon. Warfare had dented even the bones of the world, ripped apart by the force. It was as if a giant had kicked its way along the spine of mountains as it passed.

'Down there,' Xen said, pointing to what could only be

described as a stone castle perched at the top of the tallest spire. Surrounding the medieval-like walls was a ringed platform where ships docked in a circle, noses facing the keep. Atop the round towers that jutted up from the roof of the keep were a dozen missile turrets, each independently swiveling to face them, just as a call broke the radio silence.

'Incoming vessel, you have five seconds to identify or you're dead.'

Silver was on the comms line immediately. 'Allet resources,' she said. 'Blim delivery if you want it.'

There were several seconds of silence, long after the threatened five seconds, when a new voice came on the line. 'Welcome, friends, to Darkheart's castle. Land on the platform and I'll meet you.'

Calc took the ship down. Jason couldn't help but notice the turrets that tracked their every movement. Heads peered over the stone battlements eyeing the newcomers.

'You lot unload the cargo,' Silver said. 'I'll do the talking. We'll get the second payment and leave as soon as possible.'

'They sound friendly enough,' Jason said, hoping she would change his mind.

'They're savages,' she said. 'Worse than the Harken.'

'How?'

'The Harken follow the Empire's old rules, but these scum will kill a child in front of their parents to find its inheritance. Don't be fooled. They need this Blim for things more important than us.'

'Do we need suits?' Jason asked, looking at the inhospitable terrain atop the mountains.

'There's an atmosphere. The pirates paid the Seedar a fortune to make one before setting up base here.'

'Shame they couldn't afford trees,' Xen said.

'There were once,' Silver said. 'Long before the dark centuries. This place was a paradise.'

'What weapons do we have in case things turn nasty?' Xen asked.

'We haven't any. If we did, they'd tell us to leave them on the ship, or they'd steal them.'

Calc powered the engines down and Jason let Silver exit the ship first, following her to a wide hangar door leading into the new cargo bay. It opened as they approached and it again reminded him of Roo, watching their movements.

A group of ten men and women sauntered across a bridge leading from the castle keep to the platform where they had landed. Compared to the rugged fur and metal-plated outfits of the Harken that had raided Partel's ship, these seemed to be the pinnacle of fashionable audacity. They had gone out of their way to look individual in a way that made them all fit in together.

One had an armor suit made entirely of bullet shells while another wore an outlandish suit of tiny colorful plates, stitched together in a multicolored feast for the eyes that stood out against the dull ships around the platform.

All of them had weapons either in hand or strapped to a limb. They all had more than one, with several slung over backs or holsters up and down legs and arms, in the most impractical places.

Two even carried polearms that glowed blue along the edge.

They flanked the only one who did not carry a firearm or strange weapon. He wore a set of layered armor that made him an incredibly imposing figure, towering over the others in height and breadth. His bald head was capped with a blue glowing fez that hurt the eye to stare at, and his face was a mass of piercings. A strip of cartridge banks lined his neck, each holding a gold or silver-plated upgrade cartridge.

'That's Darkheart,' Silver whispered.

A woman escorted him, sticking close to him. She was dressed in a smooth cuirass, silver and unblemished. Streamers of blue light flickered around it at intervals. Gloved hands pushed back her hair. Jason knew from what he had figured out so far that it was Ancient Empire technology. She caught his eye and a knowing smile played on her purple-painted lips.

'Who is she?' he asked.

'Kalifa,' Silver mumbled. 'Second in command and a total bitch.'

'Welcome, Silver,' Darkheart said. 'I hear Partel has abandoned you?'

'He's dead.'

Darkheart shook his head, making a blue metal chain around his neck jingle. 'I think not. I hear he's looking for you.'

'Alive?'

Darkheart laughed and the others joined him in the cackle. 'Alive and coming here right now.' He pointed to the roiling clouds as a ship broke through the clouds.

25

J ason stared in dismay at the ship as it cruised down to land on the far side of the platform. The group of pirates in front of them had leveled their weapons, forcing them all to freeze. Was no one trustworthy away from Earth?

'You're a cheating asshole, Darkheart,' Silver said.

Darkheart frowned. 'I never said I wouldn't give you up. The rumor is you're each worth ten thousand credits. I don't go against my word.'

'You did,' Silver said, making Darkheart frown in annoyance. 'You told me the first time we met that the Harken would never be allowed to set foot on your keep while you lived, and that ship is full of them.'

Darkheart eyed the ship that had landed. By the piecemeal way its hull was welded together, it was clearly Harken.

'They will contact you again in the future for more jobs, but eventually they will want what you have built here or try to suppress it.'

Darkheart shrugged but eyed the delegation leaving the

ship. Captain Partel hobbled out of the ship, sandwiched between several high-ranking Harken, who wore a mish-mash of armor.

Jason couldn't tell if Partel was a prisoner or an accomplice. A dozen soldiers followed them. They were unlike the usual Harken soldiers. Instead of the ramshackle grubby garments, they wore an exoskeleton made up of thick beams of metal, like a suit of giant Erector Set parts, screwed together with heavy nuts and bolts. They all stared with hostility at the castle as if expecting an ambush.

'Harken Elite,' Xen said.

'You've done well, pirate,' the leading Harken said. His face was marred by a large black birthmark that made him seem always in the shadow of his threadbare hood.

'My name is Darkheart.'

'It is whatever you say it is, my friend,' said the Harken. 'Now you can hand them over and once we are safely away from this...' he looked around with disdain at the bleak mountain top, '*place you call home*, then we will transfer you the promised credits.'

'Up front,' said Darkheart.

The Harken leader shook his head. 'Come on. Do not take us for fools. What's stopping us taking the credits and going straight to the Vistar?'

'I'll take your head to them if you don't give us the credits now,' Darkheart growled.

The Harken elite soldiers tensed and the weapons of the pirates seemed to drift away from Jason and towards the new threat.

The Harken diplomat chuckled.

'Let me properly introduce myself, as you may be unaware of who stands before you. I am Kroth, a member of the Harken high council, *Darkheart*. I do not like violence. I detest it, if I am honest, but if I give the order, this planet and all of its inhabitants will be wiped from our galaxy before that sun rises. That is not a burden I want on my shoulders, but that is a burden I will bear to get what I want."

Darkheart gave him a strange look.

Without a word being said, Darkheart slipped a pistol from a gap in his huge armor, aimed it at Kroth's face and fired.

Chaos erupted.

The pirates turned their weapons on the Harken elite, who swarmed around Kroth, both opening fire from ten paces.

Jason dropped to avoid the flurry of shots but staggered as *Nexus One* gave out a droning whirr and came to life. Rising smoothly, it crossed the distance in a second. Hidden holes in the sides under the wings opened up, revealing weapon barrels recessed within. Flashes of blue seared his retinas as lasers blasted into the Harken elite.

A firm hand on his collar yanked him back behind the mass of pirates who absorbed the shots from the Harken elite that had returned fire.

He glimpsed Silver's fur-covered hand as she continued to drag him from the line of fire. Xen had disappeared and Calc was running for *Nexus One* as the ship landed close by. It kicked up a swirl of dust, obscuring everything more than a couple of meters around.

Captain Partel was wrestling with one of the pirates as they closed ranks on each other.

'Get on board,' Calc's voice called through the cloud as the swishing sound of doors reached Jason's ears.

The dust settled and the three of them scrambled inside, ducking as shots ricocheted around the entrance. After a few seconds more, Xen dived inside. His legs were still dangling out.

Shots arched up at them, pinging off the frame.

'Go,' he shouted.

Nexus One rose and the scruffy man cried out as he slid across the floor, the force pulling him back out the door. Jason was the closest and reached out. Xen's hands were clawing at the door frame and all Jason could grasp was the man's frizzy black beard.

Xen growled in pain, but the tug gave him enough time to get a stronger grip on the frame and flop inside like a beached seal.

Jason left him as the doors closed, and raced for the bridge.

Calc slid into his seat and instantly his panicked hands skittered across the controls. The ship was rising and Jason stared at the battle raging below them. The pirates were retreating to their keep as the Harkens backpedaled for their ship. Bodies littered the platform, both pirates and Harken. Kroth and Darkheart had survived. Even Captain Partel had made it out, although he was limping from cover to cover.

'Why isn't Kroth dead?' Jason asked, catching his breath. He had seen Darkheart fire at the Harken's face. There was no way he could have dodged it.

'Personnel shields,' Silver said.

'Very expensive upgrades,' Calc said, seeming to have calmed down.

'Just wished we had got our pay,' Silver said.

'We did,' Xen said, holding up a green glowing credit card as he staggered onto the bridge. 'Found it on the ground while everybody was busy.' He gave a sly smile and pressed a corner of the card. A small number popped up above it, a three-dimensional hologram displaying 50,000 credits.

'Whoever it belongs to,' Calc said, 'will contact the banking guild before you can transfer it out.'

Silver snatched the card from Xen, who protested until it was obvious she meant to manipulate it. 'Calc, have you got a transfer cartridge?'

Calc raised an eyebrow, but she cut him off before he could speak. 'If you have one, give it to me now.'

Calc dug inside a pocket and pulled out a small, rusty cartridge and handed it over.

'And a circuit sneak cartridge,' she said, plugging it into her console.

'They're illegal,' Calc said.

'Do you have one or not?'

Calc extracted a cartridge inserted in his arm and tossed it to her. 'They're following us,' he said, turning back to his work.

'Keep us out of their internal scanner range,' she said. 'There's a chance they don't know we have the credit card, so we might have time.' She brought up a series of programs on her screen, as Xen and Calc kept their eyes on her.

'Jason?' she said, causing him to jump.

'Er...yes?'

'Does this ship have a mobile banking system?'

Jason was about to say how the hell would he know, but something compelled him to boldness. 'Of course,' he said.

'And how do we access it?' she asked. 'Hang on...' She eyed him suspiciously. 'How did you do that? I can access it from here. It wasn't available before...'

Jason shrugged and watched her get on with it once she realised she would not get the answer she wanted.

'Once you have the credits in the ship's system, send them over to my previous details,' Xen said, casually.

They stared at him incredulously. Silver even put a hand on her pistol.

'You can take a ten percent cut,' he put in, seeing their glares. 'Er...twenty?'

'The money is ours,' Jason said. 'Or that airlock will be your permanent and last holding cell.'

Xen growled and went to posture up, but against all of them he had no choice.

'If the ship has mobile banking,' she said, working the screen like a demon, 'then we can transfer the funds from my card to it and using Calc's program cartridges I can splice the Harken's card, giving us enough time to make the big transfer. Once it is on the ship's system as a verified transfer, then the only way they can get it back is by capturing us.'

'That sounds like a problem,' Calc said innocently.

'They are already trying to kill us, so it makes no difference to the outcome,' Silver said. 'We're fugitives either way.' She set to work. 'I'll send it to my card first then to the ship. That might buy us some time, but after that, I'll be wanted.'

'You're already wanted here,' Jason said.

She looked up at him.

Calc even glanced over.

'To get me back to Earth,' Jason put in quickly, but he knew he was blushing.

26

'Right,' Silver said, cornering Jason before he could get up out of his chair. 'What the hell is up with this ship?'

'Er...' Jason stammered, but she cut him off.

'It flew on its own.'

'And fired,' Xen said.

'And suddenly has a cargo deck and banking system when we need it most?' Calc put in.

'Fine,' Jason said, not knowing what reaction he would get. He didn't need to keep Roo secret; she had chosen it herself. 'There's an A.I onboard.'

Calc couldn't keep the wonder from his voice. 'Artificial intelligence?'

Jason nodded. 'It's called Roo. She's a bit quirky but helpful, I think.'

'You think?' Xen asked.

'I've heard of them,' Calc said. 'No one ever made one that didn't explode or go mad. They're completely illegal across both galaxies. It's forbidden to even try to program one. Not that I tried,' he put in quickly. 'Although I once met a woman of, er, negotiable affection, who claimed she was one, but that's another story.'

'Why hasn't it said anything?' Silver asked. 'Or is it mute?'

'Shy?' Jason guessed. 'I don't know, maybe the fact that they're illegal? You keep asking me as if I know anything about this ship. I don't; I stole it, like you stole those credits.'

'So it won't reveal itself then?' Silver said, eyeing the bare sides of the room.

'Her,' Jason said.

'What?' Silver said, half paying attention as if trying to figure out a puzzle.

'She's a female,' he said again.

In a second, Silver had pulled out a pistol from her belt and held it to Jason's head.

'What the hell are you—' Jason said, unable to believe what had just happened.

'Steady on, Silv,' Calc said, looking up at them.

'Roo,' Silver said, looking around meaningfully. 'I'm going to count to ten and if you haven't answered, I'm going to shoot him.'

'Silver, no, please,' Jason pleaded, bewildered by her sudden madness. Had the planet contained poison air? Surely they would all be infected if so?

'Shh,' Silver said, as if to reassure him. He relaxed for a second until she said the next word. 'One.

'Two. Three.'

How could she be so calm?'

'Don't be stupid,' Xen saide. 'The ship will kill us, if it's as Jason says.'

'Four. Five.'

'Shit,' Jason said, struggling to not panic. 'Roo?'

'Six. Seven.'

Red lights flashed in the room, drowning out the normal white, joined by a blare of sirens.

Calc stood up and pointed to the inner airlock door. 'The outer door is open!'

Roo's voice echoed through them all, malice dripping in each word.

'If you shoot Jason Human, then I will open the inner door and eject you all.'

Silver breathed out, but did not continue the count. Instead, Roo's voice broke into a speedy count from zero, so fast that Jason tensed at the thought of either a bullet or being sucked out into space. 'One, two, three, four, five, six, seven, eight...'

Silver lowered the gun and the count stopped. She grinned. 'So you are real?'

They all stared at her in amazement, but she coolly eyed each of them. 'You didn't think I would do it, did you?' Her gaze rested on Jason, and something akin to fondness crossed her feline features for a fraction of a second before she turned away to address Roo. 'You have some answering to do, Roo.'

'I don't have to answer anything you ask. Your threats do not affect me.'

'Maybe some normal questions, then?' Calc said.

'I'll answer them if I so choose.'

'When we dodged those asteroids around Aquinia, was that you taking control?'

'Yes,' Roo said. 'Your evasive actions would have meant death to the crew, so I searched my database for a better maneuver that would serve in that situation.'

Jason was stunned. He had assumed Calc had done it alone, even congratulated him with the others. He expected Calc to be embarrassed, but the Humdroid gave a sly smile.

'Can you upload those maneuvers to my systems, please? I wouldn't want you to use your energy doing silly maneuvers when you could be doing more important things with your time.'

'I will create a cartridge for you,' Roo said. 'But in exchange, you will need to sacrifice a hand. Your left one, preferably.'

Calc jumped up from his seat. 'What? No!'

Roo's voice turned dark again. 'Five, four, three, two—'

'Wait!' Calc shrieked.

'She's joking,' Jason said, knowing from previous chats that the computer was toying with them. At least he hoped that was the case.

The countdown stopped and Roo laughed. 'I might have been. Who can say for sure?'

Calc sat again, a frown marring his features. 'If we get caught with this thing on board, we're done for. It'll be torture at the very least.'

'That would be an interesting thing to observe,' Roo said.

'She's mad,' Silver said, giving a slight hiss of disapproval.

'I have checked my systems for thousands of years and each time they match the original program. Give or take a few bytes of random data. All within the norms.'

Jason needed proper answers now that they had some time. 'Is it you that makes the ship change each time?'

'Me and you,' Roo said.

'I don't understand,' Jason said.

'Nothing new there then,' Xen said.

'You are the captain, Jason Human,' Roo said. 'But I also have some control over things, to my own satisfaction. My personality, you understand?'

'Not a fan,' Silver said, sitting down at the comms terminal before bolting up. 'Hey! My seat? You changed it. It's all lumpy and—'

'Welcome to my world,' Jason laughed. 'Roo, make my seat more comfortable. That's an order.'

'I do not take orders from you.'

'A request then,' Jason tried.

'I will file it away for consideration because currently you have more pressing things to worry about.'

'Really?' Jason said. He was growing tired of the snarky computer.

'We are being followed.'

'Incoming Harken ship,' Calc said, checking his nav terminal, 'same one as before.'

'Damn,' Jason spat.

'Probably want their money,' Xen said.

'And our heads,' Jason said.

'I don't understand,' Calc said, sending the ship into a tight curve and dive, making them all scramble for their seats except Xen, who held onto the back of Jason's chair. 'How did they know we were here? Every time I get us away, they find us. The odds for that are over a thousand to one.'

Jason couldn't help but join the others as they looked at Xen.

'Seat please, Roo,' Xen said, stepping back from Jason and shaking his head in disbelief. He stumbled around as the ship tilted at sharp angles, then struggled to make his voice heard above the roar of the engines. 'Why would I get them here when I just stole—when we just stole fifty grand from them? Can I at least get a seat?'

'Captain?' Roo asked.

'Yes, give him a seat.'

'Manners?' Roo countered.

Jason swore. Then, as if it hadn't happened, calmly said. 'Please, Roo.'

The Harken ship opened fire on them, forcing Calc into a series of curses and steep dives. 'Always a sitting duck. Doesn't this thing have any bloody firepower? Useless thing.'

A rounded seat molded itself out from the floor to one side of the bridge and Xen wobbled his way into it.

He almost jumped back up when a series of holoscreens popped up as a brand new terminal expanded in front of him.

'Weapons system unlocked,' Roo said.

'Ah, well, er...' Xen said, eyeing the controls. 'Not sure I can just—'

'Lining up now,' Calc said.'Take the shot, Xen!'

Xen panicked and hit multiple buttons. The bridge screeched like a banshee as a dozen missiles darted from the wings. They struck the oncoming Harken ship, blasting holes in the side and forcing them to dive away.

'Yee-ha!' Calc screamed. 'About time. No more running from the bastards.'

'Firing again!' Xen said, gritting his teeth, keen to engage and seeming to get used to the confusing display in front of him.

'Missiles out of order,' Roo said. 'Please restock.'

'NO!' Calc cried. 'Come on.'

'Would you like to use secondary weapon systems?'

'Yes!' all of them yelled simultaneously before the ships passed.

'Locked and firing,' Xen said.

Xen hit the buttons and a single missile sputtered out from the right wing. The glare of yellow thrusters behind it flickered, then died.

'Secondary weapons out of charge, Captain,' Roo said 'Please restock.'

The two ships passed so close, the bridge rumbled. Jason was jealous of the arm grips on the other's seats.

'Bitch,' Silver muttered under her breath. 'Hey!' she said, shifting and squirming in her seat, which subtly changed. 'I felt that!'

'Get us away from them,' Jason said, not willing to find out if they had any weapons other than pure kamikaze tactics.

'Where to?' Calc asked.

'Far enough away to figure out why they can find us.' Again he eyed Xen. The man had good reason to turn them in to the Harken, but he had also stolen from them. Maybe the man didn't care either way. It surprised Jason he had obeyed them so far. He was a proficient fighter, according to Silver.

'Full power to impulse,' Calc said. 'We should be able to take cover in the local asteroid field.'

Up ahead, a strip of a thousand boulderous rocks stretched across their path. They slipped between the outer clusters, merging deeper into the strange world where space clouds and the huge, silently tumbling rocks provided a natural shield and cover from prying sensors.

Calc landed on one, letting the spinning rock hide them from the Harken, if they were still in pursuit.

'Right,' Silver said, slipping her pistol from the holster. 'Xen, how are you doing it?'

'Doing what?' Xen asked.

She cocked an eyebrow.

'Okay,' Xen said, holding both hands up. 'I know what you all are thinking. But I don't even know this ship. Everything I had went down with my home. How am I possibly sending secret messages to the Harken?'

'A good answer,' Roo said.

'Shut up,' Silver said. 'We can solve this one without your smart-ass input.'

'That is what the person sending the signals would say,' Roo said. 'I am the only one who knows the truth.'

'What truth?'

'That you are the one sending the signals,' Roo said.

27

'Y ou lying sack of shit!' Silver hissed. Her finger wrapped around the trigger of the pistol she held, so tightly that Jason feared it might go off.

Calc sucked in a sharp breath. 'Outer airlock doors opening, Captain.'

Red lights flashed to indicate the proximity of peril.

'Easy, ladies,' Jason said. 'Let's think this through before someone gets hurt.'

'I'll pull her plug out and shove it in her speaker,' Silver said, searching for said plug or speaker, of which there was none evident. 'She's accusing me, trying to turn you all against me.'

'What if you didn't know about it?' Calc put in. 'I thought there was a chance I might have been hacked, but according to my system firewall, I'm unblemished. At least that's what it would make me think if I had a half-decent virus.'

'You think something is broadcasting her position?' Jason asked.

Calc checked the ship was securely docked and left his post, walking over to Silver.

'Gun away, please,' he said, pressing a finger to a metal box fused to his hip. A small door pinged open. Row upon row of battered upgrade cartridges were lined up inside. It reminded Jason of the fuse box in an old Chevrolet.

Calc plucked one out and held it up to the light for inspection. 'Roo, could you please stop the red lights so I can find something that might settle this, thank you.'

The red lights stopped flashing and Jason was sure he heard the outer airlock door clanking shut.

Calc went through several more cartridges. 'Should be the one,' he muttered.

Removing a similar-sized cartridge from the row in his cheek, he pushed the new one in with a small popping click.

His mechanical eye, usually green with a small target reticule, dimmed to black before turning yellow and displaying a small yellow fan symbol.

His eye roamed over Silver until it rested on her weapon hand.

'I said put the weapon away,' Calc said, his voice full of firm authority. Like Jason, Silver was mesmerized by Calc's manner. She obliged, slipping the weapon into its holster on her belt. 'Now, hold out your right hand.'

He stared hard at it for several seconds, turning it over for examination.

Apart from the patchy coat of thin white fur, there was nothing out of the ordinary.

'It's inside,' he said finally.

Silver's voice, usually so calm, was anxiety-riddled. 'Inside?'

Calc nodded.

Silver's composure switched to a frantic worry. 'What's inside?'

Calc looked up at her but said nothing. The look he gave her said it all.

She looked at the offending limb as if it had attacked her. 'Roo,' she said, slowly. 'I need a knife.'

'With pleasure.' A box formed from the nearest wall. Jason knew by now it was a fabricator, but the sudden appearance always disturbed him.

Silver didn't hesitate. She grabbed the knife and went back to Calc. 'Where exactly?'

Calc touched the back of her hand. 'About half an inch deep.' He had turned pale as milk.

Silver scraped the area free of fur to make a bald patch. She looked dismayed at the fur as it tumbled to the floor. 'Calc. If you're wrong about this, I'm going to sever your circuits and make you eat your hard drives.'

Calc turned even paler.

'You sure about this?' Jason said. 'There must be another way.'

She shook her head, eyes fixated on the spot.

They all recoiled in unison as the tip of the blade was inserted slowly, dividing the flesh apart. None of them could look away. Red instantly poured from the wound, but it was clear she didn't care. A sliver of transparent plastic could be seen as she dabbed the blood with her sleeve before prising the offending article out like a parasite.

It was shaped like a flat tablet, round with a series of small wires embedded inside the clear material.

'Partel, that sneaky bastard,' Xen said.

Silver seemed to wake up from her trance as if she had not considered where it had come from before. 'When we first met,' she said, shaking her head in disbelief, 'he paid for a series of operations to be done. He must have implanted it then. That was two years ago. Who knows what data this thing sent out?'

'Judging by the fact it is a series thirteen Harken tracer pad,' Calc said, 'all your vitals, locations and probably conversations.'

'Damn,' Xen said, clearly imagining the things that data might have told Partel.

'He's listening?' Jason asked. What might they have overheard?

Roo's voice came through, less full of sarcasm than usual. 'I have been dampening all outgoing signals since you arrived. They will have none of that information, except rough location.'

Silver's hand scrunched tight around the tracker, enclosing it in a fistful of uncloaked anger. 'I'm going to skin him alive for this,' she said. 'All the times I've served him, all the times—'

Calc seemed to ponder something and dared interrupt her outpouring.

'We could play a game with them instead,' he said.

Silver smirked at the idea. 'What do you have in mind?'

28

Darkheart nursed a drink in his throne room while two women draped themselves over him. Black stone cut in large slabs stretched out before the large chair made of rare T'ly wood. The darkened wood pulsed like it was alive because it was. Like a living membrane, it mirrored the owner's emotions and thoughts, twisting and warping itself, creating a chair that was like none other in existence. The planet the tree came from was destroyed in the wars after the death of the Emperor. It was even rumored that the same wood was used for the Emperor's throne. Darkheart paid a fortune for the thing to be created. Enough to seed another planet. Many had advised him against it, but what did they expect the King of Pirates to sit on?

As he took another sip from his drink, the woman on his right stroked his chin. He jerked his head away. A flash of annoyance crossed her face, but she knew better than to express it.

The woman to his left touched his biceps delicately. 'What's wrong, Dark?'

He said nothing as the throne's surface pulsed like a heartbeat, sending dark waves rippling across it.

Double doors that were wide enough to allow a small ship through parted and Kalifa walked in. Her head held high, and her purple heels echoed on the stone floor. The journey to his throne was long, but it was made so on purpose. It gave his visitors the time for their doubts and mistakes to worm through their mind before they got to him.

She came to a stop before him and gave his two companions a disgusted look. 'Leave. We have business to discuss.'

The woman on his right looked down her nose. 'Who do you think you are? We only take orders from Dar—'

Kalifa moved with a speed that would impress a Humdroid with a speed cartridge and grabbed hold of the offender's throat. Kalifa lifted her off her feet with a gloved hand, causing the woman's eyes to go wide in fear. The woman croaked one word. 'How?'

Kalifa smiled. It was a cruel and twisted thing. She pulled back the sleeve of her right arm to reveal a mechanical arm. Smooth, matte black metal worked its way up to her shoulder. 'Both arms. I would like to say I paid what the boss paid for his throne, but that would be lying. I paid enough, though, to buy a class five ship.' The arm made a sound like a soft whistle, as Kalifa continued to squeeze. The woman's legs kicked and her nails clawed against the metal arm, to no avail.

The woman to Darkheart's left squeezed his arm and looked at him pleadingly. 'Dark! Please. She's my friend. She'll behave. She'll behave!'

Darkheart frowned and rolled his eyes. 'Kalifa, let her—'

A loud crack filled the air as Kalifa snapped the woman's neck in half. Kalifa dropped the corpse to the floor, like a toddler spitting out unwanted food. 'Ah, too late,' she said in a sing-song voice.

'No, you—' screamed the woman to Darkheart's left, but he grabbed her by the arm and stared her down.

'My staff have one body to remove today, don't make it two.' Fear filled the woman's eyes as she tried to pull away, but Darkheart's grip kept her in place. He waited till she gave him a nod before he released her and pushed her down the set of stairs before him. She bounced and rolled, coming to a stop at the bottom. She held her knee in pain.

Kalifa stepped over her like she didn't exist. 'We need to discuss—' Her head snapped over her shoulder and took in the sniffling form behind her. 'Leave! Now!'

The woman didn't need to be told twice as she sprinted, lop-sided, towards the door like injured prey.

'As I was saying, we need to speak about what happened.'

Darkheart swirled the remains of his drink and knocked it back in one. 'It's a matter I'd rather not talk about.'

'Well, it's a matter you need to talk about. That is the reason I am your second, because no one has the balls to say what needs to be said. You allowed a prized possession to slip through your fingers and are doing nothing about it, apart from drinking yourself into oblivion. We both know that ship is worth more than the measly credits Partel was going to pay us for apprehending it. The fact one of the Three from the Harken side came here personally speaks volumes.'

Darkheart held the animal horn that was his cup out to the floating bot next to him. The harsh smell of brown liquid that poured out of the bot caused Kalifa to wrinkle her nose as it refilled Darkheart's cup.

'It isn't easy as all of that. You are asking me to go against one of the Six. Not only the Three from the Harken side, but the Three from the Vistar side as well.'

'The Vistar are not aware—'

'But they will be. My gut tells me this ship is more than it seems, and pretty soon everyone in the known universe is going to want it.'

'More reason for you to move first.'

'And risk everything I have worked for? Have you forgotten what we do for both sides? Have you forgotten how rich it has made us?'

Kalifa shook her head. 'I have not. But while you speak of riches, I think of power. Power to crush our enemies. Power to be seen as more than people who the Harken and Vistar throw scraps at, so we can do their bidding. Power to finally take center stage.'

Darkheart locked eyes with her while he downed his drink. Liquid poured out of the sides of the horn and splashed down his chest.

'I have power.'

Kalifa gave him a sad shake of the head. 'There are talks —whispers of your demise.'

'By who!'

'They see this loss as embarrassing. For a small crew with a little ship to land on your planet—your castle no less —and for them to not only attack you, but to escape unharmed...they say the Darkheart of old would have never allowed such a thing to happen.'

'Who are they?!'

'Your doubters.'

'I want to know who dares to think I am weak.'

'Until you crush those who are to blame, they will always think so.'

Darkheart slammed his cup down on the armrest of the

chair, turning it into bone fragments. 'I will have Silver and this Jason's head before this year is over. Put out a call to all crews. The first crew to bring me the ship belonging to Jason and Silver will be made rich beyond their wildest dreams.'

'Do you want them to bring the ship's crew back alive?'

Darkheart waved his hand at her dismissively. 'I care not. I just want the ship.'

She nodded and turned on her heel, a smile plastered on her face.

'And bring me something else to drink from and more women! The night is still young.'

29

'The Long Wait gate,' Calc said, tapping away happily at the navigation console.

They all seemed confused. Jason was glad he wasn't alone.

'Have you heard of it?' Calc asked.

'I know it,' Xen said, stuffing a protein bar in his mouth and chewing hard. 'Have to wait an age to pass through, but so what? We're going to ten-seventy-seven-five.'

'Not according to that tracker we're not,' Calc said with a smile. When none of them seemed to react correctly, he huffed in intellectual surrender. 'Fine. I'll make it simple. We set a course to the Long Wait gate. There is a two-hundred-hour wait time before a vessel can pass through that Nexus gate. There's always a queue, as it goes close enough to Vistar Prime to make it a tempting political run. We go there, find a Vistar ship that's at the front of the queue and attach the tracker to the hull. It goes through the gate and Partel and the Harkens believe we have either been captured or have taken our lovely ship to the Vistar for protection. They might follow, but it will take days for them to acquire the permits, and the wait will prevent them from just jumping through after the tracker.'

'And that's the simple explanation?' Xen said, finishing the mouthful with an effort.

'Maybe the Vistar will end the Harkens and kill Partel,' Silver said. 'If not, I'll hunt him like a Fionian Shade Mouse on a sand world.'

'What happens if you don't wait the correct amount of time before entering a gate?' Jason asked.

'Instant death,' Calc said. 'Get too close and boom, the ship is disintegrated. Some say they go to a different realm, as nothing is found of the ships that do, but I've watched more than one ship go through too early and it crumpled in on itself before it blinked out of existence.'

'How far are we from this Long Wait gate?' Jason asked.

'Three hours. You know, I once hunted a Shade Mouse on a sand world. Wasn't as easy as it sound—'

Silver hissed, cutting him off.

'Another time,' Calc said, meekly turning back to his station.

'Plot a course for the Long Wait gate then, navigator,' Jason said, sitting in his chair and feeling like a *Star Trek* captain. He couldn't be sure, but it felt like his seat was just a little more comfortable.

'Is your hand alright?' Jason asked, stepping into Silver's room after a polite knock. She was sitting on her bed, several uneaten plates of food surrounding her. Jason noticed the fish dish and suppressed a joke relating to cat food.

She nodded, attempting to preen her damaged hand. 'I just don't understand why.'

'Because he's an asshole. Some men don't deserve nice people in their lives.' He sat down next to her, sliding the plate away. 'I understand how you're feeling. He broke your trust, on so many levels, and I sort of know how that feels, especially from someone close.'

'My mother always warned me of being in someone's debt.'

'Sounds like a wise woman. Did she pass?'

Silver shook her head. 'She was taken fifteen years ago, along with my younger sister.'

'Pirates? Slavers?'

She shook her head and shrugged. 'I never found out who attacked us. We were on board a Colony ship heading for a Seedar world. We had saved for years and, with my help found a better home to relocate to. We never made it. We never found *Midway*.'

'Was that her name?'

'No. It was the name of the Colony ship.' She sniffed and wiped away a threatening tear before it could fall. His own eyes blurred. Painful memories exposed themselves to him once more. Internally he cursed his weakness. He had spent so long forgetting that—

She looked up as if seeing him in a new light.

'I had a wife once,' he said, giving in. 'And a child. A baby. But someone who I trusted took them away from me.' He suppressed a shudder at the memories trying to surface and forced them down. They needed to stay buried for his own sanity.

'I turned into a cold, calculating killer,' he said. 'They called me a soldier, but I was a monster. I did some terrible things. Things I cannot even speak about without wanting to take a jump.' He chuckled darkly. 'They even gave me a medal for it. A fucking medal. I didn't let it get to me then as I had a mission to complete.'

'What was the mission?'

'I needed to know if aliens existed. It sounds silly, but it kept me going.'

'And you want to go back?' She rested a hand on his leg to comfort him. 'To this Earth planet you spoke of?'

'I don't know. Perhaps I just want to know that I can. Instead of being out here. It feels like a dream. Sometimes a nightmare.'

'Is this Earth in the Vistar galaxy or the Harken?'

'Neither, I don't think. But how can I know for sure?'

'You're from the Black Nebula then? Through Gate two. Or The Quandau through Gate Ten?'

Jason shrugged. How could he know where Earth was? 'Maybe. But we— I mean Earth has never been in contact, at least not properly with other aliens.'

Silver's eyes went wide, gawking at the wall of *Nexus One*.

'You sure you're alright?' Jason asked, fearing he'd lost her to melancholy again.

'This ship. I know it's a Nexus gate, but are you saying it can jump beyond the five galaxies?'

'Maybe, but—' Before he could finish, she had leapt up and raced for the bridge.

All heavy feelings were cast aside and replaced with utter confusion. Jason chased after her.

'Calc!' Silver said, reaching the bridge and spinning him around in his seat. His earpiece popped out and the sound of heavy music, like death metal, blared out.

'Huh?' he said, startled and trying not to fall from the chair in surprise.

'This ship,' Silver said, sucking in lungfuls of air. 'It can jump outside of the five!'

'I'm not sure if that is correct,' Jason said.

Calc's eyes narrowed. 'It can jump without a gate,' he said slowly, 'yes. But there's no way to input new maps into the system.'

'Roo—' Silver said, then stopped. 'You ask, Calc. You're better at it.'

'Roo,' Calc said, giving Silver a withering look. 'Are you there?'

'Maybe,' Roo said. 'Who's asking?'

'I am. Can this ship jump beyond the five galaxies?'

'Yes, Calc.'

'Coat my circuits in uranium and process me. Really?'

'Maybe,' Roo said.

'What do you mean maybe?' Silver said, barging into the conversation. 'You can't say yes, then maybe.'

'I can,' Roo said. 'We were not in conversation. Were we?'

'Explain, Roo,' Jason said, not wanting another airlock episode.

'Manners go a long way,' Roo said, 'even in another galaxy.'

Jason resisted the urge to punch something. 'Please.'

'*Nexus One* is capable of intergalactic flight jumps. But the ship needs several upgrades and repairs to work at maximum efficiency. Currently, we have no Nexus fuel, so we cannot jump anywhere.'

Jason looked at Xen. 'You said you knew someone who knew someone, who could get it for us, right?'

'Yeah,' said Xen, failing to make eye contact.

Jason frowned but kept his thoughts to himself.

'It is very common in the Empire,' Roo said.

'Not anymore,' Calc said.

'It's like chatting to a hundred-year-old,' Silver said, 'with hearing problems and cataracts.'

'Happy to open any airlock doors for you,' Roo said.

'And a five-year-old,' Silver finished.

'Enough bickering,' Jason said. 'We need to get to this Long Wait gate and attach the tracker. But how? Or do we go out and throw it at them across open space or board their ship and drop it somewhere?'

'Can we fabricate a suit, Roo?' Calc asked.

'I can use the resources you purchased to create a basic one-use temporary suit.'

'Sounds risky,' Calc said.

'It is,' Roo said. 'You will have just five minutes before the suit fails and the wearer dies. Silver, would you be volunteering?'

'I said enough.' Did he sound like a captain or a petulant child? Maybe they were the same thing. 'When it comes down to working together, I need both of you on the ball. Not squabbling like spoilt children.'

'One hour until arrival at the Long Wait Nexus gate,' Calc said.

'Roo,' Jason said, 'can you make it in that time?'

'Yes,' Roo said. 'I can make two if that helps.'

'What about one that lasts ten minutes?' Calc said.

'Not possible,' Roo said.

'I can throw together a ballistic that can be fired from your pistol, Silver,' Calc said. 'But we'll need to make sure we hit a suitable spot on the target, and that pistol is not very accurate. '

'I can do it,' Silver said.

'Xen will do it,' Calc said.

'Huh?' both Xen and Silver said together.

'There's a seventy-nine percent chance of Xen hitting the

mark. Instead of twenty-eight if you do it. Revenge can ruin one's aim.'

'If I do it,' Xen said, 'then I want more credits from the split.'

'Preposterous and greedy,' Calc said.

'If I'm risking my hide, then I want something for it.'

'I'll do it,' Silver said again.

'He can have my credits,' Jason said. He had no idea what to spend it on out here, anyway. Maybe a more comfortable seat?

Silver spun on Jason. 'You don't think I can do it?'

Jason knew she probably could, but something inside him wanted her to avoid too many risks. 'Just going with the best odds.' What the hell was he thinking? This cat-like creature was luring him into a sense of... of something, and he wasn't used to it at all.

He needed to get his head in the game if he ever wanted to see Earth again.

30

'**J**ason?'

A distant village stirred inside his mind. Children hid from him and his men. He and his men were armed and seeking the fugitive hiding in one of the small shacks of the village. The man emerged from hiding, a child in his hands. Jason took the shot and missed his target. There was the expected blood. But it was innocent blood pumped from a developing heart.

Jason awoke.

'Captain?' It was Roo's voice, soft and concerned. 'Are you alright? We are coming up on the Long Wait Nexus gate.'

Jason stirred in the bed, fighting away the sinister memories. For once, he was grateful to have left Earth.

'I'm fine, Roo, thanks for asking.'

Did she care or was she just programmed to ask? Perhaps she was programmed to be a sarcastic bitch as well. He took a deep breath to calm himself. There was no need to be unreasonable. He was just lost in an infinite cosmos a trillion miles from Earth, away from everybody he ever knew and loved. Some might say he was lucky, but he knew it was a curse. One which he had engineered himself, except for the part about being forced to retreat inside a UFO and it launching him into deep space.

He had had little time to think about the attack at the base. Obviously the Colonel was a traitor, but who for? Something had been wrong with the whole thing—

'Captain,' Calc shouted from the bridge, his voice echoing into the rooms. 'The gate is up ahead.'

Jason dragged himself from the dark thoughts and went to the bridge. An immediate sense of awe struck him as he looked out through the three-hundred-and-sixty-degree window that surrounded the command room.

Ahead of them was a titanic double-ringed structure with a center of brilliant blue plasma stretching through it. The rings were positioned like nuts on a bolt, with the bolt being the cigar-shaped, neon-blue plasma. A series of tubular struts joined the two rings, lined with clear patches showing the plasma pulsing in one direction within.

A trail of ships, all different in size and shape, were lining up alongside a doughnut-shaped space station surrounded by docking platforms. The station looked brand new compared to the battered Nexus gate. Stained with eons of grime, it still implied a majestic ancestry. Intricate detailing had once been carved around both rings. It had faded with time. The endless battering of tiny asteroids had misshapen the work until it resembled an old copper plate he had once seen in a museum, beaten into shape by a thousand random hammer strokes.

'We have the tracker loaded,' Calc said, indicating the pistol on Xen's station.

Xen picked up the pistol. A large ballistic had been inserted into the end of the barrel, protruding out from the end. It was crude, but looked serviceable. 'How am I supposed to use this trinket?'

'Perhaps with my credits,' Jason said, 'you could buy a decent one.'

'A bit late for that now,' Xen said, putting on the thin space suit that Roo promised would work.

'Rope?' Jason said, running through the plan in his head.

'Here,' Silver said, helping to tie it around Xen's waist. 'I can do it if you don't want to.'

'Captain's given me his credits. I'll get it done and get back in. Which ship is it?'

'The class five Vistar freighter,' Calc said, pointing at the largest vessel close to the gate.

The Vistar ship was black and white and covered in sweeping lines and curves. In comparison to the Harken ship that had tailed them since the battle, it was a king beside a peasant. Where the Harken ships were a mishmash of girders and thick hulls of pieced-together smaller ships, the Vistar were sleek, clean and intimidating. Unlike the Harken ships, they did not wear their weapons dangling from the wings, with turrets on every side. The Vistar's were neatly recessed, like a sniper hiding behind cover inside a room and waiting patiently to strike an ambush.

'We'll be so close you can't miss it.' Calc said. 'It's going through in fifteen minutes, according to the station's schedule. So just hit the hull anywhere. The thing is full of Vistar reinforcements heading back to Vistar Prime. Will be a shock when Partel and Kroth try to board that vessel.' He glanced at a clock on his console. 'Three minutes until we're in range. Positions, everybody.'

The inner airlock door opened as Silver tied the rope to a handle that Roo had fabricated from the ship's inner wall. Xen held the gun and took a tentative step into the airlock.

The door sealed shut behind him. He rose into the air as the gravity lock faded.

'We have the ship in range. Open the outer airlock door and start a five-minute countdown,' said Calc

'Depressuring airlock,' Roo said.

They all watched through the small airlock window, except Calc, who was carefully bringing the ship into proximity with the Vistar freighter. It dwarfed *Nexus One*, like a man standing beside a mouse.

A holographic timer beamed against a wall, ticking down from five minutes. By three minutes, the outer door was open and Xen was leaning out and taking aim.

'Why's he not shooting?' Silver asked.

'The rope,' Jason said, seeing it had tangled around Xen's foot. Xen tried to shake it off, but only increased his entanglement. When he seemed to stumble in zero gravity, it hit Jason that the man was drunk.

They watched in horror as the pistol left his grip, drifting gently away as the man did nothing. 'Can we contact him?' Jason asked.

Calc just shook his head. 'One minute left.'

Xen kept up a feeble struggle, his movements weakening with every second that passed.

'His suit must be failing. He needs to grab the pistol and take that shot,' said Silver.

Jason had the overwhelming urge to snatch the second suit and put it on. Before he knew what he was doing, he had done just that. The holo-timer read twenty seconds.

'What are you doing?' Silver asked. 'You're not going out there to save him.'

'Sorry,' Jason said, 'But I can't let him die out there.'

'Bloody heroes,' Calc said to himself.

'Roo,' Jason said. 'Close the outer airlock door.'

'But the pistol is outside of the ship,' Silver said.

The airlock sealed. Gravity re-engaged and Xen flopped hard to the floor, his legs still tangled in the rope.

Jason blotted out Silver's protests and pulled over the thin helmet. He fought the sense of claustrophobia that engulfed him as the suit pressurized from the small oxygen bottle affixed to his belt. The inner door opened and he stepped through. With a swish, it closed behind him and he raced for Xen. It was a mistake. Gravity toyed with his life. The floor dropped and the ceiling came down. His head banged on the ceiling. The flimsy helmet provided no cushion, and he felt the start of a concussion. 'Shit,' he said, trying desperately to remember his scuba training. Orientate...he found his up and down and used them to find his way to Xen. His mind raced ahead, training kicking in. The man was dying. He reached out and grabbed the rope. Instead of bringing Xen back by hand, he tugged the cord and Xen tumbled towards the inner door.

Gravity came back as the inner door opened and together, Silver and Jason hauled him in. They quickly cut the rope.

Jason grabbed the frayed end, spun and raced back into the airlock.

'Wait!. What are you doing?' said Silver.

'Getting Partel off your back for good.' he said, tying the rope around his waist. He doubted she heard him, but it was almost enough to convince himself he was not doing something incredibly stupid.

This time he was ready for gravity, but not for the dizziness that hit him halfway across the airlock. Was there meant to be a subtle hissing sound in his ear? It wasn't there when he first put the suit on. He made it to the outer door just as it opened.

The Vistar ship was fifty feet away and the pistol just ten beyond the door. The size of the ship floating past increased the sense of nausea sweeping through him like having a moving backdrop to the universe.

There must have been a scuff hole in his helmet from knocking his head against the ceiling. His vision blurred, his breaths turned shallow, and the firmness from the atmosphere that pressed out against the suit was softening. His hand found the rope around him, but the universe was spinning. He stilled for a second and brought the pistol up. He tracked the moving hull of the Vistar freighter.

There was no memory of firing. His fingers went numb and he fell backwards into peaceful dark oblivion.

31

There was no dream but there was certainly a sudden awakening. It came from Silver, standing over him as he lay on the airlock floor and berating him for being such a stupid human.

'You're not a hero for saving Xen,' she scolded. 'He's a drunk and you're a fool.'

'Did I fire?' Jason croaked, hoping he had managed something.

'Yes. You got it.'

He smiled weakly.

'Incoming transmission,' Calc said, pulling away hard from alongside the freighter. 'Seems they may have taken offense to our being so close without good reason.'

'Do we have a screen or is it always audio?' Jason asked, thinking of the movies he used to watch in more civilized and less perilous places.

'Sending a video call request,' Roo said.

'Hang on,' Jason said, getting to his feet. 'Wait—'

It was too late. A man's face came on screen. High cheekbones framed a face pinched with perfection. Like a plastic surgeon with an unhealthy Barbie obsession, he was a model of beauty but tempered with freezing water to give a cold, calculated finish.

'Before we begin,' the Vistar said, 'what is your name?'

'Captain Jason Korzon,' Jason said, not caring if he had anything to lose.

The Vistar raised an eyebrow. 'Really?'

'Should it not be?' Jason asked.

The Vistar shrugged before continuing. 'You have trespassed too close to our freighter and because of this, you must surrender your ship and cargo for inspection by our trade customs officers.'

'They know the ship is unusual,' Calc whispered. 'They're just making excuses to have a gander.'

'It's out of their jurisdiction,' Silver said.

'By an entire galaxy,' Calc confirmed.

'That is out of your jurisdiction,' Jason said, hoping Silver and Calc were right.

The Vistar's perfect visage twisted into a labyrinth of rage.

'My name is High Councilor Mandar and as one of the Three, I am authorizing a search warrant for your vessel under the suspicious ship act eighteen, section four.'

Silver tapped away on her console and cut in on the comms before Jason could try and stop her. 'You have two minutes left before you need to leave this system. Come and try it, you pathetic excuse for a Vistar high negotiator, and we'll see who has the real authority.'

Silver cut the comms line and looked at them all. 'Calling their bluff. I just hope it works.'

Xen chuckled. 'They must have been waiting twenty days to be first in queue. They'll never do it.' He took a swig of his flask and tried to look embarrassed when Jason spotted him. He opened his mouth to say something, then snapped it shut as Calc brought the ship around to face the side of the Vistar freighter.

'They might be calling that bluff of yours,' Calc said. 'Five class one fighters just left their hangar with a class two shuttle in tow.' He jammed the engines to full capacity. 'Let's give them a chase to remember.'

'Can we outrun them?' Xen asked.

Calc grinned, sweeping fingers up the engine speed controls. 'Like a rock versus a bullet.'

The ship lurched forwards, pressing Jason hard back into his seat and threatening the remnants of the meal in his stomach with absolute freedom.

They glided along the Vistar hull, forcing the fighters to hold fire or risk damaging their own ship.

'Some weapons would be nice,' Xen said, twisting around in his seat to look at their pursuers.

Silver hissed. 'After that colossal fuck-up in the airlock, you can keep away from anything with a barrel or a trigger.'

'And hard drink,' Jason put in.

Xen looked guilty, but that was soon wiped away as Calc took them in a tight loop around the Vistar ship.

'I'm guessing I don't get the extra credits?'

Jason resisted the urge to punch Xen and decided to relax into the seat, letting the G-forces soothe him. Why had they kept the greedy bastard alive?

'The Nexus gate is opening,' Roo said. 'There may be a significant pull.'

'Nonsense,' Calc said. 'We're not locked to the gate. It will only draw in the Vistar shi—'

The forces on Jason's body eased, giving the sense of weightlessness as if jumping from a plane.

The gate glowed bright blue; the cigar-shaped cone of

intense neon light ran through the center of the two rings and stretched out before condensing together.

'It's dragging us with it,' Silver said.

'Engines are full power,' Calc said. The ship tilted towards the gate, ready to crash into the freighter. 'We need more power now!'

He looked at Jason as if expecting him to know what to do.

'Roo!,' Jason said, 'divert some goddamned power.'

'Mann—'

'Please!' Calc and Jason cried together.

The engines boosted as the lights dimmed and all their consoles except Calc's flickered and lost power.

The ship tore away from the freighter, leaving the small ships far behind.

'Setting a course for Gate Ten seven-seven-five,' Calc said, reminding Jason why they kept Xen from experiencing suitless space travel.

'The Nexus fuel.' Jason murmured.

Xen was close enough to hear. He nodded, but looked pale at the prospect.

'You'd better hope your friend knows where to get some from, or we're ditching you there.'

Xen said nothing, leaving Jason with a gut feeling that things would not be that smooth.

32

'The Harken have put out a dual-galaxy warrant,' Calc said. 'They must have taken the bait at least enough to piss them off.'

'Good,' Silver said.

'She has a knack for it,' Xen said, earning a dark look from the Fang, who was mid-preen.

'Where were they going?' Jason asked, taking a sip of coffee and relishing the fact they had some free time before they arrived at Xen's promised fuel friend.

'Depends on who that was,' Silver said, attempting to smooth over a patch on one arm. 'He might just forget us or...'

'Take personal offense,' Calc said. 'Which judging by the five thousand credit reward for information is the most likely by a factor of four.'

'Five thousand?' Xen asked, looking up from half-sleeping in his chair.

'Not enough to do anything about it,' Silver growled.

'Might be worth it to tip them off and be elsewhere afterwards,' he said. 'Get the reward, then slip them.'

'No,' Jason said.

'You know I was once engaged to a Vistar high lady,' Calc said wistfully.

'Really?' Xen asked.

Calc nodded. 'She needed my help to forge a series of documents for her children in exchange for some deliciously rare upgrades. In the end, she jilted me for a one-legged merchant; but that's another story. As for where they are heading, there's an eighty-three percent chance it will be Vistar Prime in the center of the Vistar galaxy.'

Jason was astonished. 'A different galaxy?' How could he hope to fathom the scale of things when he was used to being on one planet in a fixed location?

'A horrible bloody place,' Xen said. 'All high fashion, blood ties and political favors.'

'A near-perfect summary,' Calc said, giving a rare nod to Xen. 'Billions of creatures, all wanting everything that can be made or constructed, without regard for those who make them or the wanton destruction that goes into it.'

'Sounds like Earth,' Jason said.

'Don't forget the political vengeance,' Silver said.

'The Vistar are political?' Jason asked.

'Yes,' Silver said, 'and bureaucracy mad.'

'Almost forgot about that,' Xen said, shaking his head.

'Under a rock on Gedi Six?' Jason reminded them.

Silver smiled but Calc took up the tutor hat and put it on.

'The whole Vistar galaxy is a bureaucracy. Everything hangs on who you know and how well you follow protocol. Just to cross the central systems you need,' he closed his eyes as if bringing up stored information, 'a ship permit, class related. Three types of travel documents to prove the ship is yours and you are who you say you are. A local and regional space crossing license and a formal referee of high enough standing. And that's assuming you're not carrying any cargo."

'Nightmare,' Xen said, rubbing his temples. 'Tried to buy some weapons from them once. More paperwork than there were trees on Vistar Prime.'

'Don't forget the levels,' Silver said. 'Can't have our Captain be completely ignorant if we bump into them.'

'Ah yes,' Calc said. 'Every citizen is assigned a level of authority backed by paperwork, of course. With one being the lowest and, well, there isn't an upper limit.'

'Too much to learn,' Jason said.

'That was a diplomatic ship,' Silver said. 'So it's likely we just met one of the three leaders by accident.'

'Bad bloody luck,' Xen said, swigging back his flask.

Where did he keep getting the booze from? Jason would have to ask Roo.

'Five minutes until we arrive at Gate Ten seven-seven-five,' Calc said. 'Thankfully, it's not too far, or we'd have to use the Nexus system and risk the queues. Not to mention this ship is the quickest I've ever flown, even faster than a Traversai merchant prototype I found when I was ten.'

'Another story?' Jason finished.

Calc beamed at him. 'Exactly.'

'Is that it?' Jason said, seeing an extremely distant structure amidst a green and white nebula. The glow of neon blue was the first clue that it was a gate, but as they neared, the shape took on a different form to the Long Wait gate they had previously visited. Instead of two rings linked by struts, it was a three-dimensional rectangle with the ends acting as the two points.

Its frame was thick, as if hiding an interior in the shape. There was no queue of ships lining up to go through or a local space station like the last one. It was deserted. The gate itself was in a worse condition, dotted with evidence of impacts along its entire length. At several points along the rectangle, large sections stood out like buildings added onto the frame. It was towards one of these that Calc steered.

Pressed up against one was a small round ship, half the size of *Nexus One*. It was attached to the gate by dozens of tubes which, as they got closer, turned out to be tunnels.

'Do those tunnels lead inside?' Jason asked.

'Not that I know of,' Xen said.

'Hang on,' Silver said. 'I know this place. The Scribe...' She scratched her head, almost comically, trying to think of something. The comedic moment dissipated as her face turned to a dark scowl, then a furious realization. 'Wei'bel, the Scribe,' she said. 'That's his gate!'

Xen looked guilty, but tried to make it seem casual. 'Might be Wibble's home.'

'He tried to kill you,' Silver said, storming over to Xen, who attempted to look intimidating but failed in the face of Silver's undaunted attitude. 'He would have succeeded if I hadn't rescued you.'

'If anyone can find your so-called Nexus fuel, then it's him. Just a shame we parted on bad terms.'

'More than bad,' Silver said.

'What happened?' Jason asked.

'Xen tried to get a better deal. Wei'bel caught on to it. At the time we were crew together on a trade goods mission. We stopped at this gate and Mr Weapons Dealer here tried to pull a fast one.'

'Nonsense,' Xen said. 'He was cheating me from the start. Trapped me inside his funny little ship.'

'How did you get away?' Jason asked.

'Good question,' Xen said, turning to Silver. 'How did you get me out?'

'A computer virus. Although I should have left you to rot.'

'He was too obsessed with getting his hands on the Empire weapons,' Xen said. 'I would have got out, eventually.'

'What about the ship?' Jason asked.

'That's why he'll forgive the misunderstanding,' Xen said. 'He's obsessed with anything ancient. One look at this thing and he'll tell you everything.'

'He's not getting his hands on this ship,' Jason said. 'You were going to use it as bait?'

'Not in so many words,' Xen said, knocking back a swig of liquor from his flask. 'I know he'll give up the information if we have something he wants. Perhaps offer him the ship and then, once he has told us where to find the fuel, we could leave.' He looked hopefully at Calc. 'You said this ship was fast. There's no way he could catch us.'

'You're a treacherous slime weasel, Xen,' Silver said.

Xen shrugged as if it was worth considering.

'Roo,' Jason said, 'is it possible to change the exterior of the ship?'

'For a short time, yes,' Roo said.

'Make it look less Ancient Empirish,' he said, 'if there is such a thing.'

'Done,' Roo said.

'Let's hope it lasts,' Calc said, 'or he might try to capture us for study.'

Nexus One passed close to the spherical ship. The tunnels that came out were like octopus limbs, suckering onto the gate.

'Do we send out a call?' Jason asked Silver.

'We do, but let's not tell Wei'bel that Xen is on board.'

'We could use it to our advantage,' Calc said.

'Request sent,' Silver said.

They waited.

'He won't answer,' Xen said, picking at his dirty nails. 'They never do unless you have official business with them and are expected. Worse than a Vistar application office.'

'I've told him we have information regarding an Ancient Empire starship. Let's see if he takes the bait.' They didn't have to wait long. 'Return call incoming.'

'Bring it up on the main screen,' Jason said. 'Xen, make yourself scarce.'

Xen scampered away as a large holoscreen emerged from the wall in front of them.

A small brown, wrinkled creature stared at them. His brows and general features reminded Jason of the people who would purposefully scrunch up their faces to win competitions. He was like a shriveled prune with deep yellow eyes.

'Who are you and what do you want?' he said, his thin voice carrying an air of impatience like that of a schoolmaster.

'My name is Jason Korzon. Captain Jason Korzon. I am seeking an exchange of information.'

'Korzon?' Wei'bel said. 'Is that a joke or an attempt to make me believe you may know something about Ancient Empire technologies?'

'No,' Jason said impatiently at the creature's tone. 'It is my name. As for knowledge, I am seeking information from you regarding a particular chemical location.'

'How did you find me? There needs to be a proper introduction. This is highly irregular. I won't deal with strangers. If you are not in distress, then leave me alone. Well, alone.'

Silver cut in on the call. 'I am the introducer, Wei'bel.'

'You seem familiar, but I don't—' Wei'bel stopped, his wrinkled lower lip trembling. 'The gun dealer!'

'Yes,' Silver said, 'He was crew on board our ship.'

Wei'bel exploded in rage. 'You helped him get away! He sold me those useless weapons on the premise they were from the Ancient Empire.'

'You held him captive,' Silver said, getting worked up, 'threatening to kill him.'

'I lost five years of hard data from that computer virus. It corrupted everything.'

Jason tried to ease the tension. 'What can we do to make it right?'

The Scribe didn't hesitate. 'Tell me where that cheating Talahan flatworm eater is?'

'If we tell you his location,' Calc said. 'Will you promise to tell us everything you know about Nexus fuel and only if it is something more than nothing?'

Jason finally understood the literal wordage used in dealing with these Scribes. 'Can you prove you even know something of what we're talking about?' he asked

Wei'bel was annoyed. 'Of course, I know what you're talking about. How can you prove you know where that scumbag is?'

Jason shook his head. This was going nowhere.

The scribe noticed and in his rage blurted out, 'It is called Hydroxy Ethaline Microcorpius.'

Jason beamed. 'You have a deal, Mr Wei'bel.'

Wei'bel nodded, his anger appeased. 'I will arrange to have an Escrow agent join us from the nearest system.'

'How long?' Calc asked.

'At least three days, but I can hurry them up to two as I have a close relationship with them.'

'There isn't time,' Jason said. It would be a rash move, but he couldn't wait days to get the information when he was so close. 'He's on board.'

'What?' Wei'bel said. 'Say that again.'

The others stared at Jason. 'That is his location, precisely. Now give us the details for the Nexus fuel.'

The scribe turned from brown to black, in a skin change that made Silver try to adjust for interference. She stopped when she realized Wei'bel was about to explode again.

Xen chose that moment to walk in from the crew quarters and stand in front of his console. He pressed the camera option, revealing himself to the caller.

Wei'bel jumped up, 'You cheating, scrounging, lying son of a fungally poxed Fang!'

'Hey,' Silver protested.

Wei'bel ignored her. 'Give him to me now and I will personally take you to find your precious Nexus fuel once I have dealt with him.'

Jason muted the comms as Xen spoke up.

'Don't send me over to him,' Xen pleaded. For all his bravado, when it came to it, maybe the man was just a coward.

'You're only worried,' Calc said, 'because it's what you would do in our position.'

'Maybe,' Xen said. He seemed surprised that they might not feed him to the wolves. A tinge of something like regret passed over his rugged face.

'We will not be giving him over to you,' Jason said, once he re-engaged the microphone. 'He is under our charge and to let you murder him in cold blood would surely be criminal. It would hang over us all.'

'He would hang in my sleeping quarters,' Wei'bel said.

Xen smiled as if he thought they would just hand him over. He took a swig from a flask, sighing in relief.

'I lost years of data to that filth-ridden bag of Aquinian fish guts,' Wei'bel said.

'We can replace that data,' Jason said.

'I've only just caught up and—' Wei'bel stopped. He seemed to ponder Jason's words. 'You can get Empire data?'

Jason thought about it. Surely Roo must have something in the ship's computer, or they had nothing to trade. He hit the mute button again. 'Roo?' he asked, 'Can we supply him with some data that he may not have?'

'Highly likely,' Roo said. 'I have run preliminary scans on his parasitic vessel. He has been extracting data at a rate of one packet a day.'

'How much is five years' worth of data?' Jason asked.

'About three thousand packets,' Roo said.

'Send him four thousand then.'

'Of what sort of data, Jason Human?'

'What can we offer?'

'Navigation, systems, power supply, Nexus gate schematics and weapons.'

'Weapons sound interesting,' Xen said.

'Not the sort of data we want to just be giving away,' Jason said. 'Give him fifty percent Nexus gate schematics and the other half power supply information.'

Calc looked up as he always did when speaking to Roo. 'When can we get our hands on some of that data for our own use?'

Jason turned on the comms again when Roo didn't answer.

'We can offer you two thousand packets of Empire power supply data and the same again for Nexus gate schematics.'

Jason knew the creature's look of greed for information. He had been the same when seeking the UFOs, desperate to gain any advantage.

Wei'bel's look of surprise was enough to tell him they had a deal, but the Scribe continued coolly as if the greed had never entered his eyes.

'Three thousand packets of Nexus gate data and the same for power supply information.'

'No deal,' Jason said.

'Fine,' e Wei'bel said, leaning forward and clicking the off button. The screen went dead.

'Damn,' Calc said. 'What do we do now?'

33

J ason smiled. The Scribe was good. But he himself had negotiated with terrorists in Uganda and again in Sudan, not to mention the hundreds of merchants that dealt with the army during combat situations.

'Turn around and let's get out of here,' he said. 'Full impulse power, Calc.'

Calc raised an eyebrow. 'Where?'

'Towards the nearest Nexus gate other than this one.'

'We don't want to go back the way we came—' Silver started.

'We won't,' Jason said. 'Trust me.'

It was the first time he had asked such a thing of them. Would they listen? Did he even care if they did?

'Full impulse,' Calc said. 'We'll reach the destination in three hours.'

Jason sat in his seat and waited. A bead of sweat ran down his forehead. Had he got it right? A glance through the rear portion of the panoramic window showed the Nexus gate shrinking into the distance. What now then?

A buzz came through the speaker and Silver perked up. Jason smiled.

'Wei'bel on the comms again?' she said, confused.

'Perfect,' he said. 'Put him on.'

The screen switched to the Scribe's prune-like face again. Those beady yellow eyes narrowed to a competitive resignation.

'Fine,' Wei'bel said. 'Two thousand packets of each and you can keep your sneaking, cheat liar.'

'Send the data, Roo,' Jason said.

'Uploading now,' Calc said, 'two minutes.'

'Fire away, Scribe,' Jason said.

'There are two ways that I know of to get hold of Hydroxy Ethaline Microcorpius,' Wei'bel said. 'The first and most guaranteed way is to go through Gate Two.'

'The Black Nebula galaxy?' Calc said.

'There is an abundance there according to our Scribe information banks,' Wei'bel said.

'It's suicide,' Xen said.

'Agreed,' Wei'bel said, 'it might be but—'

'What is through Gate Two?' Jason asked, feeling out of his depth again.

'The Black Nebula is one of only five galaxies the gates allow travel to,' Silver said. 'Unfortunately, it might be hostile.'

'Might be?' Calc said, shaking his head. 'No one who has ever gone through has come back again. Or been heard of again. It's a one-way death ticket.'

'But we could just jump back,' Jason said.

'What?' Wei'bel said, leaning in towards his screen.

Silver hit the mute button. 'We have no idea how to make any of this work. There are rumors of enemies in the Black Nebula that have been around for centuries. We can't take the risk. This Scribe might not even be correct that there is Nexus fuel there.'

'I ain't going there,' Xen said, holding up his hands.

'Agreed,' Calc said.

'Switch it back on,' Jason said. Once the channel was unmuted he spoke. 'Go on, Wei'bel, where is the other place?'

Wei'bel seemed to check something on his computer. Jason guessed he was making sure to get all the data they were transmitting.

'The second place that you might find some will be Harken Prime B.'

'That's insane!' Calc cried, nearly standing up in his seat. 'You expect us to just waltz into System B Three unnoticed?'

Wei'bel scowled, intensifying the eternal frown on his forehead. 'You asked where to find it and I'm telling you. It's not for me to tell you exactly how to obtain it.'

'Harken Prime B?' Jason asked, muting himself first.

He saw their looks of puzzlement.

'Under a rock on Gedi Six, remember?' Jason intoned.

'Harken Prime is the Harken homeworld,' Silver said.

'A center for brutality and cutthroat oppression,' Xen said, 'with a bloody side dish of thuggish death.'

'Not to mention our lovely Harken bounty,' Calc said.

'Harken Prime B,' Silver said, unmuting the microphones, 'is one of its two moons.'

The Scribe pitched in. 'The planet is a storage yard for their... collecting.'

'One way to put it,' Calc said. 'I once bought a class five warship from them and realized it was buried under a dozen other ships. In the end, I used a royal gravity drive borrowed from a Harken princess to raise it up,' he chuckled at the memory, 'but that's another story.'

'In the depths of that moon, there will be ships that transport Nexus fuel. It was once a common trade resource. Seek one of the old Traversai ships buried there. They traded extensively with the liquid. It should be in the cargo holds.'

Jason wondered why the Harken would just leave the cargo untouched if they were such scavengers.

'A bit vague,' Calc said.

The Scribe shrugged. 'That's all I know.'

Silver inspected a patch of fur on her forearm. 'We'll never get there undetected. It would be suicide.'

Wei'bel let out a strange cough-like noise Jason could only guess was intended to indicate he could be of polite assistance.

'If you could present a false face for their comms network then you might stand a chance of infiltrating deep enough.'

'How so?' Calc asked.

'Their ship identifiers,' Silver said, catching the Scribe's meaning.

'Using a ship identifier number,' Wei'bel said, 'you could get down to the surface. As long as you don't get close enough for visual identification or get scanned too intensely, you should be fine.'

Silver scoffed. 'No one outside of the Harken military knows their identifiers.'

'For the right price,' Wei'bel said, 'anything can be obtained.'

'Except this damn Nexus fuel,' Jason said.

Silver sighed. 'How much?'

Wei'bel seemed to consider the question. 'Another four thousand packets of data. I don't know how you obtained this information, but—' He turned to look at another screen. 'This data is indeed special. I know there's more and I would be a fool of a Scribe if I didn't make use of that.'

'Take advantage, you mean,' Xen said.

Wei'bel made a hissing noise that turned to a throaty growl. 'Don't you speak to me, or about me or—'

'Enough,' Jason said, flicking the microphone off again and letting Wei'bel continue his rant in silence. 'Can't we just fake a random number and hope the Harkens don't figure it out?'

Silver shook her head but before she could explain, Calc cut in.

'They're digital signatures. Imprinted into the core of a ship's computer. Each is unique and on any preliminary scan, they show up. If they correlate to the Harkens' register, then they let you pass easily enough. Any without a number will be deep scanned but if you have a number, they let you pass through.'

Jason turned by on the microphone just in time to hear Wei'bel ask. 'Well? Do we have a deal?'

'Two thousand,' Jason said.

Wei'bel waved a hand in dismissal. 'Not negotiable. I could get into real trouble for this. Three thousand and it's a deal.'

Jason nodded. 'Send the identifier over and we'll start transmitting the next batch. He muted the comms. 'Roo, send three thousand packets over, mixed but not including weapon details. And send copies of those to the computer terminal in my quarters as well.' He saw Calc's look of covetousness and realized this was a chance to win the Humdroid to his side. 'And to Calc's terminal as well, please.'

'There is no computer terminal in your room, Jason Human. Just the standard handheld pads.'

'Then make one appear, Roo.'

There was silence.

'Please,' he added quickly.

'Of course, Captain,' she said. It was the first time she had referred to him as such. Perhaps giving orders was the key...politely, of course.

'Identifier data received,' Silver said.

'Data all received,' Wei'bel said, a huge grin stretching the wrinkles on his face. 'A pleasure to do business with you; if in the future you need—' His brown features turned black as his yellow eyes narrowed on another screen. 'You tricked me!'

'Wait, what?' Jason said.

Silver hunched over her terminal, her feline features puckered in anger. 'Harken ship incoming into the system,' she said.

'Inconceivable,' Calc said.

'How?' Jason asked.

Silver looked at her arm, scanning it either for remnants of the tracker or the tracker itself.

'I shot it,' Jason said, trying to remember the actual moment when his finger squeezed the trigger and planted the tracker on the Vistar ship.

'It's the same ship,' Silver said. 'The one Captain Partel is on. If only we had some weapons, we could take down that sneaky bastard.'

'I just can't understand how they—' Jason stopped as Xen walked in from the crew quarters. It dawned on him before the scruffy man spoke.

'I thought you were going to hand me over,' Xen said, his face guilty. He glanced at the screen where Wei'bel was still scowling... 'to him. I panicked and—'

Silver jumped up and slammed a fist into Xen's face. The

beard crumpled with the impact and he staggered backwards. Her other hand was ready to throw a follow-up.

'Wait!' Jason cried. Silver stayed her hand. It shook in readiness. 'We need to get out of here before we deal with him.'

'We must be worth more now that we've eluded them again...' Calc said, his eyes boring anger into Xen from across the room.

Xen didn't meet their eyes. 'I didn't do it for the money,' he said, 'I didn't want that Wibble cutting off my—'

The comms were still on. The Scribe had heard it all and burst into shouts, turning black in rage and throwing his hands up in utter fury. 'I will shred you into oblivion! You diseased, long-haired Yastar cow. May you rot in the eternal lava flows of Erideon Seven! I'll break you with a full-force railgun from the depths of—'

Jason clicked the mute button on. 'How long have we got, Calc?'

'Less than three minutes, Captain.'

'Can they identify us other than by sight?'

'Yes,' Silver said, 'we still have an identifier of sorts. Our energy output and systems will be obvious to any who have encountered our vessel before.'

'Roo,' Jason said, 'change the ship back to its original form, please. We need all the advantages we can get.'

'I'll deal with you later,' Silver said to Xen as he tried to stand, but she delivered another fist into his gut, dropping him back to the floor. Sitting back in her seat, she clicked off the screen with Wei'bel, who had begun violently shaking his hand in pure outrage at what had happened.

'They've launched fighters. Heading straight for the Nexus gate. Intercept in sixty seconds,' said Calc.

'Get us out of here, Calc,' Jason said, diving for his seat.

'Full impulse. Hold on, we might take fire.'

To open fire on *Nexus One*, the fighters had to fly past the gate first. Jason watched in despair as they raked the Scribe's ship with ballistics, puncturing the hull. Air burst out in gray clouds as it was rent open to the cold vacuum of space. Jason hoped the Scribe had a suit nearby. He had to turn away as the fighters closed in on them.

'Can't we outrun them?' he asked Calc.

'Sorry, sir. They're too speedy at short distances.' In response to the incoming fighters, Calc maneuvered the ship hard. Jason was forced to grip the sides of his chair.

'Incoming comms from the Harken ship,' Silver said.

'Put it through,' Jason said. It could buy them the time they needed to get away.

Expecting the Harken councilor, Jason was surprised when Captain Partel's grizzled face appeared on the screen.

'Silver,' he said, ignoring Jason. 'You there?'

A low hiss was all that accompanied Silver's look of calculation as she turned on her video feed and joined the call.

She said nothing, forcing Partel to speak again.

'I have cut a deal for you with Third Councilor Kroth,' Partel said. 'He can exonerate you of all charges in the galaxy and you can earn a split of the twenty-five thousand credits reward.'

'Is that all?' Jason said. 'You honestly think we'll all just come quietly?'

In truth, he had no clue what they could do against the Harken ship. They had no ammunition on board for the ship to use and as for personal equipment, all they had was Silver's pistol.

Partel smiled genially. 'You can all be free. You can have my word on it.'

'Lies!' Calc said.

'All the Harken want is to examine your ship,' Partel said. 'Nothing else.'

Silver let out a sudden hiss. It grew in intensity and threatened Jason's eardrums.

'You're nothing but a lowlife crook,' she said.

'Silver, why are you saying that? You served me well for three years and—'

Silver thrust her arm into view. The wound from where the tracker had been was barely starting to heal. 'Three years of you tracking my every move and who knows what else? You're sick, Partel. An ageing old captain who failed to make something of himself and for decades has manipulated others into doing things they don't want to do. And all for what? You have no ship, no loyal crew, and no friends. Just a few credits that as soon as the Harkens realized you traded behind their backs with the Vistar, they'll want returned.'

It was a well-aimed strike, making the Harken aware of what Partel had done and hoping they might do something about it.

Partel grew red in the face. 'I lifted you from that pit three years ago. I trained you, fed you and gave you decent employment! I should have left you to rot in that prison like your mother and sister before you. Instead, I took pity on a disloyal bitch of a Fang!'

'You wished,' Silver spat. She took a moment to calm herself. 'Goodbye, Partel, I will come looking for you soon...and remember, I know all your dirty secrets as well.' She cut off the link and just kept staring at the screen.

Jason felt for her. 'Don't worry about that bastard. We'll get some firepower and come back for him.'

She slowly lifted her head to look up at him. 'You mean it?'

'Yes,' he said. She reached out a hand to his, but as their fingertips touched *Nexus One* shook, staggering them all. A cluster of missiles slammed into them.

'Shields are down,' Silver said, reading her screen.

The Harken fighters had opened fire.

34

'Taking missile damage,' Calc said, still trying to outrun the smaller and more maneuverable vessels.

'How far can we make it? Before we can get away?' Jason asked.

'With our current speed and theirs, it will take seven minutes to break free from their range of fire.'

'That means?' Jason asked.

Calc gave a sour laugh. 'That they will have the opportunity to strike with four hundred and twenty-six missiles before we can escape.'

'How many can we take?' Silver asked.

'Not a clue,' Calc said, 'All dependent on where the missiles hit and their closing speed. Too many variables to calculate.'

'What can we do?' Xen asked, his voice wavering as he watched a vast trail of missiles chase them.

'Thankfully, those class one fighters only pack sixty-three missiles each,' Calc said. 'So just short of two hundred. Assuming we don't get out of the way.'

'Then get out of their way,' Jason said. The trailing wave of missiles slammed into the hull, rocking the ship. 'Now!'

'You got it, Cap,' Calc said with a grin. 'Can Roo give me more power?'

'Manners?'

'Please!' Jason and Calc cried in unison.

They were mid-bank when Roo must have made the choice to help. The turn sharpened, tugging them all to one side. The ship was suddenly much more maneuverable.

'Well, defrag my data banks!' Calc whooped, switching the turn into a barrel roll. 'This is more like it.'

Even with the dampener on, Jason's stomach threatened the floor with that strange pasta-like dish he had eaten an hour ago.

Missiles hammered into the sides and rear of *Nexus One*, but fewer and fewer hit the ship as it swooped in concentric loops, tightening until the following ships spiraled dangerously close together.

Calc jerked the ship sideways, throwing them all to one side. Two of the fighters tried to follow and slammed into each other in a blast of flames and coiling plasma. The last fighter had to sweep aside to avoid the debris field.

The lone fighter managed several more direct hits, but they were too distant to be accurate anymore and after another minute, the ship pulled back to its main carrier.

'Lost them,' Calc said, his voice a cauldron of smugness.

'Excellent flying, navigator,' Jason said.

They had all done well, except for Xen, who was hunched in his seat and avoiding eye contact with the others.

'Once we're out of the system,' Silver said, staring hard at Xen, 'we'll deal with you.'

'Setting a course for the closest Nexus gate leading to

System B Three,' Calc said. 'Hang on,' he began tapping away on his terminal. 'Power is down to forty percent of normal. I don't know why, though.'

Jason could feel the lack of momentum beneath him and the stars and local planets were not moving past the windows as they normally did.

'Maybe you pushed it a bit too far?' Silver said.

'Saved your hairy ass though,' Calc said.

'Roo,' Jason said, 'what is happening to the power supply?'

'We have overloaded the system to escape the Harken, Jason Human.'

'How bad?' Jason asked.

'We are operating at forty percent capacity, as we burnt out one of our power cells during the power diversion.'

'Replaceable?' Jason asked.

'They are a standard among class eight ships.'

'Class eight?' Silver said, eyes wide. 'We'll never get our hands on one of those locally.'

'Not for less than fifty thousand credits,' Calc put in.

'We'll have to manage,' Jason said. If they needed to infiltrate the Harken home system, then they would need to be at full power. Looking around at the others, it was clear they had come to the same conclusion.

'We might find one on the nearest trading station,' Calc said. 'It's unlikely, but still possible. We can also lose any dead weight and stock up on some weaponry for ourselves. There's a high chance we'll encounter enemies if we have to explore Harken Prime B. Who knows what we'll find in the depths of that jumbled space rock?'

Silver looked hard at Xen. 'You will be the first bit of dead weight we lose. In fact—' she stood, 'we don't even need to wait until then. Roo, open up the interior airlock door.'

The threat was enough to make Xen stagger back out of his chair, back against the walls of the bridge.

'Wait!' he said. 'Don't be so quick to kill someone who can help.'

'Help?' Silver hissed. 'All you have done is bring the Harken right to us! Roo, open the damn airlock door!'

'Manners?' Roo said.

'I can get weapons,' Xen said, backing up around the room as Silver prowled closer to him. Silver drew her pistol.

'Not good enough,' she said, giving up on the airlock and aiming down the top of the pistol.

'I can get a class eight power cell!' Xen cried.

'Where?' Calc asked sarcastically.

'And how much?' Jason asked.

'It's lies again,' Silver said. 'Just another attempt to buy more time, just like the Nexus fuel and the Scribe.'

'We're getting the fuel, ain't we? You'd still be lost without me.'

Jason couldn't believe it. Was he insinuating that they needed him? Then again, he didn't want to see another man needlessly die. 'Answer us,' he said, giving Silver a slight shake of his head. Her finger relaxed from the trigger.

'A weapons merchant in the same system as we are going to. He lives close to the B3 Nexus gate, which leads to Harken Prime,' said Xen.

'Cost?' Calc asked.

'We either use Silver's pistol...'

'You mean rob them?' Calc said.

'Or,' Xen continued, 'we promise to pay them when we get back with some good loot from the moon.'

'So,' Calc said, 'rob the weapons dealer or steal from the Harken moon.'

Silver finally lowered the pistol. 'What choice do we have?' She narrowed her purple eyes. 'But if this weapons dealer doesn't have the power cell, then I'm going to buy the weapons and use each one on you—'

'He'll have one,' Xen promised.

It sounded hopeful and Jason wanted to believe him, but fool me once... 'How long until we're there?'

Calc double-checked his screen. 'Sixteen hours at this rate.'

'Well, I'm going for a nap,' Jason said, relishing the prospect of a solid bit of sleep. He cracked his head on the doors to the crew quarters as they failed to open. 'Ow! Roo, why are the doors not working?'

'The crew quarters are out of order,' she said.

'What do you mean, out of order?'

'It will take thirty-two hours to make the crew quarters reusable again, as power was drained from that system.'

'What do you mean system?' Calc said. 'That's not a system, Roo.' He looked around at them. 'Is she broken or what?'

Jason tried to lever the doors open, using his fingers down the central gap. They refused to budge. 'Come on, Roo, just open this one up and let me use the bed. I don't care about power or lighting, I just need to sleep.'

'I had to utilize the space to make temporary power coils when we re-diverted power to increase our gyroscopics.'

Jason gave up trying the door. 'Can you explain that any simpler?'

Calc shook his head in disbelief. 'You mean you created power coils in the space where the rooms were?'

'That is correct,' Roo said.

'Unbelievable,' Calc said. 'She changed the internals of the ship. If that's true, then this is the greatest ship I have ever heard of.'

'I have a preloaded set of schematics. Which I can implement in certain areas of the ship.'

'Such as?' Calc said.

'That information is unavailable,' Roo said.

'Typical,' Jason said, 'as cryptic as ever. So there's nowhere to sleep for the next thirty-odd hours.'

'Humans are capable of sleeping in many places, Jason Human.'

The floor around the edge of the bridge curved up slowly, making a ring of beds. They were without cover or pillows but it was somewhere at least.

'I'm going to get some shuteye,' Jason said. 'Don't kill each other or summon any Harken in the meantime.' He eyed them all. 'And that's an order.'

35

Partel stroked the healing injury he'd received from the Harken scum who had boarded his ship. Ha! Boarded. More like kill everyone of use and destroy his life's work in a blink of an eye. Everything he had worked for, everything he had stolen—cheated—killed for, all gone up in smoke. Whenever he closed his eyes, he could smell the burning bodies, the throat-scarring toxic fumes from metal dissolving—the—

'I hope we shall not have a repeat performance of your failure. Or should I say failures?'

The voice woke Partel from his thoughts. He sat in a chair onboard a ship's bridge that was headed to its next destination. Bodies that smelled like a mixture of oil, sweat, and wet fur filled the space. A mismatch of metal panels, chairs and consoles littered the bridge, almost like the equipment was bolted to the floor in a hurried panic.

Partel looked to the speaker. 'If *your* men didn't interfere when I had the ship in my possession, then we would not be in this mess, now would we?'

'I hardly see how—'

'I had the ship's captain in my custody!'

Kroth raised an eyebrow.

Partel let out a disgruntled snort and turned away.

'You forget yourself, Partel. You are only alive because of my good nature and patience. Any of the other two would have you killed if they were in my position. They would have taken your failures to heart, allowing it to bruise their fragile egos. But I see it for what it is, a learning experience.'

'Maybe you are wrong... maybe, maybe they would offer me more than you have. A title and a handful of credits are hardly going to make me rich, or look after me in retirement.'

Kroth shook his head like an adult explaining something to a child. 'There is a reason I am Three. Not because I am the weakest or less able, it's because I believe there are better ways to handle business than extreme violence. This makes me an oddity amongst my people. They see me as weak because I would rather scheme and plot and make people dance to my tune, when they think their actions are their own. Instead, my counterparts would rather bludgeon and kill their way to success. Such an ineffective way of getting what you want.

'They mock me behind my back, thinking I do not know. But it has always been this way. Since I was a boy, I was different from the typical Harken. Less likely to use my fist and more likely to use my words. My parents even once told me I should have been born a Vistar. Can you imagine?'

Partel looked hopelessly at Kroth, causing the councilor to sigh.

'So, now we have lost my ship twice. Would you care to explain to me, how you will redeem yourself?'

'The situation with Darkheart was not my fault.'

Kroth looked thoughtful. 'No. No, I guess it was not. But do you expect a man in my position to take the blame? '

Partel's shoulders slumped as he turned away and murmured under his breath. 'No.'

'Good. So tell me, *Captain Partel*, how do we go about finding my ship?'

Partel racked his brains as all eyes on the bridge settled on him. He did not doubt that if he did not come up with a suitable answer, then Kroth would kill him, no matter what the Harken said about not liking violence.

His eyes drifted to the front viewing screen of the ship and took in the damaged Scribe station.

Why would they be here? Why not jump?

He knew they could, and with that kind of technology they could escape, anyway. Yet time and time again they—

Partel's eyes lit up as he made eye contact with Kroth. Kroth nodded.

'I am glad you came to the answer,' Kroth said. 'The same thought has been plaguing me. Why would a ship like that not use its full capabilities? What is the one thing every ship needs to function properly? Ammunition or fuel.'

Partel nodded, then looked lost. 'But if that is true, then where would they go?'

Kroth smiled, his teeth almost blinding. 'To the biggest scrapyard in this galaxy.'

Confused, Partel racked his brains for the answer until it dawned on him. 'If... If you knew the answer all along, then why not tell me?'

'Because I wanted to know how useful you still were. If you had failed to answer my question, then let's just say, I do not have a love for pieces of junk like my brethren do.'

36

'Coming up on the gate, Captain,' Calc said as they entered a new system. Ships were visible every few minutes, all heading in one direction—towards a vast station that sat beside a massive pyramid-shaped Nexus gate. Inside the three-dimensional framework of the pyramid was a neon blue plasma cloud that was the gateway.

Circling the pyramid were hundreds of ships, drifting in a long line to and from the station before looping around in a queue. Every minute or two a ship would enter the plasma field and in a flash of blinding light the ship would flicker from sight, leaving behind a thin blue trail in the direction of travel.

The station was a flattened circle, like a huge UFO disc, with hundreds of ships docking around the rim. Tunnels stretched out from the station, connecting to various airlocks of the docked ships.

As they closed in on the station, it became obvious that the majority of the ships were towing others behind them, either via long thick cables or a transparent yellow beam that kept anything within its radius at the same distance.

Jason stood close to the window, watching the ships in fascination. Calc and Xen were busy mid-conversation about how to get to the station and where to park.

Silver came over and stood next to him. 'Ever seen this before?' she asked.

The station ahead was like a frisbee surrounded by a swarm of busy ships. Some were tiny—those he knew would be the class one vessels as Calc had said—while others were titans in comparison, near a mile in length, but out here against the stars and multicolored nebulae it was hard to gauge correctly.

Jason shook his head at the sheer scale of it all. 'It's something I always wanted to believe.'

Silver chuckled, 'What, that the Harkens collect scrap ships?'

'Other species,' Jason said, trying to explain his thoughts. 'No one where I come from knows about any of this. They would never believe me if I told them.'

'When you tell them,' Silver corrected.

Jason turned to look at her. 'When,' he agreed.

'You don't want to go back?'

'I did,' he said; 'I do. I just don't know what to expect now that I know the truth.'

'Perhaps you could be the one to tell them?'

He hadn't considered that option. He had wanted to get back there, but there were so many unknowns. Could he just go back to living alone, drinking in bars and hunting deer on the weekends, in between chasing the best UFO viewing spots?

'Maybe,' he said. 'What will you do after?'

'Depends,' she said. 'You'll need to leave us *Nexus One*, so we can get back.'

He hadn't even considered that these three would be in the craft when they arrived back on Earth. 'I guess I should have considered that before now.'

'Maybe I can—' Silver started.

'Harken security patrol incoming,' Calc said.

Silver broke away and raced for her terminal. 'Uploading identifier frequency. Let's hope they don't scan too long.'

'We'll need to make for the station,' Calc said.

The patrol passed them without slowing.

Roo's voice echoed around them. 'I have just intercepted a news transmission and I think you should look at it.'

It came up on all their screens. It was an image of Silver with a brief article stating she was wanted by the Harken police for crimes against a Harken councillor and for theft of Harken property. There were several other similar articles about other criminals, but her face was the most prominent.

'Damn,' Jason said 'We can't hang around here for long. Xen, where on the station is this dealer of yours?'

'On the Market level. You'll need some serious credits if you're going to get weapons.'

Silver let out a small hiss, her eyes darting from Xen to Jason. 'If you leave me here with this dishonest drunk, I'll shoot him.'

'The two of us will go,' Jason said. 'You and Calc wait here for us to return.'

She sighed and fished out a credit card. 'This has five thousand on it, enough to get some decent weaponry but not enough to buy a class eight power cell. I hope you have a plan with this liar in tow.'

Xen scowled at Silver's words as he plucked the card from her hand.

'It's OK,' Jason said, as Silver made ready to swipe it back from Xen.

Jason had gone over it several times, but other than finding Xen's merchant to be extremely generous, he had failed to come up with something more than promising to bring back expensive ship parts. It was going to be a long shot.

'Will they search us at the station when we go in?' he asked.

'You'll be scanned as part of standard protocol,' Silver said, tapping her pistol in its holster. 'So I can't give you this.'

'According to my limited knowledge,' Calc said, 'there is a deep search patrol ship that circles every fifty minutes. If that thing checks us, it will flag up that we are not a Harken salvage ship. As soon as it passes on its round, I'll dock us to the station. Just get on, get what we need, and get back as soon as possible. I'll book us in for the Nexus gate so we have clearance without the wait time.'

Jason nodded.

'But if that patrol ship comes for us, Captain,' Calc said, 'we won't be able to outrun it. Or any ship for that matter.'

'I'll be ready to install the cell when you get back,' Silver said.

A black-hulled ship streaked with gently glowing red lines sailed past their side of the station. It stopped at docked ships along the way for several seconds before moving on.

'That's the patrol,' Calc said. 'I'm taking us in.'

Jason could tell that Calc tried to take them in fast, but

the ship was just not as responsive as before. They needed that power cell.

'Forty-six minutes,' Calc said, swinging the front of the ship into the end of the bay. A tunnel stretched out like a semi-rigid corridor of canvas and connected to the outer airlock door.

Jason and Xen were at the door, ready to leave as soon as the pressure equalized with the station.

'Good luck,' Silver said, handing Jason a small tablet. It had a ticking countdown timer for thirty-nine minutes and ten seconds.

'Thirty-eight minutes,' Calc said. 'Hurry. And try not to get captured or killed.'

Jason realized he was about to go onboard a completely alien place, with no knowledge of nearly anything and only a drunken washed-up soldier who had already betrayed him for company. 'No promises,' he said.

37

The doors to the station slid aside and a rugged-looking Harken soldier eyed Jason and Xen as they stepped through a scanner and a second door. Jason sighed with relief as they entered a concourse without the soldier chasing them both down, but before the sigh finished, he sucked in a breath of astonishment.

The concourse formed a wide ring that swept around a huge open space, a dozen stories high and lined with hundreds of shops that all had two fronts. One faced the walkway that ringed the station and the other opened onto the empty expanse. Both sides were manned by what Jason assumed to be merchants.

Normal pedestrians strolled around the ring concourse, taking elevators up and down to the various levels, but the open area in the center was crammed with moving platforms that drifted in set patterns to and from the shops. The shoppers would step onto a platform and it would glide out, taking them between other platforms and across the expanse to their shop of choice. The rectangular platforms were powered by what Jason could only guess was some antigravity technology or failing that, magic by any other term.

'This way,' Xen said, walking to an empty platform and opening the thin plate of railing that hemmed it in at waist height.

'I don't know about that—' Jason started.

'It's fine,' Xen said, giving an unnerving bounce up and down on the platform. It didn't sway or rock. Time was running out, so Jason stepped on, closing the gate behind him.

Xen's old leather coat had a strong whiff of alcohol about it, mixing with the man's general stench. It made the confined space, although open to the air above waist height, still pungent.

A computer holoscreen popped up displaying a huge list:

Open Merchants
Cuisine
Commodities
Precious metals
Raw resources
Ship resources
Weapons
Live animals
Clubs
More...

Jason tapped weapons but Xen quickly hit cancel.

'What?' Jason asked

'He's not a typical weapon merchant,' Xen said, 'No licenses or certificates of sale. We'll find him in the club area.'

Xen programmed the destination and, with a slight jolt, the platform drifted across the station.

It stopped at a wide entrance, full of colorful neon lights and signs that hurt the eye if Jason stared too long.

'What's his name?' Jason asked, feeling nervous that he hadn't gleaned any more information from Xen other than vague references to an old friend. The last time had been the furious Scribe Wei'bel and that had gone badly enough.

'Carlton Brisket,' Xen said. 'He'll be the fattest human in the club, just need to find him. Ah, there.'

A gallery of brightly colored club fronts and bars became visible as the platform rounded a large warehouse. The club entrances lined a wide walkway, like a pedestrian road in some eastern countries that Jason had visited.

Aliens roamed the strip like tourists. There were Fangs and Seedars, even several Scribes scurrying between places looking shady or embarrassed. The most numerous were Harken. Dressed in their usual grubby garb, they prowled in groups like drunken brawlers. Every now and then he thought he spotted a new alien that he didn't recognize, but before he could get a better view, they disappeared into a doorway.

'Which club?' Jason asked, counting at least five in between the bars and seedy-looking stores.

'Er,' Xen said, 'I couldn't say, but it shouldn't be too difficult to locate him.'

'Not a good start,' Jason muttered. He checked the tablet. Less than thirty minutes.

Jason eyed the two clubs closest. 'I'll take that one, you search that one and if you spot him, then come find me in the other. If we can't find him, then meet out here in ten minutes.'

'Search the booths,' Xen said, knocking back his flask, 'at the back of the lounges.'

'If I spot him, what should I say?' Jason asked. He

thought back to the Scribe. 'Should I mention your name to him?'

'Yes,' Xen said, 'tell him I have a once-in-a-lifetime deal for him.'

'You do?'

The bustle increased around them and Jason spotted an argument breaking out at a bar front. Within moments a group of heavily armored Harken broke from an elevator and rushed the confrontation.

'Of course not,' Xen said, with another swig from his flask. 'But that sort of talk always gets a merchant excited.'

Jason broke off towards one of the clubs. 'Let's go then.'

Inside, the club was an open room crowded with what looked like arcade games and a long bar serving a host of clientele.

A pair of Harken were standing on either side of a clear glass screen, inside a booth and surrounded by a tight-knit group of onlookers. Both were facing each other in a western-style showdown, but instead of six-shooter pistols, they had rifles. Bets were being made before a timer reached zero.

When it did, both contestants raised rifles and fired. Jason expected a bloodbath, but instead, the rifles shot out balls of light, slowly at first, then gathering speed towards the glass in the center. He watched as they attempted to shoot both each other and the incoming bullets before they hit the center screen. If one connected, then the ball of light would disappear. If they failed, the lights struck the center and lit up a scoreboard above the contestants. The sheer skill involved was frightening. A timer ticked down behind each player.

Time! He looked at the tablet. Twenty-three minutes left. He had to get moving.

He headed for a bar lined with bizarre bottles and holo-screens displaying Zero G death racing. It was a race involving small craft in incredibly dangerous places. They were battling it out in a desert canyon, trying to knock each other into the sides of the walls.

Behind the bar, a Humdroid served a few patrons, keeping glasses topped up whilst mopping up the spills from a previous crowd.

'Can I help, sir?' he asked, seeing Jason watching him.

Time was passing fast and he needed to find this merchant or leave empty-handed.

'I'm looking for a merchant who might stay in here,' he said.

'Plenty of those,' the Humdroid said.

Jason racked his brain to remember the name Xen had given him. He had been too wrapped up in awe to remember. 'Carl Brisset?' he tried.

The Humdroid glanced around suspiciously. 'Carl?' he said.

'Carlton!' Jason said, his memory getting jogged.

'Brisket,' the Humdroid finished. The Humdroid studied him for a moment and must have made a calculated decision that he was genuine. 'In the booths behind the reality slots,' he said, pointing, 'that way.'

'Thanks,' Jason said, striding off.

'Wait,' the Humdroid said, pulling down a bottle from a shelf. He poured a small glass full of the blue liquid. 'Take this to him.'

Jason must have looked confused.

'On the house.'

Jason took the offering and thanked the barman. He headed towards an area plastered with holoscreens.

Gamblers stood in front and slapped at light sequences that were projected outwards towards them.

Just beyond were alcoved booths along the back wall. Plush seats arranged in circles ringed a table. Most were empty, so it didn't take him long to locate Carlton Brisket.

The enormous bulky man was chuckling at something one of the pretty girls around him had said, before taking a large bite of a live animal the size of a lizard. It let out a shriek as it was devoured by the obese merchant.

He wore a smart jumpsuit, something akin to a suit but stained with splatters of grease from his constant consumption.

The table was overloaded with empty plates and glasses, as if the man had not moved in days. Two other men were also seated at the table. One was a scrawny man, peering over a pair of wire glasses at Carlton and laughing like a lapdog at some joke or other. A thick-built man was the other companion and his watchful eye told Jason he would be a bodyguard of sorts. The man stood when he approached, confirming Jason's hunch.

Carlton looked up from whispering in the girl's ear to Jason and stared with bored annoyance at his approach.

He must have spotted the glass in Jason's hand and the tablet in the other and assumed he worked there. 'You can take away the plates and glasses,' he said, 'and bring me another plate of Condolian trickle fish.'

'I don't work here,' Jason said. 'I'm here because a mutual friend sent me.' He placed the glass down on the table, aware that the bodyguard had a hand on something stashed in his jacket top.

'The fact it is blue means that Rick doesn't think you are law enforcement or part of a customs outfit.'

'Rick?'

'The Humdroid, and judging by how out of place you look, I'd say you're new to this sort of thing.'

'You could say that.'

'That's a good start,' Carlton said, 'but who would be our mutual friend?'

'Xen.'

'Xen who?'

'That's all I know,' Jason said, trying hard to think what he knew about him. 'Got a beard, likes shooting, was in a military group or something, drinking problem. Would sell his mother for profit.'

Carlton chuckled, knocking back the small blue drink. 'Yes, I know *that* Xen. Where is he?'

'In the next club along; I'll go find him and come back.'

'Before you do. What do you need from me?'

'Weapons,' Jason said, turning to leave, 'oh, and a class eight power cell.'

'You have credits?'

Jason nodded and looked at his timer. Twenty minutes.

'We need it in fifteen minutes,' he said and sprinted to go get Xen.

He could hear the blubber-ridden man laughing about miracles as he left.

The next club was a much seedier joint. Instead of the bright arcade-like rooms next door, this place was dark and gloomy, like a washed-out jazz lounge. Horseshoe-shaped tables lined the room and colorful coils of smoke danced like lovers in the throes of a drug trip.

Gamblers hunched over the tables, tossing strange objects down as bets. Some were lively, enjoying the bizarre games, while others wore the lifelong habitual face of those who had hit rock bottom more than once. The place smelled of stale sweat mixed with the sweetness of spilt cocktails.

If Xen was wandering among the outcasts of society like Jason was, looking for someone, then he should be obvious. Most were seated, throwing away their only means of—

A dark thought struck him like a class five warship, slamming into his chest. The sinking feeling grew into a tight knot. Xen had the five thousand credits.

38

J ason resisted the urge to panic. He scanned faces, trying to locate the scraggly long-haired man with the black beard. Jason cursed. Seated amidst a group of spirited players was Xen. He was seated between two Fang women, with several empty drink glasses in front of him.

The man had been in here only a few minutes and looked as if he had grown up within the confines of the casino.

In front of him was the credit card Silver had given them. It glowed as a dealer waved a tablet over it. Jason could only guess it was trading the credits to the table for bets.

'Xen!' Jason called loudly before he reached the table.

Xen glanced up. Through the haze of smoke, Jason saw an eyebrow lift before Xen's head lolled back and he returned to the game.

Jason marched up to him and slapped a hand on his shoulder, ready to haul him out.

'What in the shit are you doing?' Jason asked.

'Huh?' Xen murmured, eyes still fixed on the table.

Holocards with unusual symbols glowed in front of the players. 'We need to leave now,' Jason said. He looked at the tablet. Fifteen minutes.

'I hope that's your own money,' he said, tapping the card meaningfully.

Two men in his peripheral vision stirred before Xen could reply.

Some sort of pit boss or security. It was clear they were going to make sure no one interfered with the clientele.

The card on the table was the one Silver had given them.

'How much is left?'

The pit bosses had moved closer.

'You guess I'm not winning?' Xen said, taking another sip of his drink. 'This will be the winning one, though.' He slapped the card down on a symbol. 'One thousand.'

Jason pounded a fist onto the card, unable to control the fury in him any longer. 'No!'

The pit bosses were marching over.

'Xen,' Jason said, moving the half-full glass out of reach. 'We have to go see Carlton, right now.'

'Is there a reason you are bothering one of our customers?' a burly man said, rubbing his hands together as if to reinforce the idea of intimidation.

'He's drunk and playing with stol—someone else's money,' Jason said, cutting himself off. Mentioning stolen credits might bring even more unwanted attention. He eyed the two men. Should he just leave Xen here to finish and head back to the ship? Would the others understand? Silver would probably be happy but as for any chance of getting the ship up and working again, that would be impossible, especially since he let the asshole disappear with their credits. They'd never trust Jason again. He had to give it one more go.

'Xen,' he said, ignoring the guards, 'I will not leave you here to lose everything Silver gave you. Carlton will sort it out.'

Xen looked up at the Fang's name, or was it Carlton's? Clearly he was wrestling with something. It turned into a shrug and Jason sighed, ready to leave. He had failed.

Xen tried to reach the glass, failed and instead opted for his flask.

'Don't care about Car-Carlton or about you, Ca-Captain.'

At the mention of him being Xen's captain or perhaps the name drop of Carlton, the two pit bosses seemed to sag. The burly one stepped back at a nod from the other, who bent over the table and slid the credit card back to Xen.

'Perhaps you could join us again tomorrow for the tournament?' he said, looking to Jason for approval.

Jason took the card from Xen's weak grip and slid an arm under the man's. The pit boss propped up Xen's other side and together they got him to the door.

Jason didn't bother to thank the stranger. Instead, he checked the time and redoubled his efforts to keep Xen on his feet. Eleven minutes.

By the time they reached the next bar, Xen was more upright and carrying his own weight.

'Xen,' Jason said, as they passed through the entrance. 'Listen up. We have no credits except for the thousand left. I need you to help me convince Carlton to hand over weapons and the power cell in exchange for a share in whatever we can find on that Harken moon.'

'Harken Prime B,' Xen said, getting his feet to work in a straight line.

'Yes!' Jason said, relief finally giving way to hope. 'We

need a thousand credits' worth of weapons and a promise for Carlton to give us the power cell. Got it?'

Xen's hand came up, flask held loosely, but Jason snatched it away, giving the barman a nod before heading for the seating alcoves.

'We could use the credits from Silver's bounty to pay for it all,' Xen said.

'What?' Jason said, slowing their walk.

'Just a thought,' Xen said; 'she's worth enough for a down payment on the power cell.'

Jason had heard enough. 'Shut the fuck up, Xen, and do as I ask, or you're finished. Got it?'

Maybe Xen did, as he seemed to sober up on the approach to the table. 'Only joking,' Xen said.

'Xen!' Carlton said with a grin. He waved a tubby hand at the two seats opposite himself and the bodyguard. The thin simpering man and the two women had disappeared. In their place on the seats were two metal boxes each about the size of a luggage case.

The bodyguard pressed a button recessed on the seat beside him. There was a hum and the air around the alcove formed a skin, like a bubble with them in the center. The noise from the lounge became a distant dull sound, like being submerged underwater.

'It's been so long since I last saw you.' Carlton brought up a pad hidden in the folds of his ample clothing and lazily swished a finger across it. He smiled. 'I haven't forgotten the five hundred credits you owe me for those Vistar sniper rifle charges, have you?'

'Er, well,' Xen started, 'yes, I mean no—I have that here and another five hundred for some weapons.'

'Not going to get much in the way of an effective arsenal for that,' Carlton said.

'What have you got?' Jason asked, eyeing the crates.

Carlton signaled the bodyguard and the burly man pressed a second button. The surrounding air visibly shimmered, becoming so blurry it was impossible to see an inch beyond the barrier. The merchant waited for the shield to block all sight, then leant over with a groan and lifted the lid to the chest on his right. Inside was a heaped selection of guns. Some were rifles, others were pistols nestled among boxes of what must have been ammunition. There was a smaller crate inside, which Carlton opened, revealing metal cylinders. 'Stun charges. You can have two of them for five hundred.'

The only one Jason recognised in the crate was the one Carlton lifted out. 'Or one of these.' It was a Harken pipe rifle, identical to the one he had used on board Partel's ship.

'This is what five hundred will get you,' Carlton said, placing it on the table for inspection, along with two containers of ammunition. 'I'll throw in the ammunition for free.'

Jason reached for the rifle. The bodyguard stirred. A nod from Carlton eased the tension. Jason picked up the rifle, examining it as if he knew what was going to be a terrible weapon. He opened a box of ammunition and pulled out a tube. The guard stirred again and he put the weapon back down.

'We also need the power cell on loan,' he said, placing the magazine down again

Carlton laughed. 'Forty thousand or you get nothing.'

'We'll pay you back twice that,' Xen said.

'How?' Carlton asked.

'With ancient scrap,' Xen said. 'From the moon of Harken Prime.'

To Jason, it sounded like the worst proposal ever.

Carlton seemed to consider it though. Perhaps there was something to this Harken moon.

'You're not going to make it back alive from anywhere with one pipe rifle,' Carlton said. 'If you can't procure more than a thousand credits, then I doubt you're good enough to bring me anything of value. So no deal on the power cell. But you'll be taking the rifle though, no?'

Jason knew this merchant was right. If someone had come to him with a similar proposal, then he would react just the same. But he was leaving them no choice.

'Can I have a moment to confer with my colleague?' he asked.

Carlton shrugged.

Xen looked around blankly.

'With you,' Jason said, jabbing the drunk with an elbow.

Carlton chuckled but Xen seemed to snap out of it.

Jason waved an arm through the blurring barrier around them and found he could pass through. He stepped to the other side and waited until Xen joined him.

'Listen, Xen,' Jason said, keeping his voice as low as possible. He couldn't be sure the privacy barrier worked both ways audibly. 'I need to know how to load a single bullet into that pipe rifle in there.'

Xen's eyes widened as he cottoned on and all Jason could do was shake his head a fraction and open his palm so the man could just see the bullet he had taken from the ammunition box.

'Do I need a magazine or what?'

A trickle of sweat ran down Xen's forehead, his eyes shifting from side to side checking around them. Jason knew the first stages of panic better than most. He put a reassuring hand on the man's shoulder. 'We'll get back to the ship and never return here again,' he whispered, ' but I need to know how to load the thing and that's your skill.'

Xen nodded almost imperceptibly. Maybe he realized his actions had forced this.

'The magazine is the cylinder on the side. Unscrew it and press the round hard inside the opening. It will be ready to fire immediately, so only squeeze the trigger if you have to. If you accidentally squeeze the trigger as you push it in, you lose your finger and the gun will discharge.'

'Good,' Jason said, squeezing the man's shoulder. Maybe he should put the bullet into Xen and go back to the ship? No, he'd got this far, hadn't he? He sucked in a breath to calm his muscles, to not give away their intentions. Checking the time was not a good idea, it only added to the panic, but he had to know how long he had to 'negotiate.'

Seven minutes. Shit. He knew it took three to get back to the ship.

Stepping through the barrier, he didn't waste any time. He looked at the rifle on the table and slowly picked it up as if to examine it and play a game of barter.

'I think five hundred is worth two of these,' he said, making as if to check the barrel, then aim the sights at the ceiling.

Carlton scowled. 'Nonsense. Two would mean a loss, let alone breaking even.'

The bodyguard had relaxed, sensing things turning to haggling. Probably not his line of work.

Jason casually unscrewed the magazine, wiping the mechanism as if to try and attempt to wipe away an invisible blemish.

'I think four hundred would—' He slipped the concealed bullet from his hand into the gap and shoved hard with the tip of his thumb. There was a click and only then did the bodyguard show any sign of suspicion.

It was too late for that.

Jason leant right over the table and thrust the barrel of the rifle hard into Carlton's chubby forehead. The pressure would make his words much more meaningful.

'Tell him to stand down,' Jason said quickly, not turning to look at the bodyguard, 'or you're a distant memory.'

39

The guard reached for his pistol, but Carlton blustered. 'Zavar, wait!' he cried. 'Don't fire.'

Thankfully the guard was too slow or had better control than Jason had given him credit for and stayed his finger.

'Xen,' Jason said calmly, 'get the power cell.' His gaze never left Carlton, even with the bodyguard champing at the bit to his right. 'We are going to be borrowing some things from you, Carlton. Unfortunately, time is against us, but we'll pay for the goods, eventually. You have my word.'

Carlton was sucking in deep, frantic breaths. 'You'll pay with your fucking lives,' he managed between gasps. 'You have no idea—'

Jason shoved the barrel even harder into Carlton's fore-head, forcing the man's neck to crane back and the back of his skull to clunk against the wall. 'Shut it!'

'Got it,' Xen said, pulling out a large squat cylinder about the size of a small beer barrel.

'Put it in the other crate.'

'It won't fit!' Xen said, fumbling to squeeze it among the rifles and other gun paraphernalia

'Put it on the table then and take off their belts,' Jason said, using one hand to remove his own. 'And yours.'

'Why?' Xen asked, placing the cylinder down and removing the guard's gun, followed by his belt.

'Tie their hands and feet with them,' Jason said. 'Hurry.'

It took Xen an agonizing minute to complete the task while Jason held the rifle firmly to Carlton's face.

When both were securely tied, Jason stuffed several table napkins into their mouths, stifling their curses. He placed the rifle in the crate, ready for Xen to carry, and looped an arm around the power cell. It was compact but heavy.

Taking a deep breath, he gave Xen a confident look. 'Act calm out there and head for the maintenance tunnel. Remember, we just completed a deal, nothing more.'

Xen glanced at a glass on the table half full of something strong.

'Go on,' Jason said.

'Thanks,' Xen said, snatching it up and downing it in one. 'I'm sorry.'

'Too late for that,' Jason said. He eyed the wall of blurriness around the booth, forced calm into his limbs and stepped through.

The noise of the lounge struck him first—the strange stringed music and the lively chatter of patrons in the booths on either side. They hadn't been there before. He paused waiting for Xen and glanced at the tablet from his pocket.

Six minutes. He knew the journey to the dock was over three minutes. It was going to be far too close.

They strode together over the thick carpet that lined the floor and headed for the door.

Jason risked a look behind, only to see the barman watching them. He was preparing a tray of drinks and heading for the alcove where Carlton was bound and gagged.'

'Faster,' Jason said, picking up the pace, yet trying not to seem like he was running away from an armed robbery.

'Where's the maintenance tunnels?' Xen asked, adjusting his grip to carry the crate easier.

'That was just a decoy. We're going straight back to the docks via the concourse.'

They reached the vast room that housed the platforms. It was as it had been, no soldiers waiting for them, just the smooth hypnotic motion of platforms taking groups to and from market stalls.

It was a long way around the walkway that skirted the space. The most direct route was across the middle. Spotting an empty platform, he made a beeline for it and waited as Xen put the crate down and began tapping the computer to choose their destination.

His heart lurched as a group of uniformed Harken troops marched around the walkway, moving as one in a formed column. Their patchy gray uniforms boasted a belt stacked with an array of equipment, including pistols and batons. They were heading towards the lounges. The formation passed around the corner and there was no way to tell which one they had gone into.

It didn't matter; it changed nothing. Getting to the ship before they were discovered was the only thing that did. After that, the fuel and then home. Something seemed comforting about the idea of getting back to Earth. It would be a peace that he had not experienced since the day he left Area 51.

The platform juddered to life, shifting on invisible tracks across the deep black drop whilst avoiding all other platform traffic.

They took a moment to put their burdens down and gather their wits, if Xen had any at all.

They were forty feet from the landing edge closest to the docks when the troop of soldiers came racing out from the lounge section and rushed to the edge of the open concourse. One of them was the bodyguard. He looked out for them, eyes scanning the crowd, giving Jason hope they might make it across.

'Down!' Jason hissed to Xen.

Xen dropped, but the motion must have drawn the eye of the bodyguard. He pointed across in their direction.

'I guess the maintenance tunnel clue didn't take,' Xen said, peering over the top. 'That blubbering bastard didn't even bother to get out of his seat, sent his lackey instead.'

'We've still got time,' Jason said, watching as they neared the dock entrance.

Rows of red lights appeared below them, running away from the front and back of the platforms showing their hidden paths across the gap.

All the platforms shuddered to a halt.

'Shit,' Xen sighed, as another troop of four Harken soldiers came around to where he and Jason would land along the walkway. They hopped on a platform and after fiddling with the computer, they drifted over toward the pair. There were only forty feet to the edge and when the soldiers' platform was halfway, Jason acted. He crouched down, opened the crate, and slipped a pistol free.

'What the hell are you doing?'

Jason stood, pressed the pistol to Xen's head and eyed the oncoming platform.

'What the hell *are* you doing?' Xen asked, much more panicked than before.

'Trust me.'

'Why would I do that? Xen stammered. 'I just spent all your money.'

'Good point,' Jason said with a grin. Making sure the soldiers could see him clearly, he shouted at them from just a few feet away. 'Stop!'

Their platform slowed to a halt as they waited for his next move.

'How do I use the stun grenades?' Jason whispered.

'Let him go,' one of the soldiers shouted across the gap, believing the ruse.

'You're asking for my advice while you're holding a gun to my head?'

'Yes,' Jason said, 'but it's for your own good. We won't get out of here otherwise.'

'Great,' Xen mocked, 'then just twist the dial on the top halfway for ten seconds or fully for it to explode on impact or just stick it up your—'

Jason kicked the crate open, dropped down and scooped up a grenade. Twisting the dial on the top, he took a second to reflect on his training in tactical grenade use and to tell Xen to duck down.

With a jerking overarm throw, Jason lobbed the grenade straight at the platform. It hit a soldier in the chest. There was a blinding flash and a deep boom. Two of the soldiers inside tumbled over the edge, screaming until they landed on an expanse of stretchy netting beneath. The other two dropped from view as the blast receded.

Jason turned to Xen. 'Empty the crate and toss it over to

me,' he said, clambering up on the barrier and feeling it flex beneath his weight. His nerves were attempting to sabotage his thoughts, but seeing the two soldiers unconscious on the netting below gave him the courage he needed. He pushed off hard with one foot. Vertigo tried to overwhelm him, but he cleared the gap between the platforms and fell clumsily inside onto the bodies of the remaining soldiers.

Getting his feet under him, he called across to Xen, who was looking around frantically for any new threats.

'The crate!'

Xen ducked down, tipping over the crate and bringing it up to toss over to Jason.

It was light enough to make it over the gap and Jason caught it like a falling person from a burning window, staggering backwards against the barrier with it hooked in both arms.

'Guns!' Jason yelled.

Xen started tossing over boxes of ammunition and pistols.

'The power cell,' Jason said, holding out his arms to catch it.

'Don't drop it,' Xen said, heaving the cylinder onto a shoulder before launching it at Jason.

Jason braced himself and made the catch. It almost knocked the breath out of him. He placed it and the other stolen weapons inside the crate. He stood and came face to face with Xen aiming a large rifle at his face. The man must have decided that going back to the ship meant confessing and likely being left behind.

'Xen, wait,' Jason pleaded, 'you don't need to—'

The rifle fired. Its muzzle flashed in front of him as did Jason's life. A searing heat accompanied a deafening bang to one side of his head. Death didn't hurt as he had expected, instead, it was—. Reality kicked in. He was still alive. He spun to see a soldier on the landing walkway staggering backwards, a pistol falling from his hands as he collapsed.

Xen had seen the man aiming for Jason and had saved his life.

The platform rocked as Xen landed, rifle in hand, barely listening to Jason's thanks. Considering his inebriated state, the jump whilst holding the weapon was both impressive and foolhardy.

Jason fumbled at the platform controls, eventually finding the docking location just twenty feet away. As it started drifting, Jason checked the time.

Three minutes.

Would they make it?

His hopes turned to ash. He could hear racing boots coming from the tunnel leading to the dock.

'Grab the trolley.' Xen said, his eyes like that of a wired addict.

Jason spotted an abandoned trolley that someone had been using. It had no wheels and hovered off the floor. It was crammed with plastic bottles of some liquid and some poor purple animal in a cage. Its owner had abandoned it as soon as the gunshots had sounded. To Jason, it looked like a tiny purple dragon with round wings and evil red eyes.

'Load it up,' Xen said, forcing his focus away from the trolley and to the threats at hand.

They could use the trolley to get the crate and power cell to the ship much faster. Jason tipped it over, spilling the contents onto the floor. As the small cage hit the ground, the door sprung open and the tiny creature gave a "Squeep!" of delight before looping its tail to the fallen trolley like a bat ready for sleep.

Xen dumped the crate on the trolley as Jason righted it.

The power cell was delicately placed within for fear of it going off like a bomb.

'Here,' Xen said, thrusting a pipe rifle at Jason. Jason leveled the weapon as boots rang out louder and forced his sniper training to the forefront of his mind. Breathe. Relax. Stay grounded.

The formation of ragged soldiers rounded the corner and as one, both Xen and Jason opened fire. Two of the soldiers fell straight away. Two more were on the floor before the rest could scatter to find cover. Some returned shots, but just staying in one place was an invitation for death.

Half of the soldiers were down before a superior could rally them.

'Behind,' Jason said, seeing a duo of Harken take up position inside the nearest market stall, using the metal shop sides as cover.

Xen swiveled around until they were back to back.

'Push the cart,' Xen said, unleashing a storm of bullets at those in the stall.

Jason shoved the trolley forwards, stopping only to continue firing as the two of them hunkered close behind.

Several more troops descended on them. A team followed behind, but as soon as they rounded the corner to the docks, Xen ran out of rifle ammunition. They broke into a run, but halted when they reached the panoramic windows that looked out onto the exterior of the charcoal gray station. Ships were lined up outside, the tunnel connectors leading from specific doors to each vessel, but there was no sign of *Nexus One*.

'Which one did we come from?' Jason asked.

'It's not here,' Xen said, hefting a pair of pistols from the crate as the first soldiers dared peer around the bend.

Jason scanned the ships outside. The manta-like shape of *Nexus One* was gone, replaced by a ship shaped like an arrowhead. They'd left them. He checked his timer. There were still ten seconds left. He'd made it back in time, and after all of that, they'd frickin' well left him behind with a mad gunman.

The timer reached zero. There was nothing else he could do.

They were going to die here.

40

Xen didn't seem bothered by the missing ship. He was too wrapped up in combat to care about their exit strategy. Perhaps he knew they would shoot him out of the airlock if they made it.

'Watch out!' Xen said, as more soldiers piled around the corner.

Jason lobbed a stun grenade and followed it with a volley of rifle shots to match Xen's gunslinging pistols. At least they would go down fighting.

'Maybe you were right and we shouldn't have trusted them,' Jason said in a lull while the enemy was regrouping.

'Of course—' Xen said, then turned to look at the arrow-shaped ship. 'That's not Harken or anything I've seen before.' He eyed the ship, ignoring a new mass of troops entering the docks. 'It's them!'

'What?' Jason cried, unleashing a hail of bullets as a trio of soldiers dared to charge around the bend.

'That's the ship,' Xen said, sprinting for the tunnel.

'Wait,' Jason called, 'the trolley.'

Dumping the rifle into the trolley Jason pushed as hard

as he could up the incline and through the gate. The tunnel was thankfully empty and split off in two directions. Straight ahead, Xen was pounding at an airlock door. Silver's face looked out, frantically pointing for them to take the split.

'This way,' Jason said, taking the dividing tunnel. It led to the cargo bay. Both doors were wide open, ready to receive them. Silver burst in as Jason heaved the trolley inside. Xen was bent double, coughing up his last drinks as Silver shut the doors.

'What's happening?' she asked, desperation edging her usually calm demeanor.

'We got it,' Jason said. 'That's all that matters, except we're late.'

The two of them headed for the bridge, leaving Xen to throw up against the trolley.

Silver held the power cell like a lifeline as they raced to get to their seats.

'Welcome back, Captain,' Calc said, swiveling in his chair, ready to do battle with the navigation computer. 'My logical guess is that you've found our class eight power cell, but considering the number of security communications and the general upheaval of the station, I'm guessing it came at a cost?'

'We're too late,' Jason said, sliding into his seat and sucking in bitter lungfuls of air.

'Not at all,' Calc said, jerking the ship free from the docking tunnel and turning to face the local Nexus gate.

'I factored in an error margin of an eighty percent chance that you would return behind schedule and so we have a buffer of fourteen minutes to get to our Nexus gate jump,' He beamed smugness. 'We're cleared for usage in...' he tapped some holo buttons, 'eleven minutes. But please bear in mind, I didn't factor in being chased by a fleet of angry Harken stationers.'

'Noted,' Jason said, fighting the shakes that always kicked in after a serious battle. Once the adrenaline wore off, he would need something to eat. He fished out a nutrient bar from a shelf under his terminal and tore off a bite. 'Well done, Calc,' he said, stuffing the remnants into his chest pocket for later.

'We're not out of the fire yet,' Silver said, before Calc could say something witty. 'We still need to fit this.' She held the power cell.

'I thought we'd changed ships,' Jason said.

Roo's voice rang out as the engines kicked in.

'I have adjusted our visual appearance to deter the Harken patrols looking for us. And if the Fang uploads the new identifier data, then we stand a better chance at postponing capture.'

'Uploaded,' Silver said, 'a bit early but—'

'Postponing?' Jason asked, cutting her off. 'What do you mean, Roo?'

'There are too many variables to determine the outcome of your actions. I have intercepted the patrol reports.'

'And Roo, my name is Silver,' Silver said. 'Hang on—. What do the reports say?'

'Less talk and more evasion please,' Jason said, wishing he could delay the inevitable confession of what had happened.

Xen chose that moment to stagger onto the bridge.

'What happened back there?' Calc asked.

'We had to take the power cell by force,' Jason said. 'Now where does this power thingy go?'

'The unspecified report so far,' Roo said, 'is eighteen dead and twelve Harken station guards wounded after two humans fought their way out after stealing weapons from the Harken military.'

'Lies,' Jason said, secretly impressed at their total body count. 'We stole it from some fat merchant, not the Harken military.'

'What?' Silver asked, clearly unable to believe it.

'You've doomed us,' Calc said.

'You're both OK?' Silver asked, seeming angry but more concerned about their well-being.

'We will be if we can get out of here,' Jason said. 'We'll make amends later for what we did, but it was fight or be captured and there's no time to mourn or be regretful. Now, where does this power cell go?'

'Engineering,' Calc said, 'usually.'

Silver looked thoughtful. 'Roo, where is engineering?'

'There is no central engineering on *Nexus One*,' Roo said. 'Instead, all primary systems, main circuits and primary life support systems are in the maintenance tunnels that run through the ship. This saves space and reduces the chance of impacts crippling multiple vital systems. I can compartmentalize the tunnels into as many sections as needed.'

'So if we're hit,' Calc said, 'and one system is damaged in the tunnel, then it is divided to stop the damage from spreading to the next system?'

'Yes,' Roo said.

'Genius,' Calc said.

'If the power cell needs to be connected in this tunnel,' Jason asked, 'then where is the entrance?'

'Under your seat, Jason Human.'

His seat slid and shifted to one side and he hopped up, startled at the sudden appearance of a trapdoor.

'Time's ticking,' Calc said. 'You have six minutes to screw it in.'

'I'll have the identifier installed in two,' Silver said.

Jason didn't wait but lifted the trapdoor to find a ladder going down several feet inside a coffin-sized square hole. He descended into the bowels of the ship, feeling the change in temperature as heat washed over him.

Small touchscreen panels lined the tunnel walls, displaying an overwhelming amount of information. Each had block writing on it to tell what the use was. *Diagnostics, Trip fuses, Weapon calibration.* There were dozens, each more unusual than the next, until he reached the bottom and crouched to kneel at a crossing where four tunnels met.

'Which way?' he called up, wishing he had taken some sort of walkie-talkie. Did they even have those on the ship?

Roo's voice came through from some unseen speaker in the confined space.

'Tunnel three, to your right.'

Jason crawled along, shifting the power cell in front of him until he reached a tight turn in the tunnel. Poking his head around it, he froze as a purple blotch of membrane sprang from an offshoot tunnel.

It was the size of a puppy, bounding towards him on four spindly legs, supporting a lizard-like body. Round wings curved and folded across its scaly back, opened up as it scampered towards him.

'Shit! Roo, what is that thing?' Was there some invisible gas down here that was making him hallucinate tiny dragons?

It was five feet from him when it stopped, eyeing him curiously. He tried not to panic and forced himself to be still.

'My scans indicate it is a Quibble Truff from the Divide, Jason Human.'

'How do I kill it?' Jason asked, ready to block should the thing try to jump for his neck.

It gave a sniff and waddled towards him. Its beady eyes scanned him as it took a series of tentative steps closer to him. The Quibble Truff's elongated snout flared as its nostrils twitched.

It leant closer, stretching out its neck until Jason would have been able to whack it away. For some reason, he stayed his hand.

The snouted purple face extended, the mouth opening in eager silence, except for a single tiny purr, like an aged cat.

The little head poked quickly inside his breast pocket, withdrawing the half-eaten nutrient bar he had stashed there earlier. It hopped back and scoffed the bar down before scurrying away down the tunnel.

'Silver has asked me to hurry you, Jason Human.'

Jason shook the weird moment aside and crawled along the tunnel until he found a bank of power cells. There were dozens of them, all of different sizes set in groups of four, protruding from the wall. He located the largest and could see one of them was cracked wide open. Inside pulsed an orange glow; it flickered on and off.

'Do I just pull it out, Roo?'

'Yes, unscrew it and screw the new one in. There is only a seven percent chance of electrocution.'

'Funny,' Jason said, hoping it was a joke as he gripped it firmly with both hands and twisted. It came free with a ratcheting series of clicks. He quickly replaced it with the new cell. The background noise of the ship rose to a powerful hum as the engines gave a burst of speed, throwing him to one side in the tight confines.

'How do I get back, Roo?'

A hatch beside him opened and he crawled in. It didn't take long for him to find the ascending ladder. It took several seconds to get up, avoiding the pipes and cables that crowded the sides.

He emerged into his quarters, the bed having been magically shifted to one side to make space for the secret exit hatch.

The ship was pulling some serious g-forces as he stumbled towards the bridge door. It automatically opened in front of him and he took in the situation.

Calc was taking the ship directly to the nearest Nexus gate just ahead of them.

He turned as Jason walked onto the bridge. 'We have one minute—' He stopped mid-sentence. 'Erm, OK.' He studied Jason.

'What?' Jason asked. 'Did it not work?'

Silver rose from her seat. Slowly, she slipped her pistol from its holster, her purple eyes never leaving his body. She raised the weapon.

'Really, what?' Jason said, ready to dive aside. Had she gone mad?

'Why do you have a Quibble Truff attached to your waist?'

A chill spread through him. He gradually looked down. The purple dragon-like beast was dangling from the hem of his jacket, claws hooked into the fabric.

When did that get there?

The contented little creature must have sensed the silent tension surrounding it as it craned its neck up from preening a delicate round wing and eyed Silver.

'Don't move,' she said, cocking her head to sight down the length of the pistol.

The ship lurched suddenly, throwing them all off balance.

'The gate is pulling us in,' Calc called, holding on to his station.

The Quibble Truff let out a sharp 'squip!,' dropped from his jacket and flapped towards the crew quarters.

Silver tried to get a shot off, but the jerky movement from the ship meant she risked hitting one of the crew instead.

The creature disappeared around the corner.

The Nexus gate was surrounding them. A blue plasmodic wave expanded in front of the ship, wrapping around it and dragging them inside the swirling, neon vortex.

Prickling tingles shot through Jason as it dragged them into the wormhole.

Here we go again.

41

J ason gripped his seat as the sensation of suddenly stopping tried to throw him from it. He took a few seconds to calm his beating heart and relax a fraction.

The system they'd entered was almost beyond belief. In front of them were three stars, seemingly in a dance about the center. One was the same as Earth's sun in color but smaller, the second and third were blue and deep red. Nebulous clouds stretched like a painter's brush stroke across the background, bringing to life hues of pink and purple.

Several planets stood out against the backdrop—a large gray gaseous giant ringed with a yellow circle and two smaller planets, one black and riddled with shadows and the other red like Mars in full sunlight.

Ships were zipping away from the Nexus gate, heading to their destinations, each of them towing a second, smaller vessel. A large freighter, as big as some of the ones in the battle he'd arrived in, was towing half a dozen, linked by yellow beams that kept them from drifting off into the void.

In all directions around them were long lines of

stationary lights dotting the sky and demarking zones and boundaries. They stretched as far as the eye could see, crossing each other and changing colors.

'Welcome to B Three,' Calc said, bringing up a holo-screen at the front of the bridge for them all to see. He moved his fingers across his terminal screen and a projection of the system appeared on the larger one. It zoomed in towards the three suns, gliding past the planets from the outside in. Some asteroids had been turned into colonies, several barren planets had been mined to exhaustion. The gas giant dominated a light brown planet closer to the three suns with a pair of moons orbiting it. The view stopped on the brown planet.

'Harken Prime,' Calc said. Patches of gray outlined vast cities on the surface as it slowly rotated. Calc brought the view around to one of its moons. It was the smaller of the two and the surface was speckled with shades of gray, like some of the digital camouflage the mountain forces used when Jason had served with them in Peru. It hurt the eye to try and pick out a particular point.

'What is the surface like?' Jason asked.

'It is entirely composed of decaying space debris.'

'Asteroids?'

'Old ships and stolen stations,' Calc said. 'I once bought a series one explosion resistance cartridge found here for only five hundred credits. I could have been sitting on top of an explosive charge and it might have just warmed my butt, but that's a story for another time.'

Jason tried to imagine such a place, but tiredness struck him like a sudden fog, rolling in over his mind and dampening any such thoughts.

'How long until we are in orbit?' he asked.

'Four hours,' Calc said. 'Assuming we can cross these

damned scrapyard territories without being scrutinized too closely.'

Jason looked out at the ships still spreading out from the Nexus gate. 'We're just missing something,' he said.

Calc looked around through the window and shrugged. 'What?'

'We're not towing anything,' Silver said.

'Exactly,' Jason said. 'Tow something and we'll fit right in.'

'Genius,' Calc said.

Jason grinned. 'Even a genius needs rest,' he said. 'I'm hitting the hay, so wake me when we're close.'

'Hitting the what?' Calc asked, confused.

'Sleep,' Jason said.

'Not until you find that Quibble Truff,' Silver said. 'That thing will eat through every wire on the ship unless you catch it and flush it outside.'

'Wires?' Jason asked.

'It's their favorite,' Calc said. 'That and microprocessor chips.'

'Maybe he'll take a bite from you,' Xen said, eyeing Calc's menagerie of droidy bits.

'Good point,' Calc said, missing the dig. 'Better find it first, just to be sure.' he glanced around at the few dark patches on the bridge.

Jason shook his head. How tired was he? A creature that eats wires? He didn't know why this surprised him, considering everything he'd seen and done.

'No sleeping until you catch that little bugger,' Silver said. 'In the meantime, I'm going to inspect those weapons, get them cleaned and ready for use. I still don't know how you got all of those and the power cell.'

'With difficulty,' Jason said. 'Calc, do you have a spare microprocessor chip somewhere that I could borrow?'

'That's like me asking to borrow your fingernail.'

'More like the old clipping of a nail.'

Calc poked his fingers in a pocket and pulled out a small, faded copper-coloured chip about the size of a die. Jason plucked it from his fingers and made his way to the cargo bay.

He snatched up an empty crate and headed for his room. He would get his sleep and the little Quibbly dragon-thing be damned.

Jason woke, cold sweat beading his face as something made a gentle purring noise in his room. He peeked an eye open to see the Quibble Truff creeping across the floor towards the crate, which was precariously propped up with a short metal rod.

The creature's nose twitched as it homed in on the microprocessor that had been placed neatly under the angled crate.

Jason had left an open nutrient bar as a backup prize and regardless of what Calc had said, it was this that it scooped up first in its elongated little snout. He tugged the thread attached to the metal prop, and it dropped, capturing the monster.

Jason sprang from his bed and tossed the light covers aside and landed hard on the crate, dropping his weight on it.

It was the wrong move. The creature hissed and bucked, rattling the crate under him. Its strength was startling for such a small creature. It wasn't the wrong move because of the dragon being underneath, but because he had no way to trap it. As soon as he got up, the creature would break free with ease. There was no cage to toss it in and no lid for the crate within his quarters.

He tried to think his way through the situation, but he was interrupted by shouting from the bridge. The argument grew more savage as the seconds passed and when it was clear this was not a normal debate, he eased his weight off the box.

In an instant the Quibble Truff bucked the heavy box off and rose on its haunches, facing Jason as he stood up.

The little creature looked indignant as Jason backed up, giving it no chance to think he was attacking it.

There was a moment of stillness as they faced off before the purple dragon lowered itself and sprang away towards the open hatch to the maintenance tunnels.

Jason turned to head for the bridge when a scuffling noise made him turn around. The Quibble Truff had looped around when his back was turned and now made off with the nutrient bar clamped firmly in its mouth.

'Little trickster,' Jason said, unable to stop a grin at the creature's cheek as the end of the tail swished down into the tunnels.

The bridge was in chaos. Xen was hunkered behind his terminal, eyeing Silver who stood aiming a pistol at him. Calc had found cover behind Jason's chair and watched the scene like a hawk.

'What happened?' Jason said. 'Ease up, Silver, what is going on?' Was she always this quick to bring guns to bear?

'We know what happened,' she said, 'in the casino.'

'Ah,' Jason said. 'Yes, well, I don't know if—'

'It's time to finish him,' she said, readying herself to shoot.

Xen had backed up to the wall and was edging along towards the cargo bay entrance. 'Wait,' Jason said. 'No one needs to die here. We got the guns and that stupid class eight power cell.'

'He should have been out of that airlock days ago.'

Calc gave a small nod of agreement. 'The odds of us making it through this alive are severely lowered with him around, Captain, given his track record.'

'I got you the power cell though, didn't I?' Xen said, his eyes flickered to each of them. 'As I promised I would. Have you no honor?'

'You dare talk of honor,' Silver spat. 'After what you did. After what you *keep* doing? That's it,' she raised her pistol, 'no more putting it off. It's either wait around for you to get us killed or do what we should have done the first time you turned us in. Sorry, Xen.'

'Wha—wait no!' Xen said, throwing his hands up as if to ward off the weapon.

Jason sprang forwards and backhanded the pistol from her hand.

The weapon discharged as it left her grip.

42

J ason was too late. The bullet ricocheted off the ceiling of the bridge. Calc was thrown back as it skimmed his arm, taking out a bank of cartridges set in his skin.

He cried out in agony as the wound both bled and sparked from the broken circuits. As he staggered back, his eyes shot wide in fear and pain.

Silver put her head in her hands and slumped to the floor as Jason closed the gap and knelt beside Calc. 'Roo, I need a first aid kit right now.'

A box expanded from the floor beside Calc and through the transparent door set in the top, he could see a roll of material. He opened the lid, took it out, and unrolled it before the box had melded back into the floor.

Xen had gathered his wits and retreated towards the crew quarters.

'Roo,' Jason said, 'block any transmissions from leaving the ship. I won't have him calling the Harkens again.'

'I'm so sorry,' Silver said. Though whether to himself or Calc, Jason couldn't tell. She looked thoroughly exhausted.

'I haven't had time to process what leaving Partel and that ship meant.' She wiped at a rogue tear. 'Calc, I'm sorry.'

'Just leave me alone,' he said, his eyes not leaving the wound on his arm.

Jason scanned the first aid kit and began trying to sort through what would be useful.

'That one,' Calc said, pointing to what looked like a sheet of gray paper. 'Press it on the wound and it should dampen the sparks and stem the blood loss.' He still stared at the wound, thoughts adrift.

'What is it?' Jason asked, pressing the sheet against the skin and misfiring circuitry.

'Trying to figure out what cartridges I lost,' Calc said, pressing the sheet so Jason could let go. 'Maybe you should check on her.' He nodded to where Silver had slumped against her terminal and was staring blankly into space.

He walked to her and crouched down.

'Sorry,' she said, before he could find the words to soothe her. 'I've got some issues, I know.'

He sat. 'Don't we all.' He nodded to Calc, who was using his bad arm to desperately pick through the cartridge pieces on the floor. 'Him, Xen and me. We are all one messed-up little family.'

'I just got so mad at Xen; issues or not, the man is a piece of Harken—' She shook her head. 'He gambled it almost all away. How did you not kick his ass there and then?'

Jason chuckled, making Calc look up from his search for a second.

'Believe me, I wanted to. More than anything, except getting that power cell and getting back here.'

'Not to your Earth?'

'Maybe. I don't know. This ship isn't so bad. It's growing on me.'

'Thank you, Jason Human,' Roo said. 'I feel the same.'

Jason looked up. 'If we are so familiar, then you can stop confirming that I'm a human at the end of every sentence.'

'I will end the experiment,' Roo said.

'Experiment?'

'To test your patience and eventual madness level,' Roo said. 'We are growing on each other.'

He looked back at Silver with a grin. 'See what I mean? We've *all* got issues. But I'll admit that you, Calc and Roo are growing on me.'

'Stop sucking my circuits,' Calc said, having stopped the bleeding and sparks.

'And Xen?' Silver asked.

It was Jason's turn to sigh. 'He saved my life in there, Silver. I mean really saved it, more than once and that, to someone who has been fighting all their life, means something.'

'Even if he put you in the situation in the first place?'

Reluctantly he nodded. 'Yes, I think so.'

Roo's voice sounded again, stopping Silver from replying.

'Incoming call.'

Jason instinctively glanced outside through the window, expecting to see Partel's and Kroth's ship hunting them down after a call from Xen to hand them in.

The remnants of dozens of ships and unknown vessels floated past like fish in an ocean.

'Is the call safe?' he asked, wondering if the derelicts were secretly occupied.

Silver had made it to her console. 'It's coming from a local station, not an official link, so possibly just a nearby resident.'

'Put them through,' Jason said.

The craggy face of an old Harken appeared on screen. His features were human enough, but there were subtle differences in the facial bone structure. To Jason, they always seemed bonier, almost emaciated.

'You be trespassing on me boneyard,' the Harken said. The man's speech patterns were a mix of Victorian gutter wench and the hacking cough of a plague victim. 'And you ain't not declared what you're doing or forwarded any suitable certifications of movements.'

'Forgot to apply for one of those,' Calc said.

Jason gave a dry laugh.

'No, really,' Calc said. 'Would have been easy enough to get hold of.'

The Harken seemed to ponder their words, a look of stupid effort on his face. 'If yer be crossing my yard space, then ya need to either bring summin, which I sees you ain't, or ya need to do me a favor, see?'

Jason had had enough of gallivanting off to do favors or find things. He wanted the Nexus fuel and he would damn well get it this time. 'No,' Jason said. 'We'll go around. I don't need your permission for that and don't think for a second we're not armed.'

The Harken seemed baffled at Jason saying no, and somehow calling the bluff worked. 'Ah,' he said, giving in. 'You can pass through, see, but perhaps you'd be a'towing a few of the derelicts across to me on ya way past? It's on ya way to the capital if that's where ya heading.'

Jason flicked the microphone off. 'Should we do it?'

Calc seemed to have gotten over his wound, now that the damage was stemmed. 'Might avoid some suspicion,' he said, 'if we're towing something through this system. Seems to be the fashion.'

'Can we do it, Roo?' Jason asked.

'Yes, Jason Captain, we can use a collider beam to drag debris.'

'Fine,' Jason said to the Harken, reactivating the conversation. 'We're heading to Harken Prime B. If we stay in your territory, how close can we get to the planet?'

'All the way,' the Harken said, looking suspicious for the first time. 'Ya ain't been here before, have ya?'

'No,' Jason said. 'First-time tourists.'

The Harken nodded. 'It be like the spokes of a wheel, see. All slats of space stretch from the center of the system, some thin, some wider than others, but mine stretches from the star to the exterior rim, all owned by me, for my yard. Some sell off but I've held on for six generations. It's Harken law.'

'You have a deal...?' Jason let the question hang.

'Morgar,' the Harken said. 'Just bring one of those ships with you and leave it when ya pass. I'll be grateful. A passing fee, see.'

'We appreciate the offer, Morgar,' Jason said.

'Can I ask what ship ya have there? Very unusual.'

Jason didn't want to arouse suspicion. 'It's nothing special. We'll see you in a few hours, Morgar,' he said.

Morgar nodded and ended the call.

'A friendly Harken?' Jason asked.

'Always in return for something,' Silver said, preening her arm and seeming to relax for the first time since they had last encountered Partel.

'What happened to the Quibble Truff?' Calc asked.

She looked up, interested.

Jason shrugged. 'I caught it, but the shouting meant I had to let it go.'

Silver sagged and stopped her preening.

'It went down into the maintenance tunnels again,' he said, slightly embarrassed. 'Roo, can we trace it?'

'I can only confirm that it is still on board, Captain. Somewhere in the maintenance ducts.'

'Really helpful,' Silver said.

'If it eats anything important,' Calc said, 'we're not in the best system to get a recovery frigate out to us.'

'Roo,' Jason said, 'use the collider thing to gather whatever we can tow without impairing us too much.'

'Too much would be more than five percent, Roo,' Calc said. 'Please.'

'Got it,' Roo said.

There was a sharp hum that faded to a droning background noise. The nearest derelict was part of an old station. Much larger than *Nexus One*, it was suddenly lit up with a yellow beam that widened in a cone shape, engulfing the entire station.

Calc flew the ship closer, his fingers tapping and sliding through the holoscreens that curved from the top of his terminal. 'Well, defrag my data banks. That station has added a drag of nought point five percent.'

'Which means?' Jason asked, not understanding.

'That, again, this ship is beyond the usual. That station section would have dragged a class six freighter down by more than three times that!'

'Pick up some more en route then,' Jason said.

Within an hour, *Nexus One* was towing three sections of stations and four class three vessels coming in at well over a hundred feet, close to the size of *Nexus One*.

They traveled until they came across a collection of giant stations. Each one was shaped like a cigar with a hollowed-out interior. Within their hollows were hundreds of ships and partial pieces of debris, some piled into corners and others lined up in neat rows.

The rows were a hive of activity and movement. Small ships, a few feet across, were cutting the pieces up in bursts of sparks and reconstructing new ships from the parts.

'One hell of an operation,' Jason said. He had assumed Morgar was a loner. 'Is this the right place?'

'The coordinates are for that station over there,' Calc said, pointing to a large, tidy-looking rectangular station. Compared to all the other Harken stations, it was immaculate. Large, one-way windows looked out onto a ring that curved around the station. On the ring were a dozen ships, all looking complete. Space suited people were walking around them like a used car sales lot, inspecting the vessels.

'I thought he was a hermit,' Jason said. 'Seems he has company.'

'Those are for sale,' Calc said. 'More like *a* company.'

'A successful one,' Silver said. 'You don't last six generations out here without solid finances.'

'And the ships in the hangars?' Jason asked.

'Automated construction robots,' Silver said.

'A ton of credits invested here,' Calc said.

'Make the drop, Roo, and we'll continue on,' Jason said. 'We don't need any more hang-ups or to be seen by his clients.'

'Disengaging collider beam,' Roo said.

'Hang on,' Xen said, coming into the room. He'd been missing since the incident with Silver. 'That collider beam looks like a weapons system. I believe that's my position?' He moved to his terminal and sat down, looking expectantly at them all as if the previous confrontation hadn't happened. He seemed nearer sobriety than usual.

'We could arrange that,' Jason said. 'Roo? Please.'

'Are you seriously suggesting that we put him in charge of weapons?' Silver asked.

Xen looked meaningfully at Calc, who, at the mention of weapons, gave an unconscious rub of his shoulder. 'Some are better than others at it.'

Silver winced.

'That's what we asked him to do in the first place,' Jason said, 'and that's what we'll do going forwards.'

'Incoming call,' Silver said. 'Our Harken friend again.'

Jason clicked the screen on and took up his seat. 'Morgar,' Jason said in greeting. He didn't have time to bandy words. 'We have delivered on our promise and will be on our way now. Thank you for the safe passage.'

Morgar came on with a look of astonishment. 'I don't know how ya got so much here, so fast, without blowing a power cell. But I'm bloody grateful. Perhaps you could—'

'No more,' Jason said. 'We need to be on our way—'

'Wait!' Morgar said, looking in confusion at his computer. 'There's a ship coming in at the far end.' He disappeared from the screen.

'Trouble from the sounds of it,' Silver said. 'I'll try to run a long-range scan to—'

Morgar came back on. 'Seems ya stirred up a jitter nest. A diplomatic one at that. One of the Three, no less, Kroth, if the idents are accurate. Not the worst, but not the friendliest either.'

Jason gave Calc a 'be ready to run' look.

He nodded, sliding a finger across his holoscreen. The engines hummed to a higher frequency.

'Are they coming?' Calc asked.

'Ya got about ten minutes until they're here,' Morgar said gravely. 'They're coming wicked fast.'

'We didn't want to bring trouble to your yard, Morgar,' Jason said.

'Seems a bit late for that,' Morgar said, but his countenance was far from angry. 'Ya did me a good turn so I'll do you one in return and says you came through so fast I couldn't stops ya.'

'Thank you,' Jason said. 'If there's anything we can do…'

'Head off,' Morgar said, 'and if ya pass again in the future, without one of the Three on ya ass, feel free to drag some more behind ya.'

Jason ended comms immediately. 'Punch it, Calc.'

'Punch what?' Calc asked, giving a raised eyebrow. 'This is no time for physical violence, Captain.'

'Just get us out of here,' Jason said. A glance behind and he could see the Harken ship as a speck in the distance. The only thing distinguishing it from the scattered wrecks was a thin trail of blue behind as they pushed their ship's engines to the maximum.

Nexus One's engines roared as they skimmed past a row of old ships, swooping close to the station to conceal themselves against the gray hull.

Once they were past it, Calc headed towards the planet in the distance. Beside it was a duo of moons, much smaller but still daunting. They were now heading straight into the enemy's mouth and it was fast closing on them.

43

The planet overshadowed the moon, like a maroon beach ball beside a mottled gray marble.

Nexus One had gained a lead on Partel's and Kroth's pursuing ship. Calc assured the crew they were at least an hour ahead of the pursuit, giving them a good chance of finding the fuel first.

Looking at the surface below them, it was clear it would not be easy.

Surface wasn't quite the right word. It implied something either flat or solid, of which it was neither. It was closer to the inside mess of a child's toy box, upturned and spread across the planet's terrain, assuming the child only played with broken spaceships.

'Looks like someone smashed a moon station into a million pieces and scattered it over the top,' Xen said. 'Why haven't the Harken done anything about it?'

'It's strictly off-limits,' Silver said, 'a well-guarded secret and patrolled by hunter seeker drones. All set to Sucrash mode.'

'Sucrash?' Jason asked.

'Suicide by crash,' Calc confirmed.

'Kamikaze?' Jason said, wondering if they would make it out alive.

'Never heard of it,' Calc said. 'But damn, it's a dangerous place. Get spotted by one of those drones and all within a click come racing in to take you down. Not to mention the Harken treasure runners and their constant shadowing from the Zip droids.'

'Of course,' Jason said, ' which means what, exactly?'

Calc seemed to remember. 'Ah yes, Gedi Six. The treasure runners are kind of like us, sneaking in to seek the hidden depths of the moon and the Zip droids are down there to pursue and kill them, again using Sucrash tactics or close enough to make no difference. Nasty little things.'

'How many of them are down there?' Jason asked.

Calc's eyes drifted away as if to check some mental list. 'Five thousand hunter seeker drones,' he said, 'and eight hundred and forty thousand Zip droids to patrol between the wrecks.'

'Well, at least we have weapons this time,' Silver said, her voice oozing with sarcasm.

Xen looked ready to say something, but Jason eyed him down. The last thing they needed was another argument.

'Get us down there, any way you can to avoid them,' Jason said.

'Where do we start the search?' Xen asked.

'There's no telling where we'd find it,' Calc said. 'If at all. Nothing is certain about that Scribe being right.'

Jason didn't want to believe there would be no Nexus fuel. He felt frustration gnawing at him. 'Well, use those damned cartridges and modules you're so proud of to figure a way we can find the fuel without getting Sucrashed to smithereens.'

Calc unplugged a cartridge from his chest, looked inside, then blew it out like some old computer game, before reinserting it. It hummed as he turned his attention to his screen, which was scanning the surface.

Jason left him to it, turning to Xen, who was examining the weapons they had stolen, between swigs of his flask. 'Are they any good?' he asked.

Xen looked up and gave him a crooked grin. 'Even though we got them for free, I'd say that pig Carlton got the better deal.'

'That bad?'

'Could be better. We got two grenades left, three pipe rifles, two pistols and a sniper rifle with jamming issues.'

'Ammunition?' Jason asked. They could have all the guns in the galaxy, but without ammo, they'd be dead far too soon to find anything. He'd learnt that the hard way in Siberia.

'Plenty. Except for the sniper, we used quite a lot back on the station, but we made 'em count, huh? Only got twelve rounds left.'

'I've got it,' Calc said.

'More rounds?' Xen asked, looking up hopefully.

'The optimal location, you buffoon,' Calc said.

'The fuel?' Jason asked, moving over to Calc's station. They had been circling the moon for almost an hour, staying just out of short range scan distance. It seemed their identifier was working.

'Here,' Calc said, using the holoscreen to zoom in on a particularly dark patch of the surface. 'There's a high concentration of particulate soot from some event, but it has blocked several potential routes to the hollows beneath. This one here.'

He showed a large cavern tucked deep below. The scan

showed tunnels that led up to it but fell short of the actual location.

'If we can force a way through these corridors, then judging by the initial scans, I would guess there might be some old Empire ship down in that cavern.'

Silver had come in from her quarters and was eyeing the three-dimensional display with suspicion. 'Why hasn't it been plundered before? And what about the drones?'

'The soot would have meant fewer patrols due to intakes being clogged,' Calc said. 'Those drones may dive bomb anything that moves, but they are programmed to last, which means avoiding potential hazards. As for treasure runners, I calculate only a twenty-one percent chance that they would have made it past the blocked tunnels without explosives, which would show them as being open, not blocked like this.'

Silver had moved to her console. 'Did you not bother to set up a trip scan for Kroth and Partel?'

'Hardly my job,' Calc said, 'but no, the drones kept setting it off so I—' he froze, 'why?'

'They're coming right towards us,' Silver said.

'They shouldn't. Isn't the identifier change working?' Jason asked.

'Could have guessed,' Calc said. 'It wouldn't have been difficult to figure out we needed some ship part or other, and this is the best place to find anything for a strange old ship like this.'

'I have taken offense, Calculator,' Roo said.

The holoscan Calc had been looking at flickered and faded, as if the power was being drained.

'I didn't mean you, Roo,' Calc said quickly, trying in vain to keep the image from disappearing. 'I meant how the

Harken might perceive us. You know, I think this ship is incredible.'

'Flattery accepted,' Roo said.

'Take us down then, Calc,' Jason said as the Humdroid sighed in relief when his screen reappeared.

Calc found a spot on the surface and descended.

'Picking up a spike in radiation,' Silver said. 'Directly below us.'

As the ship tilted downwards, Jason could make out an immense crater amidst the jagged surface of broken spaceships.

'It's an old impulse engine blowout spot,' Calc said. 'At some point, a plasma drive exploded here, causing the radiation. It also caused the hole, which goes down a thousand feet and is our entry point. After that, it narrows before joining a canyon buried deep inside the crust. We need to join that canyon and find our way to a blocked-off cavern at about twenty thousand feet.'

'Twenty thousand!' Xen said.

Jason tried the math. It was over three miles down. The sheer scale of the debris suddenly hit him. Who knew what they would find down there?

44

'Clear,' Silver said, as they waited for the hunter-seeker drone to pass above them. They had dipped below the level of the debris crater and were slowly dropping into the abyss of piled ships. Light from above illuminated the side walls, showing the jumble of spacecraft and discarded stations. There was no pattern to it, no ship was at the same angle. Some were upside down, some with shattered holes in their sides from the weapons that had defeated them, but most were crushed under the weight of those above.

'This radiation is playing havoc with the scanners,' Silver said.

'Same for weapons,' Xen said. 'I doubt I could get a lock on anything down here.'

'That's why it's our best shot,' Calc said. 'No drones would risk the long-term effects from extended exposure.'

They passed caves and wide fissures in the sides of the sinkhole. The size of the ships varied, but mostly it was the largest that didn't succumb to the weight of those pressing down from above. Creaking noises and groans, like the beginnings of earthquakes, echoed around them.

'There's an atmosphere?' Jason asked.

'Yes,' Roo said. 'Breathable for about twenty minutes before you would show signs of lung damage. I have prepared more oxygen bottles for you to take with you.'

'We're not going out there,' Jason said. 'Are we?'

Calc gave him a shrug. 'Might have to. This ship can't pick up small crates without using the manipulation bean, and that could easily disrupt the distribution of the debris.'

'And we'd struggle to get a lock on down here,' Xen added.

There were strata of vessels now. As they moved deeper into the sinkhole, the construction of the ships changed subtly, like the difference between a truck from the nineteen fifties compared to a modern-day SUV. The colouration changed as well, becoming dirtier and more twisted. There were fewer small caves in the sides now, but they passed several wide canyons that tore through the wrecks and boggled the mind in size.

It changed again, but this time the walls narrowed suddenly.

'Getting close,' Silver said, warning Calc of the proximity.

'This isn't even tight,' Calc said, twisting the ship down into a fissure riddled with thick cables stretching across the expanse. *Nexus One*, twisted under or over, giving Jason's stomach a stability check.

'Bottom of the sinkhole,' Silver said.

The light levels dropped significantly as they slowed to a stop just inside one of the cave entrances. Unlike the canyons they had passed, it was an angular hole, through the center of a vast starship about twice the width of *Nexus One.*

Calc slowed the ship to a stop just inside.

It was a strange world down here. Darkness covered every crevice of the surrounding wrecks, making the walls almost appear black. Touches of gold and silver shimmered, revealing semi-precious metals used in the construction of whatever was buried in this elemental graveyard. Most flat surfaces were smeared black. It looked painted.

'What's with the paint?' Jason asked.

'Oil,' Silver said.

'To be precise,' Calc said. 'Hydraulic oils, congealed plasma and water from all the ships above. Dripped down over centuries. They say at the bottom, below all the ships, is a black ocean of oils and chemicals.'

'I heard there are creatures swimming in it,' Xen said.

'Nonsense,' Calc said, 'the odds of that are ridiculous, well over a million to one.'

'I've heard the same,' Silver said.

A dark streak of oil, which was oozing over a huge engine part, suddenly twitched.

'It moved?' Jason asked.

'What did?' Calc asked, turning around to look in that direction.

'The oil running down that engine,' Jason said. 'I swear it moved.'

'Oilsnake,' Silver said, pointing to another oozing line among the hundreds of dripping gunk lines. It moved slowly from one to another, pausing every few seconds to blend in.

'They live down here?'

'Evolved down here,' Silver said. 'The Seedars terraformed this place thousands of years ago. It was an

Eden when they finished, bursting with life. It was turned into a dumping ground long before the unfathomable split of the Ancient Empire.'

'I heard the original inhabitants displeased the Emperor, and so he ordered all the empire's toxic waste and decommissioned ships to be brought here until the planet was irreparably ruined,' Xen said.

An alarm sounded from Silver's terminal. She furiously swiped fingers through her holoscreen as it flashed red. 'Something's out there. Up ahead, coming out into the cave from a side chute.'

'Roo,' Calc said, 'shut down anything that makes us obvious. Let's hope it's not a hunter-seeker drone.'

The engines dipped to a barely audible tone and all the holoscreens on the bridge dimmed as the power was cut off.

Calc slowly swung *Nexus One* to the side of the cave, taking partial cover behind the wing of a battered old fighter.

'There,' Xen hissed as a small craft, speckled in a gray color scheme, curved out from a tight hole in the hull of a ship that was riddled with bent and broken turrets.

The craft was using a spotlight to scan the turrets one at a time, moving closer to inspect them, then sidling to the next one.

'A class one scouting vessel,' Calc said.

'Treasure runners. Vultures,' said Xen.

'Behind us,' Silver said, her voice rising in panic. 'Hunter-seeker.'

Jason spun to look through the rear section of the window and spotted a set of red laser beams, like eyes projecting out from the front of one of the arrow-shaped drones. It glided past them.

'It hasn't picked us up,' Calc said.

'Too interested in them,' Xen said.

He was right. The drone headed straight for the treasure runners' ship, both lasers moving like spotlights over the turreted battleship.

'It shouldn't be down here,' Calc said.

'It might have picked up our signal and followed,' Silver said.

The treasure runners must have spotted the drone, as they'd turn their lights off, but it was too late. Red lasers narrowed in on the runners' scout ship and the drone sped up. The noise of a high-pitched engine grew in intensity, speeding for the runners. There was a rattle of minigun fire from a small opening at the front of the drone before it crashed into them.

It struck the turret on the wreck where the scout was about to land. The runners' pulling away at the last second had confused the drone. They sped off towards the bottom of the sinkhole and had just entered the lit-up area when three more drones swooped down through the hole above, opened fire, and then slammed into the ship. The impacts were a trio of bright blasts, like grenades popping. It left only another wreck to crash down and join the others.

There was a loud clattering from above. They all jumped at the strange sound. 'Collapse from the roof above,' Silver said.

All across the tight tunnel, chunks of metal and pieces of old ships were crumbling from the roof. A large portion broke free, just in front of *Nexus One*, forcing Calc to quickly jerk backwards to avoid a twisted shuttle as it plummeted past. It was like watching a deadly rain as chunks of debris, cables and compressed parts were dislodged until the tremors subsided.

'Hold position,' Silver said. 'There's another one coming down the sinkhole.'

They waited in silence until after a minute a single drone came to inspect the remains of the runners' scout ship, which was visible as the cloud of dust around it settled.

The newcomer swept past, red lasers scanning the fresh wreckage for movement. There was none. It scanned the surroundings in a final pirouette, its beam stopped on them for a split second longer than the rest. Jason held his breath, heartbeat loud in his ears, before the drone continued to spin and zoomed away through the sinkhole, back up to the surface.

'Gone,' Silver said.

Jason gave her a nod. 'That was close. Give it a second, then let's get moving.' He eyed the walls for more drones sitting in ambush and felt the weight pressing down from above. 'This place is a deathtrap.'

Calc took *Nexus One* deep into the fissures of the tunnel. It grew tighter as the minutes ticked by until they were flying inside ships. Following wide corridors, the only time they saw any openings was between two vessels as they exited one for a moment and entered another.

Nexus One was the only genuine source of light in the near-constant darkness of the passageways. Some ships must have had a tiny fraction of power remaining, as LED lights flickered from unidentifiable computers, screaming out their ancient injuries through blinking warning lights.

No matter how tight the turns became, Calc could pilot *Nexus One* skillfully through the maze. They came to a halt in front of a large metal sheet, completely blocking the way. Old fracture lines could be seen, like lightning strikes running through the rusting metal.

'That's the plate,' Calc said. 'If my calculations are accurate, which they are, then it should only be a thin wall. The cavern is behind it and in there we might find a small ship from the Ancient Empire that survived the millennia, or at least old enough to be unplundered, that would have been carrying Nexus fuel in their cargo bays.'

'That's a lot of mights, shoulds and coulds,' said Xen.

'How deep are we?' Jason asked.

'Three point two miles,' Silver said.

'Out you go then,' Calc said cheerfully, eyeing them all in expectation.

'Out?' Jason asked, wondering what the crazy droid man meant.

'Yes, outside. To place the last two grenades on the plate and blow it from a distance with a rifle.'

'Just ram it,' Xen said. 'Use the ship.'

'You think it works like on the holoscreen?' Calc exclaimed. 'Ships just crashing through things and no thought for equal and opposite reactions? Such an impact would crumple the front of this ship and if it did not, then the best-case scenario is we damage any front-facing sensors, rendering us essentially blind. So time to get outside.'

'You're not volunteering?' Silver asked, giving him a withering look.

Calc spun in his chair, making Jason envious of the comfortable seating. 'See this,' Calc said, tapping the patched wound where the bullet had struck him. Silver shrank back as if trying to blend in with the walls. 'This means I stay. Anyway, I'd be much more helpful here.'

'Doing what?' Xen asked.

Calc turned back to his console. 'Monitoring. Now get going.'

'Or what?'

Roo's voice came through as if to back up Calc. 'Or the ship that has been following us will catch us up,'

'What ship?' they all asked.

45

Without a face to stare at in incredulity, they all looked at each other.

'What ship?' Jason repeated.

'There's too much interference for a clear picture,' Roo said, 'but it is much larger than a drone.'

'Why the hell didn't you say anything, Roo?' Jason asked.

'I just did.'

'Sooner,' Silver added.

Roo seemed to ignore her. 'You have eleven minutes and six seconds before they reach us.'

'I'm picking it up on scans now,' Silver said. 'It's coming fast.'

'Let's move then,' Jason said, grabbing up a pipe rifle and pistol. 'We'll talk about this later, Roo. If we're not all killed due to your inability to inform others about imminent danger.' He stuffed a few magazines in his pockets and eyed up one of the oxygen tanks beside the airlock door. 'What are those for?' he asked, as Silver and Xen joined him.

'You can survive unaffected outside for seven minutes,'

Roo said. 'After which you will need oxygen tanks to breathe, to stabilize your mental faculties.'

'And if we don't?' Silver asked, snatching one of the tanks and examining it.

'Then after the dizziness and nausea, you will faint and the air in your lungs will be flooded with—'

'Enough, Roo,' Silver said. 'Maybe we don't need to know that much detail.'

Jason was surprised Roo didn't continue.

Xen shouldered the sniper rifle and repositioned the last pistol into a fabricated holster on his belt.

The airlock closed on the inside, sealing them in.

Jason had the remaining two explosive grenades strapped to his belt, as well as a pistol tucked in beside them. It was an unusual design, seeming to be made of just two parts with a side loaded cylindrical magazine.

He completed his look by clipping the small oxygen tank beside them. The tank was the shape and size of a small fire extinguisher with a fixed mouthpiece at one end.

When the doors opened, Jason raised his rifle, his heart leaping into adrenaline-fueled panic as his finger squeezed the trigger. A long black snake swung in front of his face. It took a fraction of a second to realize it was just a long cable, drooping from the roof of the tunnel. He thought it had been an oilsnake.

Xen chuckled, reached over and clicked the safety off on Jason's rifle. 'Might be useful to have that off, unless we bump into more mainline cables.'

'Don't tell Calc,' Silver said, 'or he'll think you've got it in for electronics.'

'Don't tell me what?' Calc's voice broke through from a band on her wrist, something she had acquired on one of the stations they had visited.

She looked at it. It showed ten minutes on a timer. 'Nothing, Calc, we just need to hurry.'

'Be careful of firing down there,' Calc said. 'There's a chance you may cause a cave-in or alert a nearby Zip droid.'

Xen swatted the cable aside and stepped onto the cracked glass cockpit of a small fighter ship.

Jason eased his weight down, perilously aware of the precarious footing, as the glass creaked and groaned beneath him.

Xen was bounding off over girders and contorted metal panels, staggering only slightly from the usual belly of liquor.

Silver didn't even look down at the mishmash that was the ground. She navigated the hollows and dark cracks like a gymnast, eyes up, scanning the walls of the tunnel as her feet blindly found footing on the thinnest pieces of rusting junk.

Nexus One's spotlights illuminated the flat barrier that separated the dead-end tunnel from the cavern beyond. It was fifty feet away, but the undulating floor of crevasses and jagged scrap made it seem like a hundred.

Jason clambered down from the fighter, landing on the sea of compacted scrap. He sprang forwards as something he stepped on moved and shifted, causing a small cascade of ironwork to tumble down to the lowest point. A black coil writhed and hissed as the ironwork landed on a concealed oilsnake in the shadows.

A second snake slithered up towards Jason, trying to escape the danger, its eyes yellow against the pitch black of its long snout.

Jason lashed out a boot, connecting with its head and sending it rolling back down.

It merged with the shadows below. He didn't wait for it

to come for revenge, instead he took a short jump across to a crumpled wing and focussed on reaching the wall.

Xen and Silver were already waiting and discussing where best to place the explosives.

'Put them in that crack and that one,' Silver said, pointing out two broken parts of the wall.

'How do we detonate them?' Jason asked, placing the first in the lower crack.

'Good point,' Silver said.

'Shoot them,' Xen said. 'There's a chance the first won't set off the second, so we'll need to shoot them both at the same time.'

The second crack was much higher; even at full stretch and using a rusted girder as a ladder, Jason couldn't get the grenade to rest in the crevice.

His head was fuzzy. Each attempt became harder than the last when it should have been easier.

'Oxygen,' Xen said, using his own and seeing Jason steady himself on the wall.

Jason unclipped the bottle and put it to his mouth. The world became clearer, like a fog parting to a warm wind.

'Give it here,' Silver said, using her own breather and thrusting out a hand to take the grenade after Jason failed for the fifth time.

She took it and eyed the wall like a determined free-climber. Using the girder as a springboard, she leapt up, stretching out her free hand to the crack. She gave a short grunt of effort as she clasped the lip and dangled there like a fish on a line. Another grunt and she heaved her weight up on one hand and planted the grenade in the gap.

She dropped and accepted the astonished cheers of Jason and Xen.

Calc's garbled panic through her watch cut all of them short.

Silver shoved Jason, knocking him against the wall as a red beam slashed the air where he'd been standing. He used his hand to soften the impact and instinctively unslung his rifle. He couldn't see what had shot them at first, then he spotted the spider-like legs raising a robotic body from a nearby pile of scrap. It blended in so well that there was no way to tell it had been there before it moved. More movement around the walls and floor made his skin crawl as half a dozen raised themselves from dormancy.

'Zipper bots,' Calc said, his voice coming through Silver's wristband before she opened fire with her rifle. A bot dropped from the ceiling in front of her, landing with a ringing metallic crunch. Jason aimed and fired automatically. His shot was true, hitting one of the legs, blowing it into fragments and toppling the spider over. It flailed wildly as it tumbled down a slope, firing random red shots around it.

Xen took down two more with his sniper rifle and switched his pistol as the closest ones scuttled towards them over the rugged ground.

Silver dived aside as a pair tried to flank her. She kicked the legs out from under one and fired point blank at another, dodging lasers the whole time.

To Jason, it seemed like the lasers were slow to land, almost easy to predict, but there were so many it became more difficult by the second.

He blew apart three more, seeming to make a dent in the numbers. But further back in the tunnels behind the ship, dozens more were coming out from the shadows, drawn by the fire and noise.

'Back to the ship!' Jason called, sensing the situation

getting more and more out of hand. A wave of sickness forced him to his knees. He threw up. Damn, he needed to get a grip on himself. It was a brutal effort to get up again, fighting waves of spinning and dizziness.

'Oxygen,' Xen called from a few yards away. He was firing behind Jason, stemming the constant tide of spider robots.

Jason grabbed for his tank but his hand clasped on thin air. He tried again and vaguely he knew he had lost it in the chaos. His lungs burnt and blackness closed in on his vision. He could just make out Silver shouting and the noise of her rifle getting closer before fading away.

He needed air, proper air. What a place to die, he thought, giving in to the sensation.

Xen was over him. The cool ring of the mask cupped his dry mouth, and he sucked in a deep breath, hoping it wasn't too late.

His vision returned with the feeling of the rifle barely gripped in his hands. His fingers tightened around the warm metal and he brought it up, ready to take vengeance on what had caused his suffering.

He put the hatred to use as soon as he could stand, joining in the fight until they had cleared the immediate vicinity. The lights from *Nexus One* illuminated the wall in front, leaving mostly shadows behind, but from the darkened areas more droids crept towards them. They seemed sluggish and creaked as they moved, yet they came on inexorably towards the light and noise. Some fired lasers, while others had long ago lost the use and seemed intent on trampling over them.

'Take the shot!' Silver cried. 'I'll cover you both.'

Jason turned to face the wall that had the two grenades in position. The noise of the clanking Zip droids behind him was unnerving. He wanted to turn and fight, to make sure they weren't about to jump on him.

He fought the urge to turn and aimed at one of the grenades.

Silver kept up the fire, shouting for Xen to join Jason.

Xen finally sidled in beside him, taking a sharp breath from his tank, followed quickly by a swig from a flask.

'Not the time,' Silver growled, between shots that were just holding back the tide of machines.

'Three,' she called out, rattling off a series of shots. 'Two!' He heard the click of her rifle running out of ammunition.

There were too many for her to stop. It took all of Jason's willpower to not turn around. He realized in that second that they had not agreed on who would shoot which grenade.

'One!'

Xen was kneeling, so Jason jerked the barrel up and squeezed the trigger just as Silver yelled out, 'Fire!'

It was a fifty-fifty chance.

The explosion tore the huge panel apart, sending shock-waves through the ground as both grenades exploded simultaneously, making them all stumble to stay upright. Silver was the only one who didn't wobble, seeming to ride out the tremors.

Debris and black trickles of oil rained down from above. A hard piece struck Jason on the shoulder, throwing his aim off from targeting the closest Zip droid.

'Back to the ship!' Calc called to them from Silver's bracelet.

The three of them didn't wait. They sprinted for the ship, leaping gaps, and dodging large metal pieces that hailed down on them.

Calc twitched *Nexus One* from side to side, shaking off the remaining spider droids that had climbed over the ship or fallen from the tunnel ceiling. It slowed, spinning so the airlock doors were open to face the three of them. It hovered at head height from the ground.

Jason dived in first, followed by Xen. A large chunk of debris crashed down on the hull just as Silver sprang up to get in.

She cried out as she missed the lip and tumbled back down to the jagged ground below.

46

J ason was at the back of the airlock, ready to enter. He watched in horror as the ship jerked up and Silver hit the rim. He was too far away to do anything but cry out. If the fall didn't kill her, then the swarming Zip droids would.

Xen threw himself down on his belly, both hands extended over the edge. He let out a winded "huff" as Silver caught his hands. The ship rose and he slid forward, as Silver's weight pulled him along.

Jason scrambled forwards and wrapped his arms around Xen's legs, bracing himself as he tried to hold them both. Xen hauled Silver back, easing the sharp pain in Jason's arms as they both dragged her up and inside the airlock.

She stood, dazed, sucking in a breath from her oxygen tank. 'Thank you,' she managed between gasps.

Xen bent double and threw up over her boots as the outer door sealed shut.

'No problem,' Xen grunted, heaving again.

∾

'Took your time,' Calc said, as they entered the bridge. 'The ship which has been following us is Kroth and Partel's. I just received a confirmed ident on it a minute ago and they've already reached the bottom of the sinkhole.'

Smoothly, *Nexus One* glided through the hole they had made and into the pitch-blackness beyond. There was nothing to see inside, just an engulfing darkness that surrounded the ship like a blanket.

'The scans must be wrong,' Silver said. 'There's no way this place can stay hollow if it's this big!'

'How big?' Jason asked. 'Why can't we see it? Are the lights still working?' The darkness was unnerving.

'Eighteen hundred yards ahead of us is the closest surface,' Silver said.

'Over a mile?' Jason said, astonished.

'Switching on side lights,' Calc said, clicking on another set of exterior lights. All it did was increase the glare around the sides of the window.

'Roo,' Jason asked, 'can we get more power to the lights? Please?'

'We have sustained damage to our power reroute modules.'

Calc looked away from the blackness outside. 'How? When?'

'Internal damage to the circuits in the maintenance tunnels,' Roo said.

'Did one of those Zip things get inside?' Xen asked.

Calc looked perplexed, his frown of confusion turning to red-cheeked anger. 'Curse my cartridges! That damn Quibble Truff is still down there.'

'Correct,' Roo said.

'Obviously,' Calc said. 'I don't need you to—'

Jason put his hand up as a flare of blue far down in the distance pulsed on and then off. 'What was that light?'

They all looked out the window, then at him.

'I saw a blue light down there, like a ring or—' he tried to think what the glare had reminded him of or where he'd seen it before, then it came to him, 'like the ring of an impulse engine.'

'Very improbable,' Calc said.

'There are ships in here?' Xen asked, peering hard out the window.

Instead of wasting time looking out, Silver had gone to her terminal. 'I'm picking up a faint radiation signal. Just a blip, but it was there. Hang on.' She tapped away on the holoscreen, swiping and palming through lines of data. 'It's warm out there. Thirty degrees, compared to just ten in the sinkhole and tunnel.'

'An engine warming this place up?' Jason asked.

'Over a very, very long time, perhaps,' she agreed.

The flash appeared again, a pulse of blue in the infinity of black.

'There!'

'I said improbable,' Calc said at Jason's smug look. 'Not impossible.'

'Well, you shouldn't be so damn sure all the time,' Jason said.

'I'm not,' Calc protestedf. 'If I didn't calculate every—'

'Turn off the lights,' Xen said.

Calc continued to rant: '—and I know if you only bothered to listen— He stopped. 'What?'

Xen slid his flask out. 'Turn the ship lights off,' he said, unscrewing the top.

Jason remembered a night on an oil rig in the Mediterranean. In order to see an incoming stealth boat, they were ordered to turn off all lights, like reducing the glare in a city to see the stars at night.

Xen put the flask away and stepped to the window, cupping his hands like a child playing with binoculars.

'Roo, kill all exterior lights,' Jason said, then realized what he had said. 'Wait! Not kill. Just turn off, simply turn off! Please,' he added.

'Of course, Jason Captain.'

The lights dimmed off, leaving behind nothing but somehow a darker blackness, if there were such a thing.

'Pointless exercise,' Calc said. 'Why don't I navigate using sonar and some simple mapping software I keep around for such times? Then...'

His voice trailed off as he stood from his seat and walked to the window.

Jason joined him, mouth agape at what he saw.

47

The darkness of the cavern gave way to speckles of light at first. Dotting the entire surface, yet clustered together, they morphed into patches of color. Greens, yellows, and subtle blues popped out. The closest were on the walls of the cavern. It was a lichen of some sort, luminescent and covering almost every surface.

The distant surfaces grew brighter the longer the crew members looked. The cavern slowly revealed itself. It was just as colossal as the scans showed, like ten football stadiums fused together and covered with the junk from a million failed space programs. Several large ships hunkered down on mountains of metal, perfectly preserved.

In the very center, surrounded by these, like a king among lesser nobles and raised high above the others, was a titanic vessel. It perched on the largest mound of scrap and rubble and was surrounded by a doughnut-shaped moat. The ship was an elegant form, curving yet vast and growing in size from front to back. It ended with a series of massive strutted engines, one of which was the firing culprit. It flared as they watched, illuminating the cavern further, revealing patches of huge fungi clustered around it. Being so close to a heat source must have encouraged the growth.

'Well, defrag my databanks. That is something special.'

'Class nine?' Silver asked. There was no response. The find enraptured each of them.

Calc got back in his seat and took *Nexus One* down towards that largest one. 'It's old,' he said, excitement barely held in check. 'Look at the turret towers.' Jason spotted where the turrets might be mounted, platforms set high above the roof of the ship like flat, silvery pedestals.

'There aren't any turrets,' Xen said.

'They are yet to be formed,' Calc said.

'Formed?' Silver asked.

'Look around us,' Calc said, 'that should give you a clue,'

Jason eyed the silver plates where the turrets would be, then around at the shimmering surfaces of *Nexus One*. Then it hit him.

'They're like this ship?'

'Exactly,' Calc said, bringing them closer to the enormous ship so they could make out the squares of mercury-like metal. 'They form the turrets they need, in the same way Roo can change the shape of this ship. They'll have presets they can use depending on the situation.'

'What does it mean, then?' Xen asked, 'that it's Old Empire tech?'

Calc nodded. 'Yes, most ships weren't like *Nexus One*, being a hundred percent malleable, but certain sections were. Such as turrets or wings.'

'You will not believe this,' Silver said, back in her seat. 'But I've got a crude ident on it.'

'Must be some residual power still in the reactor,' Calc said. 'That's why that engine keeps firing off.'

'It's called *Jupiter Six*,' Calc said.

'Weird name,' Xen said.

'It's almost fourteen thousand years old,' Silver said, 'according to the first creation date.'

The name Jupiter made Jason uneasy. His gut told him there was more to the name than first met the eye. Was it just a coincidence? Perhaps it was a common name back then, or was it related to Earth?

'What is it?' Silver asked, eyeing him suspiciously.

'Nothing,' Jason lied. 'It's just so old and perfectly preserved down here.'

'I'll take us in there,' Calc said, maneuvering *Nexus One* towards a large open hangar door on the far side, which had not been visible before. The curvature of the ground around the ship was odd. It seemed far too smooth compared to the walls and ceiling, which were jagged like crumpled foil paper. Had the lichen and algae eaten the circular area around the ship smooth? It had to eat something. There was a small run of oil flowing through the moat, coming from a sickly black falls a few feet across. It must have flowed in from outside of the cavern. Jason could imagine the years of draining from everything above to pool at a point somewhere overhead before slowly cascading in.

Silver turned around to face the back wall, where they had entered just before they dropped behind the crest of *Jupiter Six*.

'They're here,' she said.

Kroth's Harken ship had entered the cavern. It was incredibly bright, like a north star, blinding everything nearby.

'Same problem we had,' Xen said. 'Will they figure it out?'

'Well,' Calc said, easing the ship just below the rim to avoid any scans or the possibility of the others seeing *Nexus*

One. 'We will not wait around to find out. You guys get in there and bring out that fuel. Chances are you'll find it in a cargo bay. Won't be too far from this hangar entrance, unless ship design was much different back then.'

'Staying behind again?' Xen mocked.

Calc raised his arm, winced and then seemed to fight back the pain. 'No, I'm coming in with you. Can't have you running around inside an Ancient Empire ship on your own. Who knows, you might get hurt, or worse, lost.'

'You mean we might miss the cartridges and treasures on board?' Silver said.

'Exactly,' Calc said, ignoring the sarcastic tone or missing it entirely.

'They'll figure the lights out eventually,' Jason said, taking a second to stuff a nutrient bar into his breast pocket. He glanced around for the Quibble Truff. He'd get the little nonsense sometime. 'So let's park inside, find the fuel and get back quick.'

It was empty inside the hangar. No small ships as they had expected and no cargo containers half loaded for easy pickings. Only mold and lichen competing in the open space to dominate. Calc brought *Nexus One* to a stop beside an interior door, facing out, ready to speed away through the open hangar door.

Jason joined the others, grabbing up a rifle and ammunition and getting into the airlock. Each of them carried the small oxygen tanks attached to utility belts.

It nagged him that their ship was so obvious. They couldn't risk Kroth getting *Nexus One* before they came back out. As soon as Kroth made it inside, he would spot the ship.

An idea came to Jason as the inner airlock door shut with a click. 'Roo?'

'Yes Jason Captain?'

'Can you pilot this ship alone?'

'Of course, Captain.'

'When we're inside, take the ship outside and park just below the *Jupiter Six* in the trench. Disguise the ship as scrap, using the shape change thing that you do, and wait for us to come out again. Can you do that, please?'

'Of course, Captain, and be careful.'

'So she has a pleasant side,' Calc said, tapping away on a computer pad instead of carrying any weapons. They all knew he was a terrible shot.

As one, they stepped outside and looked around the hangar. It was a strange construction from the usual Jason had seen, although he'd be the first to admit he hadn't seen the interiors of many ships. There were no corners, it was all curving, giving everything a rounded appearance. Even external corners were rounded like the edges of work-benches and the door frames around the outside of the room.

'This one,' Calc said, leading them across the open space to a battered door. He pressed the open button by the side, but it refused to budge.

'Is there power?' Silver asked.

'Intermittent. The same with the flaring of the engine, which is happening every thirty-eight seconds.' He tapped away at his pad. 'If we wait for just five seconds, then...'

The ship gave a trembling vibration and with Calc's hand on the button, the door slid open, revealing a dark corridor in front of them.

'Lights on,' Xen said, clicking a torch he had attached to the side of his rifle. Jason and Silver followed suit.

Calc had a light installed on the front of his chest, which he flicked on, giving a wide angle of illumination.

The corridor leading away from the hanger was circular, its floor lined with mesh tiles. The tiles were laid over dozens of pipes that followed the corridor. There was no light inside and no lichen either. It seemed the life in the cave had yet to flourish on the inside of *Jupiter Six*.

'Where are we going then?' Xen asked, scanning rooms as they passed. They were all following Calc's lead.

'Most cargo bays are connected to the dock by a short walk, so,' he paused at a closed door with some runic symbols on it, 'here.'

The ship vibrated and again the double door slid open with Calc's hand firmly on the button.

It was an expansive cargo bay, vast and layered with floors overlooking a wide loading area, like a mezzanine of a small skyscraper. Lifts lined the open floors, ready to take cargo up to the relevant level before it was stored for the journey. There was only one problem.

'Shit,' Xen said.

'Improbable,' Calc said.

It was completely bare of any cargo.

'So that's it then,' Silver said, keeping her back to the room and watching the corridors for any pursuers.

Calc sped off towards a rusted terminal on the wall and set to work on his tablet.

"What's the plan, Calc?" Jason asked. Calc was calm, considering the monumental screw-up ahead of them.

'I'm going to access their storage system,' he said as Jason followed him.

Xen said nothing as he went to search the ground floor.

'Why the storage system?' Jason asked Calc, whose face was glued to his screen.

'I can use it to search the records for any Nexus fuel on the ship.'

'Checking the roster?'

'Exactly. But with only a fraction of a second to run the search as the power turns on and off, I won't be able to type in the query quickly enough. So I'm making a quick program to upload a search query and quickly download that roster to find out where it is.'

Jason was near useless with computers but he was following the explanation well, all things considered.

The vibration shook the ship and the screen flared to life. There was a cascade of strange angular symbols.

'You can read that?' Jason asked.

'I can read many languages courtesy of my galactic language cartridge, similar to your universal translator, but it works with most writing instead of just common.'

'My what?' Jason asked. 'I own nothing like that.'

Calc laughed, but when Jason still looked perplexed, he matched him. 'You don't know, do you?'

Jason was getting uncomfortable. 'Know what?'

'That you have a universal translator in you.'

'*In* me?'

'At some point, you must have been implanted,' Calc said. 'There's no way you know my home language of Kalleed and there's no way either of us could know Xen's Harken sub-dialect of Draag.'

'So?'

'So you have a chip in you that does all the hard work. Most babies in the galactic colonies get one, but I'm guessing not where you're from.'

Jason had wondered about the fact that all species spoke relatively good English. Sometimes it was off a bit, but nothing more than a foreign student midway through a course. It explained a lot. 'But how?'

The vibration through the ship had died and the terminal they were using had gone blank, but the program seemed to have worked. Calc's comp pad was scrolling through a mish-mash of data, seeking something.

'Have you had any medical procedures since you left Earth?'

Jason shook his head. 'No.'

The search finished on the comp pad and he began something new. 'I wonder...'

'What?'

'Were you by any chance injured on board *Nexus One*?'

Jason thought back to the time just a week or two back. 'Yes. I was injured when *Nexus One* left my galaxy.'

'Yes,' Calc said, looking at the pad, 'here it is. I've linked this pad with *Nexus One* to use its computing power, with Roo's permission, of course, and it shows here a pair of small medical procedures completed while you were in an induced coma.'

'I was in a coma?'

'Could just be unconscious from the pain. But I'm guessing Roo hooked you up with such an upgrade during that time.'

'Upgrade?' Jason said. He felt violated.

'Indeed,' Calc said. 'Access to ten thousand languages and derivatives is what I'd call an upgrade. Speaking of which, I've found a stash of them on board this ship.' He grinned darkly.

'And the fuel,' Jason asked, not liking the tone in Calc's voice and unsure what he meant.

'In the same place, against all probability, an officer's storage room on the floor above. There should be a maintenance tunnel here somewhere that we could use to climb up.'

'So Roo chipped me,' Jason said, 'like a dog?'

'Not sure what a dog is, but I get your meaning. Yes, but could you understand her before that happened?'

It was a good point. Jason couldn't remember. It had seemed like an age ago. Perhaps it was needed for him to communicate with her and without that initial ability to ask him, then there would be no proper way for her to do it with his permission. Still, he wished she had said something about it. It came across as deceptive.

'Here,' Silver said, moving deeper into the room and to a pillar set to one side of the room. She took a breath of oxygen, then cranked a handle on a small hatch set in the pillar.

Jason did the same, making sure to firmly clip the tank back onto his belt this time.

Xen had returned. 'Nothing in the entire hold. No weapons, no ammunition, nothing of value either.'

Calc shook his head, then explained about the stash above. Xen perked up at the prospect of finding some actual loot and he was first inside the maintenance tunnel.

Jason went after Calc, letting the Humdroid's navigation skills work outside the realm of atmospheres and space. Silver followed, pulling the hatch in behind her and leaving it slightly ajar in case they needed to retreat quickly.

The tunnel was hexagonal, a strange change from the smooth curves in the decks below. A ring ladder curved in a circle around the tunnel with hand holds all the way around so that no one side was the right one. It was wider than a single person and allowed two people to pass each other if needed, in the tight confines.

'Better designed than the ones on most ships,' Silver

said.

'It's strange,' Jason said, 'to imagine a previous point in history when ancestors or even aliens were more technologically advanced than now.'

Calc's comp pad gave a buzz and he stopped mid-climb to look at it.

'We've got a problem,' he said, looking in fear at the pad.

He held it out for them to see. It was a live feed of the hangar from the perspective of *Nexus One* just outside. Kroth and Partel's ship was already inside. A troop of soldiers, led by Partel, were forming a circle whilst Kroth yelled at Zip droids. Not just a few of them, but hundreds had made it inside the cave and were swarming up into the hangar. They flowed around Kroth; he gave orders to them as they scurried for the open doors.

'I don't want to alarm you,' Calc said as a scuttling noise echoed up the ladder from below. 'But this is a delayed feed because of the magnetic interference from this ship.'

'Shit!' Silver hissed. Jason looked down as she opened fire below them. The swarm had found the entrance and was clambering up the ladder, their legs spread across the space or clinging to the rails. The noise of Silver's pistol in the confines was deafening. Broken Zip droids piled up below them until one fired back. The shot blew open a panel on the side of the tunnel, sending sparks showering out and partially blocking the view.

'Go!' Jason cried, heart thumping in his chest as he reached one sweaty hand over the other. He felt the heat as more shots made their way up until so many Zip droids were below them they blocked each other except for the lead two.

Calc punched open a hatch to the side of the tunnel and threw himself out onto the deck above. Jason followed, feeling a shot skim his leg as he tumbled out onto a steel floor. It burned fiercely, making him grind his teeth together to fight the pain. It was like someone jabbing a burning stick into his flesh.

Xen was next, twirling around to grab Silver's hand as she came out last. He thrust his rifle down and blindly opened fire. 'Get moving!' he cried, peering back down the tunnel.

Jason scanned the room with his torch. They had emerged from a pillar at the side of an engineering deck. It was two stories high, with a series of walkways above. Strange machines built into the walls lined the perimeter, coated in dust and a thin sheen of grease. It was all centered on a cylindrical glass-like tube as wide as an SUV and stretching up from the floor to the ceiling two stories above.

Inside the tube a small glimmer of gold plasma coiled and writhed, like a contorting mist trapped within.

'Captain,' Calc said. He had his comp pad plugged into a door across the room. 'We need to get through here.'

Silver joined Jason as he sprinted across to him.

'How long?' Jason asked, glancing back at Xen, who was still leaning into the tunnel firing down with a pipe rifle. He had the sniper rifle strapped to his back, which was wedging him and stopping him from falling. He was drunk again, but Jason didn't care.

'I can't force it open,' Calc said. 'Not even slightly compatible. I could reroute the operating system from *Nexus One* via this pad, but it will take an hour or more.'

'We've got about a minute. Wait for the power,' Silver said.

Calc raised his head from the screen. 'You're right. Why didn't I think of that?'

'You would have,' Jason said. 'When's the next one?'

Calc closed his eyes. A small green glow flared behind one, then he opened them. 'Three minutes and four seconds. They're getting longer between flare-ups.'

Jason could see several spots in the room that would be better to defend than by the door, but they had no choice. They had to keep close or risk missing the opening.

Xen fell back from the hatch as a dozen smaller Zip droids spidered out from the opening. He fired wildly before getting to his feet, kicking one away before hitting it with a shot. Jason fired at the others, stepping left and right to avoid the small laser shots.

'Silver, get in close!' he called. 'Xen! Get back here and defend. We need three minutes to get the door open.' The two bunched up and together they destroyed most of the small droids, leaving only a couple to scatter before the first large Zip spider clanked out from the hatch. They all fired together, and the bigger droid burst open in a shower of sparks and oil.

Three more crept out, a slow and steady stream of death.

They killed two before another trio emerged. Their numbers rose, increasing every time one of the crew needed to reload or a shot went astray.

'One minute,' Calc said

By the time there were ten in the room, they were scuttling across the floor and their lasers were forcing the four to dance around, dodging and hopping aside.

'There's too many,' Silver said. The tip of her rifle was red hot from the constant shooting.

Twenty came towards them now and an endless stream behind. They were locked onto them, and Jason decided a new tactic was needed.

A stupid one.

But surely they always worked.

48

The spider droids came on relentlessly, the smaller ones fanning out to encircle the crew as their larger brothers clunked forwards, firing a steady stream of lasers.

Jason fished out a magazine from his pocket.

Xen noticed the movement.

'Can you hit it?' Jason asked, making a throwing motion.

Xen nodded, unslinging the sniper rifle across his back.

Jason eyed the hatch across the room behind the core and imagined the arc it would take.

He tossed the magazine underhand and watched as it soared over the mass of spider droids climbing across their dead comrades to get to the four of them.

Just before it landed amidst the Zip droids, Xen fired once. The shot was impeccable. It struck the tumbling magazine and the resulting explosion rocked the room. The Zip droids closest shattered, and it blew the rest outwards in a rolling splatter of oil and metal parts.

The four of them hunkered down, feeling the heat and taking the hits from a few far-flying pieces of metal.

'The core,' Calc said as the smoke cleared. The stream of spiders had nearly ceased. There was now a carpet of broken droids, but between the door and the hatch the core had changed. A thick crack ringed the giant tube.

The core flared, and the small glow grew to an intense blue light, rippling and flashing like lightning-covered clouds inside the tube.

The door opened, throwing Calc inside as he had been leaning on it in desperation. The others leapt through as the power was restored for just a second. Jason couldn't help but turn and stare back at the core. The crack grew like tree roots do over decades, splitting into smaller fissures.

'It's going to blow,' Jason said.

'It might take one more flare-up,' Calc said. 'But after that, it will end this ship and probably this entire cavern.'

'Can we shut it down?' Jason asked.

'Yes,' Calc said, 'I can use the terminal in there to—'

The doors closed automatically, hiding the reactor from view and sealing them off from it.

'Damn,' Jason said. 'Guess not.'

'How long?' Silver asked, rolling up a torn and bloody sleeve to inspect several burnt patches of fur along her arm.

'Five minutes,' Calc said, marching down the corridor away from them.

'Give or take what?' Xen asked, as they trailed behind.

Calc stopped at a junction for a split second before making a choice and taking one. 'About five minutes,' he hissed as Xen asked again.

'So five minutes or no minutes?' Xen said. 'Very precise.'

Calc turned into another corridor, stopping to look at his comp pad in frustration. 'You try doing the calculations for warp core instability in a ten-thousand-year-old ship, buried under—'

He froze, turning down a noise-riddled corridor. Jason rounded the corner and skidded to a halt as well. Thirty feet away, the corridor was crawling from floor to ceiling with Zip droids all swarming towards them like angry ants in a tunnel. Shots swished past their heads.

Calc ducked, nearly dropping his comp pad as they all opened fire. 'This way,' he yelled, leading them back to another fork before racing into it. A different route was also blocked by a second swarm. They were being hemmed in and surrounded.

'There must be thousands pouring into the ship to find us,' Silver said.

'Tens of thousands,' Calc said unhelpfully. 'The odds are they'll find and trap us, eventually.'

'Like a giant game of Pac-Man,' Jason said.

Calc halted suddenly and turned into an empty corridor with a single, heavily set door at the end. 'This is it,' he said, double checking something on the comp pad.

They faced the door, with Silver and Xen covering them from any stray droids that might find them. They had stayed ahead of the main infestation, but that couldn't last for much longer.

'We can't afford to wait for another power surge to open it,' Jason said.

'No need,' Calc said, 'The damage to the core has scrambled most available circuits, so—' He pressed the button beside the door and it slid open, slowly at first and screeching in protest at a millennium of hermetic closure.

They all stared at the rows of boxes and containers lining the shelves stacked floor to ceiling. The hoard was lit by just a few remaining lights set in the walls and ceiling, slowly fading to near uselessness over the years.

The door slid shut behind them, creaking less this time

as they had exercised the sliders. There was a solid clank. Calc cursed and turned to bang a fist on the open button. Nothing happened. 'We'll have to find another way out,' he said 'or—' He stared around again at the storage room, unable to finish. He jumped up in excitement and skipped to a terminal, and began scanning the haul.

They all took a second to use their oxygen bottles in a strange moment of silence.

'Hydroxy Ethaline Microcorpius,' Calc said, resuming his tappings, 'is in zone four, blue shelf. And the other—' He began muttering to himself, searching for something else. Silver and Jason began the hunt while Xen moved over to Calc, staring hard over his shoulder.

Silver had strode into the depth of the room. Although only a few hundred square feet, the room was so stacked with flaking boxes and sagging shelves it made it a warren of tight spaces and shadowy dead ends.

'Got them,' Silver said, standing on a faded blue line and reaching up to a high shelf. There were two chrome cylinders, each about the size of a water bottle. They were just out of reach.

'Here,' Jason said, kneeling beside her and interlocking his fingers.

Silver didn't hesitate, slipping a boot onto the foothold and pushing up. She came down with a cylinder in each hand. She smiled at him. It twisted to panic as a loud creak issued from the shelf.

She said nothing, just shoved him backwards out from the tight space. The last thing he saw was her dropping to her knees, arms raised to protect her face as the shelf lurched over her and an avalanche of boxes and containers crashed down.

'Silver!' Jason cried, jumping back in, yanking out boxes

and dragging heavy objects away, trying in vain to catch a glimpse of her.

Xen and Calc rushed to join the fray, rolling canisters and debris out from where she had been just seconds before.

Calc stopped helping and disappeared, returning with a small box in one hand, the other plunged inside it, pulling out cartridges. Jason ignored him and kept digging through the pile.

'Her arm!' Xen called out, finding an elbow.

Jason assessed the situation, trying to figure out how best to free her. The shelf was firmly on top of her, weighted down by a huge metal box accessible only from the row behind.

He barged past Calc, who was fiddling with a bank of cartridges on the side of his chest.

Jason made it around to the crate and tried to heave it off. It was impossibly heavy. They needed leverage to get her free.

A loud bang hammered the door they had come in by, startling them all. A second and third bang pounded the metal, shaking the frame, then a constant stream of sizzles and hisses issued from behind.

'They're breaking in,' Xen said.

Calc ignored the threat and joined Jason, clambering up on the angled shelf to better reach the top of the metal crate.

Jason hoped that at least Calc's slim frame would help him free Silver, but he doubted it.

Calc reached over to the shelf still standing behind the one that had fallen on her. He hooked a hand around a strut and stretched across to slip a hand behind the crate. He was spread between the two like a spider in the center of a web.

He grunted, his face turning red, and with a supreme effort, he slowly tilted the crate away from the shelf.

'What the—?' Jason couldn't work it out. The crate must have weighed a thousand pounds.

Xen gave a tug, and with most of the weight off the pile, Silver was dragged free, her face scuffed but relieved.

Calc pulled free a cartridge, looking drained and pale. 'Found some real treasure in here,' he said.

'What was that?' Jason asked as another bang reverberated from the door.

'Strength module,' Calc said. 'You're looking at paying a minimum of half a million creds from a Traversai merchant for just one.'

'The door,' Xen said, as Silver brushed herself down and offered a thank you.

The door was glowing red hot, turning white in the center.

'They're burning through,' Calc said, tucking the box with his find under an arm and slinging a large bulging bag over the other. He nodded towards the dark areas at the back of the room between the remaining shelves. 'There should be another maintenance tunnel leading down to the canteen and through to the hangar from there.'

Xen slung a bulky bag he had found over an arm, sipped his canteen and raised the rifle to the white-hot door. The metal sagged like water sprayed onto a brown paper bag as it broke, drooping down into a molten pile of white-hot slag.

The smallest Zip droids scurried in first, their spidery legs melting as they attempted to cross the scorching pile. Those that clung to the sides of the door were picked off by Xen before the larger droids scurried through, firing red lasers into the dark storeroom.

'Wait! Silver said. 'The fuel's still under the shelf.'

Jason nearly turned back. He had the other one, but would it be enough?

'Go!' Xen shouted, picking off the larger droids as the smaller ones made a sacrificial bridge over their comrades, allowing the largest to pour in unhindered.

Jason didn't go back. It was difficult to fire his rifle with the remaining Nexus fuel cylinder under his arm, so he bolted for the rear of the room where Calc and Silver were ducking into another tight shaft. As he descended, he caught sight of Xen dropping his empty rifle and turning tail to follow them.

It was a much smaller shaft than the last. Only one of them could descend at a time, but even with Silver's injuries, they got down much quicker. They were driven by fear and the need to escape.

Xen slammed the hatch shut above. Jason glanced up, looking past him to see it already glowing red from the lasers.

Minutes passed before they reached the right level. Each second, Jason's anxiety grew, knowing that the core would breach at any moment. The heat from the droids firing at the door above cascaded down, making his forehead bead and drip with sweat. It stung his eyes, threatening to blind him. He didn't want to die in this coffin-sized tube like some prisoner in a medieval oubliette.

There was a draft of cool air as Calc kicked open a hatch and sprung out.

Jason sucked in a desperate gasp and clambered through into a huge table-lined canteen, glad to feel the open space around him again.

'This way,' Calc said, threading his way through the tables and chairs to a nearby door.

Jason glanced behind to see Xen sprinting, chased by a

dozen Zip droids, who had been so fast that he could not close the hatch behind. Several smaller ones sprang up on the tables, leaping from table to table, scattering ancient cutlery and gaining ground at a frightening speed. A pair simultaneously leapt onto Xen's back. He shook them off, yelling as the lasers seared his skin and beard.

Calc skidded to a halt, clearly undecided whether to leave him behind, and began fishing inside his box again. Jason pulled his pistol from his belt and fired. A third leapt onto Xen. Jason aimed down the pitiful sights, but his shot connected, throwing the droid clear off Xen's back, freeing Xen up to close the gap between them.

One of the agile larger drones had raced along the ceiling and dropped to cut him off. Jason raised his pistol and fired. It gave a series of beeps.

'Shit!' he cursed, fishing in a pocket for a spare magazine. But it was too late. The droid turned from Xen and sprang at Jason.

Calc leapt in front of him, launching a kick at the droid. It was a feeble effort, but as it connected, a shower of sparks and eye-piercing lightning burst from the droid.

Stunned, they all froze.

The droid recovered, leaping at Calc. Calc grabbed it midair, the weight toppling him backwards onto a table. There was more lightning as he pressed a hand into the underbelly of the droid. The droid's legs crumpled up like a dead fly's before it was flung back by the mysterious force.

Calc jumped up, invigorated for a second, his eyes wide, showing the array of tiny reticules imprinted in his pupils. He put a hand around a cartridge on his thigh and jerked it out, stowing it away.

The supernatural light in his eyes died and he sagged. Xen looped an arm around him as a prop before he fell. It took Calc a few seconds to come back to life before the three of them made it to where Silver was waiting at the far end of the room.

'What the hell was that back there, Calc?' Jason asked.

Calc grinned. 'Found some Ancient Empire upgrade cartridges in storage. Should come in handy if my calculations are correct.' He straightened his back, seeming to get his strength again, and took the lead again.

Two corridors later and they came into a tunnel that led straight to the hangar.

They halted at the door and peered out, expecting to find a sea of Zip droids still pouring in from the cave but it was empty.

'Bringing *Nexus One*,' Calc said, using the comp pad.

'You can do that?' Jason asked.

'Put a little code into the nav system just in case something like this happened.'

'Wasn't Roo meant to meet us here?' Silver asked, scanning the empty hangar and the piles of debris outside.

'She should have picked up this pad and intercepted it,' Calc saidd. 'Could be the interference from the ship or the droids making connections hard from outside.'

Something was off. A niggling feeling in his stomach made Jason wary. His instincts were good, and he'd learned to trust them over the years.

'Come on,' Calc urged, seeming to struggle with the comp pad.

'What is it?' Xen asked.

'Just being difficult,' Calc said, jamming the end of his little finger against a socket on the device. 'There.' He pointed at the rubble visible outside and like magic, the manta ray shape of *Nexus One* materialized. It had been expertly camouflaged, blending in with the debris to near perfection. Rising, it swiveled to face them and cruised into the hangar.

'Let's go,' Calc said, making a beeline for *Nexus One*.

Silver followed. She looked dazed as she stepped out, with Xen by her side. Jason held back a second, then, with the cylinder in one hand and pistol in the other he made the crossing to the ship.

The airlock was open and inviting.

Before they could reach the door, the sound of heavy footfalls echoed in the hangar. A squadron of Harken elite troops filtered in from the other doors. Flanking them were a dozen large Zip droids who had been hiding underneath the lip of the hangar entrance.

The Harken wore heavy exoskeletons, thick frames of scrap-like metal that lent them a menacing air, along with enhanced strength and speed. Their weapons looked in better condition than most things Harken and Jason could tell the soldiers knew how to use them.

They were outnumbered and outgunned.

'Drop everything,' one of the Harken said, his voice guttural and crass. Jason let his pistol fall and waited as Silver and Xen did the same with their weapons and gear. He slowly slipped the canister onto his belt, making sure that the Nexus fuel canister was next to the oxygen tank. Perhaps their similarity would avert any extra investigations.

From behind the mass of soldiers stepped Kroth, his face marred by the black birthmark that darkened his features to a devil-like intensity.

Partel, dressed in a new outfit, smarter and more pompous than his old one, stood beside Kroth. Sweat beaded his balding head, the droplets running into the constant frown upon his wrinkled forehead. A dark grin stretched his face into a sneer of gloating at their capture.

'Well, isn't this nice,' Kroth said, looking around at the hangar as if they were out for a stroll in a park.

'I knew you would find us,' Xen said. 'I sent you the transmissions before we entered—'

Kroth shook his head in disappointment.

Xen doubled over as one of the soldiers stepped in and rammed the butt of a rifle into his stomach.

'You have led us on quite a chase,' Kroth said, a smile twisting his lips at Xen's coughing. He turned around to face the ship, hovering with its airlock door open. 'Ever since I laid eyes on your rather unique ship, I've wondered what it was. Its very existence kept me up at night. The moment I laid eyes on it, I knew.' He turned back to face them. 'I knew it was different. The way it just appeared out of nowhere during that war. I guessed what it could do, but I needed proof and answers to my questions. Why could you not just disappear at will when we were close? Why could you not jump?'

He said the last word with near reverence.

Partel caught Silver's eye, then scanned her battered body. 'Please just tell him, Silv,' he said, stepping forward.

'Why do you care?' She sneered through the pain.

Partel opened his mouth but stopped himself before looking to Kroth. The Harken gave him a nod.

'I've been awarded a new position,' he started.

'You're a lackey,' Silver spat. Jason noticed the red in the spit as it hit the rusted floor.

'Maybe,' Partel admitted. He seemed to sag. 'Since we last spoke, I realized you were right. I had nothing to my name. My ship was it. Old and battered, a bit like myself. But I've been offered a proper position now, among the Harken. A new ship, a salary and a pension. I'll be a made man, but to make it happen, we need that ship from you and to know how it jumps. So just tell him, Silv.'

'You'll get nothing from me,' she said. 'Except a knife in your eye.'

Two of the soldiers began rummaging through the quartet's gear. They checked Xen's bag and Calc's box of cartridges, scattering them in their efforts to find something. Jason didn't even blink as they checked over the oxygen tank and then the Nexus fuel canister, but his adrenaline gave a jolt. He had to master his reactions and be ready for whatever Kroth wanted.

Kroth smiled, coming back between them from walking around the ship.

'We don't need you to tell us anything,' he said, slipping a golden pistol from his belt. He raised it slowly to Silver's head and tilted his own towards Jason. 'He'll tell us instead.'

'Fuck you,' Jason said, a sinking feeling of utter failure spreading through him. 'You'll kill us all, anyway.'

Kroth shrugged. 'I just want your ship. All this violence was so unnecessary. I detest it, if I'm honest. But when needs must, needs must.' He pressed a button on the side of the pistol. A high-pitched noise rose, indicating the pistol was ready to fire. 'Now, I'll ask again. How does your ship jump?'

'And you'll get the same answer from me. Fuck. Off.'

'Fine,' Kroth said. 'Have it your way.'

His finger moved to the trigger. It squeezed.

49

'It's in the cylinder,' Calc blurted, gesturing to the cylinder in the pile beside the oxygen tank. 'The hyperdrive needs the fuel. We don't know how much.'

'Good boy,' Kroth said, lowering the weapon and eyeing the canister. 'See, that wasn't so hard. No violence. No bloodshed. No pain.'

Jason understood Calc's desire to stay alive, but did the Humdroid not understand that this Kroth would kill them all once he had what he wanted?

'So that's what you were doing down here,' Kroth said, staring back out to the cavern beyond. 'This place holds a lot of secrets, even without this ship of yours. The other two were foolish to ignore this place and cordon it off. There are years of research down here. The things our people could do if we were more patient and used our brains, instead of relying on our base instincts.'

He turned back, his gaze roaming the pile of objects they had scavenged. He bent to pick up the scattered box of cartridges Calc had discovered.

Calc looked ready to jump forward and take them back,

but the soldiers noticed his anxiety and shook their heads in warning.

Behind *Nexus One*, dozens of kamikaze drones waited, hovering motionless, ready for a signal.

Kroth placed cartridges down, also noticing Calc's reaction. 'Go on, Humdroid.'

'You'll need us to show you how to fuel the ship,' Calc said. 'By the time you figure it out, the core of this ship will blow. We fractured the core on the engineering deck. It won't be long now before it gives out.'

As if in confirmation, the hangar floor shuddered, making them all stagger. Had the core blown? Surely it would have been an explosion rather than just a tremor.

Kroth ignored the motion, gesturing to one of the nearby soldiers. 'Take the cylinder. Bring the Humdroid and kill the others.'

The soldier wasn't paying attention to Kroth. Like all the others, he was staring out into the cavern. It was moving.

The floor of debris surrounding the ship was shifting slowly, spinning in a circle around the vessel. Something was moving inside the trench around *Jupiter Six*.

It was enormous.

A slithering giant with a mishmash of metal-like scales covering its body.

The thing was at least fifty feet long.

It moved with the calculated slowness that all apex predators had.

Jason looked upon the monstrosity, dumbfounded. How had they not seen it when they first entered— it dawned on him. The heat from the engine was keeping it warm.

This was its nest.

Partel looked around and raised his rifle at the monster beyond the open door.

'We need to go, Kroth,' he said. 'Now! Just leave them here and take the Humdroid.'

Kroth spotted the moving mass, stepped forward and snatched the cylinder from Jason's pile. He stood and their eyes locked just inches from each other.

'Pity. It seems you never lived up to your name, Korzon. Think you can steal the Emperor's name, fly one of his ships and not stir up the Hidden Alliance? More fool you.'

The Emperor's name? Jason had wondered why so many had scoffed when he had told them his surname.

Korth smiled, bright white teeth standing out against the black birthmark on his face. 'You could have been useful, Mr Korzon,' he said, plucking the nutrient bar from Jason's breast pocket. 'Now, like the relics your body will bleed on, you will be forgotten.'

Kroth's ship rounded the corner, coming to a stop. Its airlock opened and a ramp slid out, leading up inside.

Calc was frog marched towards *Nexus One*.

Kroth peeled open the nutrient bar, content in the madness around them, and turned to board *Nexus One* as Partel and several soldiers raced for their ship.

'What do we do with them?' one of the last soldiers asked.

Kroth turned to stare at the three, glanced at the cylinder in his other hand, took a bite of the bar and said, 'Kill them,'

50

"No!' Calc cried, trying to fight the two men holding him.

The soldier in front of Jason raised his rifle and shrugged as if to say life was unfair.

Damn right it was, Jason thought, watching as Partel headed back to their ship. It was obvious he didn't want to see Silver's death.

As Kroth turned back to *Nexus One*, the smile vanished as a small flying bundle of purple launched itself from inside the airlock. It latched onto Kroth's face as the man screamed in terror, spinning around trying to swat the thing away.

Jason dived forwards in the confusion, wrestling the soldier in front of him to the ground.

Beside him, Xen crouched, snatched up a pistol and in a split second took out two soldiers trying to help Kroth beat away the Quibble Truff.

The cylinder dropped from Kroth's grip, bouncing hard on the floor before rolling towards Jason. Jason reached for the cylinder. His fingers curled around it as Partel spun back and opened fire with a rifle. Jason scrambled for the open airlock of *Nexus One*.

Partel closed the distance, reaching Kroth and kicking the Quibble Truff away as it lined up for another jump. He grabbed the councilor and raced to their ship as their men gave covering fire.

Xen kept firing until Calc broke free from his captors and they all reached the airlock.

'Close it,' Silver said.

Calc moved to press the button, but Jason put a hand out to stop him.

Jupiter Six rumbled, a grating noise that grew into a thunderstorm in their ears.

Jason sprinted out to the hangar again and scooped up the purple bundle, cursing himself for doing so even as he raced back inside.

'Idiot,' Silver said.

The door closed as they sprinted to the bridge.

Calc took to his seat, maneuvering the ship around, but Kroth's ship was already making for the only exit, the small hole that they had come in by.

Jason dumped the unconscious Quibble Truff and looked out at what could only be described as a surreal moment. Jason absorbed it all in a flash, time seeming to slow in the overwhelming tide of chaos.

Snaking through the cavern was the huge slimy cavern worm, raising its oil-slicked head to snap at the hunter drones waiting in the air around *Jupiter Six*. It ate them whole, consuming the explosives, which detonated in its mouth without concerning the beast.

Thousands of spidery Zip droids moved like a swarm around the large ship, scuttling over the hull even as a huge portion collapsed and caved in where the core was disintegrating.

The hunter drones in the air chased *Nexus One*, forcing Calc to bank hard left and right to avoid those waiting between them and the exit.

Jason dropped into his seat, unable to tear his gaze from the flying drones as they followed like the tail of a comet.

Xen emerged from the crew quarters, staggering to his seat and getting busy behind the weapons terminal.

Jason eyed him suspiciously. Was he communicating with Kroth's ship again?

Calc pushed *Nexus One* to its limits to catch up with Kroth's ship, but they were too slow. They were gaining fast, but as Kroth's ship passed through the small opening, it unleashed a barrage of ballistics that tore the sides down, making it collapse into a wall of debris.

'Shit!' Calc jerked the ship away, raw power surging through the engines to stop them from being caught up in the fall. Debris cracked the hull as they skimmed through it, banking around to circle the cavern again.

Jupiter Six was a glare of light now, burning with a harsh blue plasmodic glow that illuminated the giant cavern worm as it came straight for them. Like a demon, it rose on its hind body, mouth open to swallow *Nexus One*. Savage rows of teeth snapped shut like the doors to hell, encasing the entire ship in its maw.

Jason and Calc froze. 'Lights,' Silver said calmly beside them, powering up the exterior lights to see the undulating insides of an oily mouth all around them.

There were a series of beeps from *Nexus One*.

Xen looked up with a grin as Calc slowed the ship to a stop, riding the movements of the creature they were now a part of.

'Ready to fire!' Xen cried triumphantly as they all turned to stare at him. Had he gone mad?

Jason looked at the small computer screen in front of him and tapped *"Weapons."*

"Loaded."

Had Xen done something?

'Roo?' Jason asked, 'Do we have weapons?'

'Affirmative, Captain Jason.' she replied.

'Fire?' he said, unsure.

Xen pushed something and the front of *Nexus One* lit up like a furnace. A trio of missiles surged from the front, surrounded by a rainbow of lasers.

A deep squelch was followed by a hideous roar of thunder and a burst of light as the flesh of the creature ruptured open.

Calc urged the engines to full and they soared out through the sickening flaps of broken flesh. He had to bank hard as they encountered a dozen kamikaze hunter drones waiting beyond.

The drones locked on and tailed them like hawks on the wing, giving the crew no time to celebrate the bizarre set of events a second before.

Calc circled even as *Jupiter Six* finally blew. The plasma raced outwards, the roof of the cavern collapsing on top of the now dead worm.

'Hit the exit hole with the missiles,' Jason said, seeing the faint hope that might get them out.

He glanced behind. The roof was sagging down in a tide of metal ships and twisted parts. The cavern shrank behind them as Calc powered forward at the blank wall.

They were fifty feet away.

'Xen?' Jason asked, wondering why he hadn't fired.

'It's loading,' Xen said, confused.

They were going to hit the wall or be crushed by the falling world from above.

Calc swerved around tight again for one last look back into what had been the cave. It was now a falling tide of metal surging towards them.

Jason glimpsed the hunter drones still following them before the wall was back in view.

'Use the drones!' he cried.

Calc understood and turned the bottom of the ship towards the wall as if to land on it.

'Roo, help,' Calc cried, needing an extra boost as they had before.

There was a second of nothing, and then they all screamed, 'Please!'

Extra boosters fired, turning the vertical landing into a drag race. The ship pulled away along the wall, leaving the drones to impact the thin spot. They ignited in a series of explosions, tearing the hole open, and Calc flipped the ship up in a loop and soared out into the tunnel beyond.

'Weapons ready,' Xen said.

They glared at him.

51

'No one will believe that tale,' Calc said, wiping the sweat from his forehead before it set his circuits off. 'Mind you, I don't think they usually do.'

The force of the blast had propelled them forwards at a breakneck speed, allowing them to clear the damage radius and plunging them into the dark tunnels.

There was no sign of Kroth and Partel's ship in the gloomy tunnel. The overall shape had changed since they last came through. The tremors from the collapse of the cavern had contorted the shape. It was squashed, as if the weight of the world above had settled down again. Calc slowed the ship to squeeze through ever tighter gaps, navigating the darkness, following scans and relying on the lights from the ship to illuminate hazards.

The walls were even more blackened by a fresh excess of squeezed-out oil that oozed down through the layers.

'Xen,' Jason said, taking a second to trust Calc's skills, 'I think you need to explain—'

Jason looked around but Xen was unconscious on the

floor beside his chair, a large bump growing on his forehead.

Silver moved over to him, checking his pulse and vitals. 'He'll be alright, needs some rest though.'

'I think I can piece it together,' Calc said. 'He checked the roster in the officer's storage and must have seen some old ammunition cases. I guess that's what he had in the bag and was probably down in the maintenance tunnel leading from your room to install them. Not communicating with the Harken. We seem to have some firepower now. Let's hope he pulls through enough to help us.' He looked slightly guilty. 'Probably took a beating in the maintenance tunnel with me flying like that.'

Jason felt bad for thinking Xen had been conspiring again. He hadn't forgotten that the man had saved him in the firefight.

Jason helped Silver carry Xen to his quarters, the only place where there was a comfortable spot to lay him down.

'I could carry him myself,' Silver said.

'I know,' Jason said. 'I just wanted to check in on you after what happened back there.'

'I'll manage. As long as we get out of this alive.'

'What do you mean?' he asked.

She gave him an exasperated look. 'You think Kroth has just run away, leaving us with the ship and the fuel? And if I know Partel, he won't let us tarnish his newfound fame. This won't be over yet.'

Jason realized what she meant. Kroth would be waiting for them. Partel too.

'I'll get the fuel loaded,' Silver said, plucking the canister off her belt and lifting the trapdoor to the maintenance tunnels. 'We might bypass them if we can get it working.'

Jason headed back out to the bridge. It was just him and Calc.

'How're you doing?' he asked, relishing a moment where there was no real peril or guarantee of sudden death. Even his stomach had settled after the rollercoaster ride needed to escape.

Calc nodded, his eyes scanning all the screens. Jason was sure another screen had appeared since he last looked, increasing the constant glare that lit Calc's face up.

'Nothing to report yet,' Calc said. 'I see Silver is attempting to load the fuel. It won't be instant, though. I already quizzed Roo and she said we won't have capabilities for at least an hour, due to an algorithm update. The ship's holding up though, even after such a beating. Probably blew a few smaller power cells, but nothing we'll miss at the moment, and having weapons now is comforting. I've extrapolated several options for what will happen when we make a jump and there's only a fifteen percent chance of failure or death.'

'I asked how you were doing,' Jason said, 'not for a situation report.'

Calc shrugged. 'Sorry, just a habit.' He took a second as if to evaluate his feelings. 'I'm pissed I lost those cartridges,' he said, subconsciously pressing a finger to a slot where one had been. 'Not for the value, although they were worth enough to live off for a lifetime, but for how much it would have helped us in the future.'

Jason hadn't considered a future with them still around. Somehow he kept imagining Earth, being at home with a beer and the game on.

'You used them to get Silver free,' Jason said, placing a hand on Calc's shoulder. 'That was more than enough.'

Calc nodded but with just a little conviction.

'It felt amazing having all that power, all the strength, or the ability to shock things. It's what most Humdroids set out for in the first place. I do not know what some of the other cartridges could have done.' He chuckled at his longing. 'Spoken like an addict.'

'Spoken like someone who is still alive enough to speak like an addict,' Jason said, slipping his fingers inside a pocket. He pulled out a small silver cartridge and placed it on top of Calc's terminal.

Calc sucked in an excited breath.

'How? Where?'

Jason laughed lightly. 'Found it when I picked up that Quibble Truff. It was in its claws. Must have wanted to keep it for itself.'

Calc smirked at the irony. 'And how is the cute little beast?'

Jason had forgotten. He looked over to where he had left it after finding the cartridge. The purple creature was gone.'Somewhere eating important things, probably.'

Jason looked at the gift. 'Sorry I couldn't get one of the bigger ones for you.'

Calc examined the small cartridge and raised an eyebrow. He plugged it into an empty socket on his damaged arm. The top of the cartridge popped open and a second later, three tiny tripod robots scurried out and examined the damaged skin and small bits of circuit showing through the injury. They ran tiny blue lines over the areas before performing some sort of operation.

Jason was astonished. Speechless.

Calc buzzed with excitement. 'It's a self-repairing cartridge. These are *so* rare. I've only ever heard of them as a myth.' He beamed at the creatures like a proud parent and tickled one as it hovered over a damaged circuit.

'Do they work on humans?' Jason asked.

Calc looked thoughtful. 'I wouldn't say so, but they performed organic repairs on my flesh parts, so maybe to some degree.'

'Worth investigating,' Jason said, rubbing at one of the dozen burns he had sustained.

Silver joined them. 'The fuel is processing,' she said, taking a seat at her terminal and running a scan. 'And we've got a problem.'

'Go on,' Jason said.

'The scans coming from the sinkhole ahead are full of radio chatter.'

'Meaning?'

'Meaning that there are ships waiting for us. And they are from different factions. I'm picking up Harken, pirate and several others.'

'Looks like our bounty has got ahead of us,' Calc said.

'What can we do?' Jason asked. 'Fight?'

'Although Xen found ammunition,' Calc said, flicking through a digital list on a holoscreen, 'there's not enough for a full-on attack.'

'Diplomacy?' he asked, eyeing Silver.

'It's possible,' she said. 'One faction or ship may offer protection from another, but the real problem is we are in Harken territory. They control everything here.'

'Roo?' Jason asked.

'Yes, Captain?'

'Any suggestions?'

'There is a gateway on the far side of Harken Prime. At full speed, we could get there in five minutes.'

'And use it?' Calc asked.

'Yes,' Roo confirmed.

The ship angled upwards as they reached the sinkhole and ascended into the light.

'Thanks, Roo,' Jason said. 'Maybe we can use the weapons enough to get us through to the gate.'

'I could try to avoid them,' Calc said, 'until the gate lets us through. It's only a two-minute queue time. Assuming Roo helps like before. We'd need serious maneuverability. That may mean no weapon systems or even shields.'

'I will aid you, Calculator,' Roo said. 'As long as you don't override my systems again, as you did in the hangar. That virus was measly.'

'Then why did you come?' Calc asked.

'I had had enough of your prodding around in my algorithms and so wanted them to kill you,' Roo said. 'To eliminate a parasite.'

'Then why—' Calc started.

'So no matter what we choose,' Silver said, interrupting them. 'It's suicide?'

'Not if we're quick enough,' Calc said. 'It's our only advantage against Kroth's ship.'

Jason nodded slowly. 'Slim odds.'

'About forty to one,' Calc said.

'I've won on worse odds,' Xen said, stepping into the room, flask in hand.

'Reassuring,' Silver smirked, 'considering your idea of winning is usually cheating or coming out slightly worse off than when you went in.'

Xen took a swig and steadied himself at his terminal. 'It's the coming out that's the important part. Alive, that is.'

'Well, alive is all we need here,' Jason said, holding up a hand to stop Silver's imminent retort.

The top of the sinkhole appeared, sunlight gleaming in from the nearby star. Calc slowed to a near stop and like the head of a rabbit poking out of a hole, he raised the ship just above the rim.

'Erm,' Silver said, 'those odds, Calc. Care to calculate that again?'

Jason sighed.

It wasn't just Kroth's ship and a few rogue captains that had joined the fight and were waiting for them.

'T-that might just be the entire Harken royal fleet,' Calc stammered.

'And every other ship in the sector,' Xen said.

52

They had expected to be confronted when they left the sinkhole. Kroth would have been there in his ship waiting to take revenge on them and maybe a dozen others, all after the bounty that had accumulated on the ship and its crew.

Jason didn't know whether to laugh or cry.

Ships filled the star-studded system. Fleet upon fleet, lined up or bunched together in battle formations, blocked all view of anything behind, including the entire Harken homeworld. There were hundreds of them. Small ships lined up for combat and dozens of titans, dominating the vista, waited like predators at a prey hole.

It was as if all the ships piled up on the surface of the moon had risen in defiance, eager for revenge.

'Well, shit,' Calc said. 'That's a nice welcome party. Those odds I gave back there, they may be a little outdated.'

'We don't want to know,' Xen said.

'Can they see us?' Jason asked.

'We have thirty-eight incoming calls,' Silver said.

'That's a yes then,' Jason said, trying to get comfy in his seat before death rained down on them.

'We're sticking to the plan,' he went on, feeling a surge of defiance in him. He hadn't come all this way to die here like a rat in a barrel.

'What?' Calc asked.

'You're the best navigator in the galaxy, yes?'

'Er, of course,' Calc said, staring out at the vast array of enemies.

'Best calculator in this system?'

'There's a high probability of that,' Calc said, his voice wavering.

Jason eyed the formations. 'Then calculate how the hell to get us through that, using those skills. Xen?'

'Huh?' Xen was barely listening. Like the rest of them, he stared out the window.

'Xen, weapons!' Jason yelled, bringing them all back to attention. 'We're going to need your new-found weapons to break through here. But we'll also need them to hold back these bastards when we reach the nearest Nexus gate. So split it fifty-fifty as best you can. I saw what this ship did back there, and even against those scum out there I have confidence.

'Silver, any chance we can make them think we're giving up? Maybe buy us some time or get us close enough so that Calc can break us through the cordon?'

'Sure,' she said.

There was some hope there, but Jason needed them to understand they could make it.

'Listen! All of you. We can do this. They are stupid. Greedy. Fighting amongst each other instead of coming together. Their greed will make this easy. All we need to do is to allow them to get in each other's way and it's home free for us.'

Calc looked up at that. 'True,' he nodded.

'And,' Jason went on, 'we are small and they are big and cumbersome. We can dance around them while they fall on their asses.'

'Is that Sun Tzu?' Roo asked.

'Sun who?' Calc asked.

'Sort of,' Jason said. 'So, are we ready?'

Calc nodded. 'I need five minutes to examine their formations and account for each ship's individual turning speed and thrust vectors, compare them to ours and set a rough course based on their expected movements.'

Xen seemed to choke on his drink as Jason turned to him. 'And I'll aim my barrel things—squeeze triggers—er....systems?'

Jason frowned but didn't want to lose the momentum he had gathered. 'Do your best, Xen.'

'Establishing contact,' Silver said.

Kroth's face appeared on the screen first before a line split the screen in half with another joining the call. It then halved again and again until there were a dozen random faces on at one time.

'We are ready to give in,' Silver said. 'But who of you can guarantee our safe passage? If our ship is destroyed, then everyone misses out on the bounty and opportunity to see the technology we have on board.'

A hooded and masked figure spoke first. 'We, the Traversai, will guarantee safety for your crew.'

'Captain Larnis here,' one said, 'representing the Merchant Guild. We will see that you pass safely—'

'I can promise—' another said, cutting them off.

'You have our word that—'

'Enough!' Kroth shouted, going red in the face. 'As councilor in this territory, *I* have jurisdiction over you all. Cease your attempts to—'

Silver gave Jason a nod.

'Roo, I need a little static on this line,' he asked. 'Just after my fourth word.'

'Got it,' Roo said.

Jason pressed the microphone on, overriding Kroth and all the others. 'I accept your proposal—'

There was a burst of static; '—and as such we will make our way to you now under your supervision. Thank you.'

There was a chaotic uproar as every single one of them tried to clarify what had been said.

'Who did you say?'

'Confirm your choice or—'

'Repeat that please...'

Kroth had disappeared from the screen. He must have known something was up.

'Calc,' Jason said, keeping himself muted. 'Take us towards the main bulk of the waiting ships. But take it slow until we can gain cover from one of the larger ones.'

'Programming route now,' Calc said.

Nexus One glided forwards as if to supplicate before one of those facing them. None of the ships dared intervene, in case it was them they were heading for to seek sanctuary.

As they neared the largest carrier, Kroth's ship raced out from the sidelines towards them.

It was enough to start a space stampede. A hundred ships engaged full power at nearly the same time, plunging forwards together in a mass, like the start of a marathon.

'Full power, Calc,' Jason said, gripping his seat hard.

All of them were pressed into the rear of their seats, heads absorbing the g-forces as *Nexus One* twisted wildly, running along the side of the nearest carrier, using it for cover.

'Oh no,' Xen said.

'What?' Jason asked.

'Someone just opened fire.'

There was a second of silence as a rogue missile, fired from within the tight mass of chasing ships, tried to lock onto them. The single missile slipped past the hull as Calc threw the ship into a spin. It struck the side of the huge carrier. A fraction of a second passed, and then a dozen other ships all opened fire simultaneously.

The system turned into a chaotic storm of firepower.

Ballistics tore out from under wings in flashes of yellow and white. Missiles spread away in arcs, each trying to weave complex paths around the packed vessels.

Small craft poured out of the largest cruisers and added their lasers to the mix.

'Holy shit!' Xen cried, shielding his eyes from the flashes.

Turrets swiveled to track speeding targets or take out incoming missiles. A dozen anti-missile systems engaged, each overpowering the next until the surrounding space was a searing dance of explosions, colors and plasma blasts.

Some weapons were aimed at *Nexus One*, but most were targeting whoever had fired first, and those after targeted whoever had fired second. It was utter chaos.

'Perfect,' Jason said, his fingers turning white as he held onto his terminal, riding the stomach-churning twists as Calc urged Roo to force more power from particular thrusters as they skimmed the side of the colossal ship. Calc threw it into a dive, ducking underneath and making a beeline for the Nexus gate in the far distance.

There were several bangs as the rear of *Nexus One* was hit.

'Kroth is on our tail,' Silver said.

Jason glanced back. Kroth's and several other ships had broken free from the war zone and were tailing them, ignoring each other for the chance to win the contest of catching them.

'Xen?' he asked.

Xen understood. 'I need a clear frontal shot. We're not loaded for chases. There wasn't enough ammunition. Calc, can you bring us around?'

'I can do a single loop,' Calc said, 'but we would risk being hit by those damn heat source missiles.'

There were several more bangs. 'Shields at forty-nine percent,' Silver said. 'They're hitting us anyway.'

Calc ran a palm around a screen as if wiping the grime from it. Jason noticed he was sweating on it. *Nexus One* banked around, pulling a tight circle to come in facing the side of their pursuers. There were four ships, including Kroth's.

Xen grinned as a barrage of blue and green missiles burst from the sides of *Nexus One*, followed by an eye-watering ring of lasers.

The missiles instantly destroyed one ship, disabling two more and forcing them into a death spiral that ended with both slamming into each other.

Kroth's ship flared as its shields absorbed the laser fire, flickering as if struggling to find the power to resist.

They returned fire, but Calc was already lining up for the Nexus gate again.

Silver's worried voice came through between more bangs and rattles. 'Shields at twenty-four. Calc, you're using too much for acceleration. We need defense.'

'Speed is our best bet now,' Calc said, teeth gritted.

'More incoming fighters,' Silver said. Half a dozen more

ships had disengaged from the conflict around the carrier and were in a fresh race to reach *Nexus One*, ignoring each other as they attempted to close the distance.

The Nexus gate was a double helix with a series of rings in the middle. Blue plasma streaked through the center.

'We've got three minutes until we can enter,' Calc said.

The ships had caught up. Missiles came at them, followed by the shorter range of ballistics and lasers that seared past the windows.

Calc began a series of sharp twists giving Xen a chance to open fire, taking out several of the closest ships, but more were joining the fray, sweeping in from all sides.

'We need more shields,' Silver said, as another bang shook the bridge. 'Five percent!'

A searing flash lit up one side of a large Harken cruiser, drowning out the other weapons fire. Dozens of missiles shot out from a bank of turrets.

'Heat hunters,' Calc said.

It suddenly became a race of endurance. The heat hunters tracked their every twist and turn, locked onto the lingering temperature in the cold of space. Calc tried to force a path away from them, but they closed in as time went on.

'How long until the gate will accept us?' Jason asked, eyeing the construction that would be their salvation or death.

'Ninety seconds,' Silver said.

'Impact in twenty,' Calc said.

'There's too many for the shield to absorb,' Silver said.

They all waited in silence as Calc tried to dodge the inevitable, but they knew it was going to happen.

Death was coming.

EPILOGUE

The heat hunter missiles were gaining on them every second and even Calc was tiring, swaying more and more as he entered each sharp maneuver.

Roo's voice startled Jason. It was louder and more forceful than usual.

'Enter the gate, Captain.'

'What?'

Calc broke concentration for a second on his terminal, allowing the missiles a further gain. 'It's locked!' he said. 'We can go through. But I don't understan—'

'Just go for it,' Jason said. Then he remembered what Calc had said about ships entering early. They all perished.

Calc wove a final tight spin and headed straight for the blue plasma at the center of the gate.

One of the heat hunters struck the shields, and then another hammered the hull, but just before the bulk of the missiles hit them, there was the familiar feeling of being pulled into a Nexus.

'Doesn't this ship need wait times?' Xen asked just as the center of Jason's being turned into a thousand different physical feelings and they completed the jump.

They came out on the far side in a blue flash. They hadn't died or been disintegrated into oblivion. Jason took a breath, feeling life in him and relishing the moment.

It faded when he looked out of the window.

There were ships everywhere. They waited deathly still, in a deep formation, making a near-perfect sphere around the gate and hemming them in on all sides. They all had the same cobbled-together look as Harken ships.

'I would hazard a guess,' Calc said, his voice small in the moment's quiet. 'That is the entire Harken military.'

'He knew,' Silver said. 'Kroth knew we'd get through.'

'Or he played it smart as a backup,' Calc said, sagging. 'It's what I would have done. We've got two minutes until they come through behind us. Not that there isn't enough already.'

Jason stared in awe at the display of power that had gone into hemming them in. Hundreds of little class one fighters were diving away from the big carriers and forming an inner circle closer to *Nexus One*. It was like a synchronized drone show that he'd seen at an Air Force base during a Thanksgiving celebration. This time there was nothing to celebrate though.

The fighters held position, then slowly closed in on the gate and *Nexus One*, tightening the trap.

'They're charging holding beams,' Silver said.

A dozen transparent yellow beams shot out from the

biggest ships. The yellow encased *Nexus One*, giving the ship an aura that shone through the window on all sides.

'Can we break it?' Jason asked.

'Possibly,' Calc said, his hand ready to engage the engines again.

'Wait!' Silver said as her console beeped. 'The Nexus fuel has been loaded.'

Beside them, the gate opened up in a sprawl of blue plasma as Kroth's ship came through.

'Incoming transmission,' Calc said.

Jason nodded.

Kroth's marked face came up, a smirk of satisfaction on his face.

'You've lost,' he said. 'I won't ask you again to give up. I'm eager to see what defense that ship of yours can offer. And honestly, I'm tired.' He pressed something in front of him and leaned forward. 'All ships, this is Councilor Kroth. Open fire on the fugitives.'

A thousand missiles and ballistics streamed towards them in an ever-closing sphere of light and death.

'Roo?' Jason said, as time seemed to slow around him.

'Yes, Captain?' Roo said calmly.

'Engage the jump drive!'

'Destination?'

There was a moment's hesitation.

'Earth!' Jason cried. His voice was drowned out as Silver and Xen both joined in.

'Alcanta!' Silver screamed.

'The Emperor's armory.' Xen said.

They all looked at each other in surprise, then at the incoming blaze of death.

'Manners?' Roo asked.

'PLEASE!' they all echoed.

There was a soul-sucking pull and a blinding flash of golden light.

Nexus One jumped.

53

Please leave a review, reviews help sell books and allow us to create more stories like this. The more reviews we get, the faster the stories come.

As always, if you want to join my mailing list do so by clicking here. There is even a free book or two in it for you.

Or join me on Facebook in a secret group. Link below.

https://www.facebook.com/groups/913118699871413/members

And if you are reading this in paperback form send an email to Writer@dominiquemondesir.co.uk and I will add you to the emailing list.

Till next time

Books by Dominique Mondesir

Beware The Dog: Junkyard Dogs 1

Breakout: (Space Outlaw 1)

The Elements of Home: Space Elemental Book One

. . .

About C.W Tickner

C.W Tickner launched onto the science fiction book scene with the Humanarium series. A unique world set inside a terrarium, owned by a titanic alien imposing its will on the inhabitants.

The last remaining humans trapped inside, live a savage and intriguing life of unknown imprisonment. One man wants out of the box and that is where our story starts.

Living in rural Cambridgeshire, where love for all things small led to the creation of the unique glass sided worlds, imprisoning the last humans in the galaxy and the makings of a legendary story unlike anything seen since Attack on Titan.

His latest dive is deep into expansive Space Opera, bringing to life worlds and species in new and fantastical ways.

Start reading the first book in his series by clicking the link below: *The Humanarium: An Epic Science Fiction Action Adventure Series*

Printed in Great Britain
by Amazon

32722169R00191